the waiting

regi claire

Published by Word Power Books 2012
43 – 45 West Nicolson Street
Edinburgh
EH8 9DB
www.word-power.co.uk

Printed and bound by Martins the Printers, Berwick upon Tweed.
Designed by Leela Sooben

British Library Cataloguing in Publication Data.
A catalogue record for this book is available from the British Library.

ISBN 978-0-9566283-8-1

Cover photo: detail from *Lucy 2* by Mike Knowles

The publisher acknowledges support from Creative Scotland towards
the publication of this title.

ALBA | CHRUTHACHAIL

Regi Claire is Swiss. She is the author of *Inside~Outside*, *The Beauty Room* and *Fighting It*. Her work has twice been shortlisted for a Saltire Scottish Book of the Year Award and has won her a UBS Cultural Foundation Award. She teaches creative writing at the National Gallery of Scotland and is currently the Royal Literary Fund Fellow at Queen Margaret University. She lives in Edinburgh with her husband, the writer Ron Butlin, and their golden retriever. *The Waiting* is her second novel.

www.regiclaire.com

Thank you to the editors of the following publications, where extracts from this novel first appeared: *Orte 140: Schweizer Literaturzeitschrift, Variations 13: Literaturzeitschrift der Universität Zürich* and *Gutter 07*.

Heartfelt thanks to Dorothy Harrower for inspiring me, and to Sally Harrower for continuing the tradition of conviviality and for all her help and support.

Thank you also to Chrissie Dewar, Pamela Smith and Colin M. Warwick MBE for their time, knowledge and memories.

Grateful thanks to Pro Helvetia and the Scottish Arts Council (now Creative Scotland) for bursaries which allowed me time to complete this book, and to Union Bank of Switzerland for a Cultural Foundation Award.

Any inaccuracies, historical or otherwise, are my own. For the sake of the story, Edinburgh Royal Infirmary and the Royal (Dick) School of Veterinary Studies remain in their original locations near the Meadows.

for my mother and Ron
and in memory of Dorothy

'Now that we've done our best and worst, and parted,
I would fill my mind with thoughts that will not rend.'

— from 'The Busy Heart' by Rupert Brooke

1

'Yes?'

'Oh, hello. Is this Mrs Fairbairn?' The girl's voice was foreign-sounding.

'I don't want a new kitchen, thank you. I'm too old and I hate courtesy calls.'

A giggle. 'You don't understand. I'm calling about Marlene.'

And that's how it all began, three days ago: with a misunderstanding. Why did that girl have to interfere with things? Why couldn't she just let me trundle on as usual? Keeping in touch with my stepchildren. Walking Yoyo in the Meadows. Singing to myself for company as I watch the diseased old trees get the chop. Gazing into the gaps left behind, into an always indifferent sky.

'My name is Rachel Keller,' she went on.

But all I could think was, Marlene? That was years ago. Decades. I've learnt to live without her since – without her acts of glory and disgrace.

'I'm Marlene's granddaughter, from Switzerland.'

I said nothing.

'And I'd like to visit you – to hear about her.'

A straight talker. . . I hesitated, then told her I wasn't feeling too well (sure enough, my head was starting to ache again).

Told her I had my Christmas cards to do. That I'd promised my granddaughters a shopping trip (a blatant lie, and my ears burnt as I tried to imagine myself trailing, purse in hand, from Miss Selfridges to Gap to God-knows-where-else on Princes Street).

In the end we agreed on Monday afternoon and I hung up, glad for a few days' reprieve.

Then at teatime yesterday – I was in the middle of frying some lamb cutlets – the doorbell rang. Yoyo shot off yapping down the hall, almost falling over his fat legs. I followed on tiptoe to have a peek from the bay window in the front room.

The streetlights had come on and there she was, Rachel, it had to be her, right on my doorstep: smaller than Marlene, with a scarf round her neck and coat tails whipping in the wind. I couldn't make out her face, but I watched her for a moment. Watched her bend forward and lift the flap of the letterbox to peer inside, then drop it with a clang. Which set Yoyo off again.

When she rang a second time, I tiptoed back to the kitchen, to the cutlets that couldn't wait any longer. I was emphatically and, perhaps a little cowardly, not at home.

~

I never played with dolls except to execute them. I'd heard grown-ups talk of hangings in low, secret voices – in those days the death penalty was still very much a fact of life.

It was during my last week at infant school, just before the summer holidays, that I arrived home one lunchtime to find the wireless on at full volume, reporting an execution.

They were all listening to it: Hamish lounging on the sofa, my mother through in the kitchen, cooking, Audrey at the table behind her, picking up ladders in one of her precious silk stockings.

As soon as my mother caught sight of me, she called to Hamish to turn it off. '*Now*, Hamish!'

My brother finally unslumped himself, and the gruesome description of a hangman's duties faded away.

I stared at the silent wireless. 'Why do people get *hanged*?'

Hamish shoved past me into the kitchen and helped himself to a cigarette from my mother's packet of Passing Clouds. 'Because they've murdered folk, slit their throats, cut them up or strangled them.' He waved the cigarette about as he mimed the deeds, down to the phantom knife and axe, to scare me.

'But why *hang* them? Is it to drain off the blood?' When Mr McDougall, our neighbour, killed rabbits, he always strung them up on the washing line – skinned and beheaded.

Audrey giggled, 'Don't be daft. There's no blood.' Pursing her red mouth (so red I could easily picture her as a vampire sucking all those murderers' blood), she sewed up a thread, scissored it off and slid the stocking egg on to the next ladder.

'Why not shoot them with a gun?'

'Shush. Don't talk about shooting, Lizzie.' My mother looked at me over her shoulder, her face like a mask all of a sudden, stiff and unfamiliar. The wooden spoon in her hand dripped bits of mince and onion slivers.

Hamish didn't take any notice. 'Good question, wee one. Myself I'd opt to be shot.' He grinned and blew a smoke ring – quite unaware he had just pronounced his own death sentence.

'Shush, Hamish. Don't talk about shooting, I said.' Sweat was beading my mother's upper lip. She clawed at a pan and it clattered to the floor, spilling boiled tatties.

Audrey sprang to her feet, knocked the cigarette from Hamish's fingers and shouted at him to shut up.

Later my sister told me that Grandad, our mother's father, had shot himself – not died in his sleep as I'd been led to believe. He'd gone into the woods one morning to fell some trees and hadn't returned. Dervish, his dog, had found him. That night I dreamt of my grandfather dead in the woods. They were dark and still. Nothing moved. No bird sang. The trees were enormous. They reached into the sky and tore it apart.

I never shot my dolls, for the simple reason that I didn't have a gun. Instead they got amputated. Limb by limb I explored their insides; I shattered Parian porcelain, drained sawdust, destroyed elastics, wires and rod-and-lead-ball mechanisms. Afterwards I stuffed the various body parts into Audrey's discarded stockings and laid them to rest in the old rabbit holes under the hedge at the bottom of our garden, the graves marked by broken slates.

One particularly sickly specimen, with huge, stupid eyes that lolled like a drunk's and eyelashes long enough to wipe its nose, I ceremoniously hanged, minus its arms, from the McDougalls' lilac tree. I'd just given the bootlace noose a last tug to test its soundness and was ready to jump down and crawl back through the hedge when a voice yelled:

'Hey, what're you doing up there?'

I twisted round in alarm.

'Only ch-checking on a b-bird's nesssssss–' The word flew off into the air as I lost my balance and crashed to the ground. Life had started in earnest.

I tossed my hair, straightened my frock and the freshly ripped three-quarter hose, then glanced about me. No sign of Mrs McDougall. The garden was empty. It had to be someone in the street, on the other side of the wooden fence. Someone *small*. I grimaced to myself and climbed over.

And there she was, about my age and size, perhaps slightly shorter, her face half-buried in the fur of two tiny puppies.

'But it's August,' she said, continuing our conversation as if nothing had happened. 'No baby birds around.' She kept nuzzling the puppies. One of them was speckled white and bluey grey, like Stilton cheese, the other was the sleekest, wettest black.

'Please, can I hold the black one?'

Flaring her nostrils, the girl looked me up and down. After what seemed at least five minutes, she smiled a gap-toothed smile. 'If you tell me what you were really doing up that tree.'

'You'll have to cross your heart and hope to die first.'

'Cross my heart and hope to die.' She clapped a hand to her chest, quickly, so the puppies couldn't squirm out of her grasp.

I paused for several seconds, then said, 'I hanged my doll. I hate dolls. Dogs are much more fun.' I inched closer, to stroke the black puppy.

The girl took a step back. 'Is this where you bide?'

'N-no. I stay across the hedge. My dad's the plumber and slater.'

She glanced from me to the lilac tree.

'It's Mr and Mrs McDougall's garden,' I whispered. 'He always strings up his dead rabbits on the clothesline. . .'

The girl pulled a face, then waggled the black puppy at me. 'Here. You can keep it if you like.' And she put the furry bundle into my arms. 'I'm Marlene.'

The puppy had begun to lick my throat and chin and I could feel its muscles twitch under the glossy coat. Its eyes were as shiny black as liquorice.

Until I met Marlene, I was a solitary child. I hadn't made any friends at the local fee-paying school, where my parents had sent me from when I was four and still wet my knickers. Born on an April Sunday in the middle of our kitchen, at the very moment the meat was ready to be carved, I'd slipped out 'just like another hot roast', as my mother was fond of saying, proud of herself, and me. And from my parents' bedroom upstairs I bawled all through that disrupted meal, providing a soundtrack – it was the year of *The Jazz Singer*, after all.

I was the youngest of three by seven years and my mother indulged me from the start. 'Come here, my pet,' she'd call from under the pend of the slater's shop, her voice carrying across our big yard, past parked vans and cars to the plumber's shop with the garages at the far end. Obediently I'd stop my games and trot up to her. 'Good girl,' she'd say and stick a custard cream into my mouth or, even tastier, a piece of raw meat. Fresh lamb and beef I adored to the point of salivation (one *clop* of the cleaver and I'd be in position at the kitchen table, my upturned face barely level with it).

I loved rummaging among the old taps my father kept in a brassbound seaman's chest. Rusty or verdigrised, they did nicely as one-armed pirates. Leaning them together, hot and cold in matching pairs, I crowned them with downy thistles, dandelion clocks and overblown roses, then blasted their heads off in a storm of puffs. Other times they became water pistols I aimed at the cabbages, the grimy window of the yard WC, our cats and the workmen. Pete, the young apprentice with five sisters of his own, would laugh and pretend to give chase; the older one ignored me. But the journeymen and Red Ray, the fiery-haired foreman, all swore they'd dunk me in the Tweed.

Besides the taps, there were heaps of cut-offs from copper pipes, not really good for anything, or anyone. I planted them in a jagged circle in the earth of the yard – my magic circle – and played at organ pipes, striking the metal lengths into a ringing frenzy as I sang at the top of my voice:

> 'Mary had a little lamb
> You've heard this tale before,
> But did you know she passed her plate
> And had a little more?
>
> Mary had a little lamb,
> Her father shot it dead,
> And now it goes to school with her
> Between two chunks of bread.'

People said I was a 'rum one'. They asked, 'Why don't you play with a nice wee doll instead, like a nice wee lassie?'

'Because I'm *not* a nice wee lassie.' And I'd bash the pipes extra hard.

They'd frown down at me, shake their heads and walk off. But the scarecrow wifies with their baskets, bat-wing hats and quivering wattles would press closer to peer at me, rheumy-eyed. 'A naughty thing to say, Lizzie. You don't mean that.' And they'd wag their gouty fingers before hobbling off in a flap of skirts that almost swept the yard.

'I hate dolls! Hate dolls! Hate dolls!' I'd cry after them, whirling in my circle, rapping the pipes like so many knuckles.

Then one evening after the workmen had left and my father had gone to the pub with Red Ray, a woman in a mouldy greatcoat and a faded beret stepped from the shadows of the pend – and into my magic circle. She grabbed my arm and pulled me towards her. Fastened to her beret was a gold chain with two front teeth, each set in a tiny gold frame. They dangled hypnotically. I could smell the camphor in her clothes and something else, faintly sweet, decayed.

The strange woman looked down into my eyes for so long I forgot to scream. Forgot to struggle. Her face was webbed with wrinkles, ancient, but her eyes seemed to dance. They danced from misty blue to grey to silver to the palest shade of pearl green. She had what I've come to call seawater eyes – eyes like Dafydd's. Without a word she lifted my right hand, palm up, studied it for a moment, then, nodding, vanished into the thickening dusk.

'Tinker Jeanie, damn her!' my mother exploded when I told her about the stranger. 'She's no business snooping around our yard. If she's put the jinx on you, I'll kill her!' She clutched at me. 'Lizzie, pet, she didn't touch you, did she?'

I mumbled something and wriggled free.

My mother had a thing about travelling folk, especially gypsies. Tramps she fed and occasionally let bunk down in the slater's shop, but she refused point blank to buy Chivers jam, saying it was 'the tinks' who picked the fruit in the Perthshire fields and made it 'rot on the spot'. I myself rather fancied their wooden wagons with the big wheels, fairytale shutters and dainty henhouse ladders, fancied the shaggy ponies, the sooty, bulbous pots that hung over their fires and, most of all, their songs that floated in the air like promises.

It was shortly after my encounter with Tinker Jeanie that I fell from the lilac tree and met Marlene. My mother was sifting flour into her bread-making bowl when I got home. She never noticed the fresh rips in my three-quarter hose because the puppy had run up to her, snuffling.

'Lizzie! Where on earth did you get *this*?' And she pushed Liquorice away with her foot, glaring at me, but the puppy ran back again as if it was a game.

All I knew was the girl's name and that she had wheaten hair, bright blue eyes and was generous to a fault.

'Marlene!' My mother thumped the kitchen table so hard the bowl tipped over in a flurry of white. 'Must be Mrs Gray's youngest – a wee horse face, they say. Changed her name as if that could undo the shame. Illegitimate she is.'

I didn't understand the half of it and tried to catch Liquorice, who'd just peed under the table, to escape with her into the yard. Wagging her tail, the puppy fled into the sitting room, up to the closed office door and, in one quick crouch, produced a lurid yellow offering. It was a Friday afternoon and I could hear my father talking inside as he sorted out the wage packets with Miss Hunter, the secretary. By the time I'd cleaned up the mess, my mother had started to fondle Liquorice, murmuring, 'Pretty girl, darling girl . . .'

In future it would be Liquorice, not me, who'd get enticed across the yard with a biscuit or a tasty cube of fresh lamb. Meanwhile, I had to be taken to Doctor Jolly's for the after-effects of eating raw meat, referred to as 'noodles' by my mother.

My pet days were over.

2

Yes, Marlene did have a horse face, but a curiously attractive one: long, narrow, with a straight flat nose and nostrils so wide they could hold a farthing each (I know, because I lost that bet, like many others later in life and more disastrous). It was her eyes that were her best feature. Large and forget-me-not blue, edged with spiky, dark lashes that threw star shadows on her face, they allured with their I-don't-give-a-damn look. And it must have been those eyes and the child-blonde curls that led to wee Milly being called Marlene at the age of three, after her mother saw Marlene Dietrich in *The Blue Angel*.

Everybody knew Mrs Gray had got pregnant again, as a widow. Twice she was rumoured to have placed the newborn baby on the doorstep of the alleged father's house in Jedburgh, and twice the screaming bundle had been delivered back to her by return.

Many years later, when Marlene got married, secretly, with me and the cab driver for witnesses, she filled in the blanks in the registry book with a flourish. Rank or Profession of Father: 'professional footballer'. I bit my tongue as I wrote down my name, Elizabeth McLean, but my signature was like a burst of flyaway laughter. Marlene kept a straight face – and no one, not even her new husband, queried her entry.

~

'Yoyo, what is it now?' I know, I know. Time for a walk. But there's more tea in the pot and it's such a dark day. 'Go and find Squeaky.' Dark and dank, with layers of mouldering leaves on pavements and paths. Birds flitting between trees like shrivels of burnt paper, the park squirrels in their lairs gorged on the rotting insides of litter bins. The year sloughing off its last few weeks in half-darkness, spattered by rain, sleet and mud. On days like this I prefer dozing in my rocking chair by the gas fire, a cup of tea at my elbow and some biscuits, the *Scotsman* crossword on my lap. Today, though, that's just an excuse. It's the thought of Rachel that makes me put things off.

'Two more minutes, Yoyo. Let me finish my tea. Here's a chocolate digestive.'

~

Now that I went to the same state primary school as Marlene, I began to share my snacks and sweets with her – she never seemed to have any of her own, poor soul. Gratitude lay at the heart of our friendship: her gratitude to me for feeding her, my gratitude to her for that initial gift of life, *real* life, pulsating, whimpering, affectionate. Perhaps that's what was wrong with our friendship all along.

Most afternoons she and a few other girls from class met me in my father's yard. Liquorice and Stilton, their names made official at a torrential christening under the outside tap, would scamper about as we bounced a ball against the walls in a contest of claps and jumps, including a rather daring 'frock-up, knickers-down' bum show. Our skipping drove the puppies frantic, and they often got themselves lassoed into the air, yelping.

If the coast was clear, we'd sneak through the pend door up into the slater's shop. My friends would line up at the big barrel filled with lumps of chalk for roof markings and I'd dish out a piece to each. Afterwards we'd have a game of hopscotch on the cement floor under the pend or daub figures on the yard walls, mostly ourselves, exaggerating knobbly knees, fat bellies and stick-out ears until we resembled cartoon characters. Sometimes Pete joined in and impressed us with drawings of lions, tigers and giraffes – he seemed far too gifted for an apprentice plumber and slater.

Best of all were our 'performances' in the arena of the yard. Perched on the corrugated iron sheet that sloped down over a heap of slater's batons, the audience would pass round a bottle of sugarallie water and a bag of sweeties while being entertained by cartwheels and handstands, dog fights (courtesy of marrow-bones tied to strings), songs and dances, poetry recitals (Isobel loved declaiming Burns) and the mimicry of my private elocution lessons. My speciality was a deadpan rendering of 'Christopher Robin goes hoppity, hoppity, hoppity, hoppity, hop', which always earned me shrieks of 'encore!'

It was Marlene who rewrote the script.

'Wait here,' she ordered us one murky November afternoon as we stood about the yard, trying to decide what to do. Then she clambered up on to the corrugated sheet, tugged at her clothing, squatted and squirted a steaming rivulet down one of the troughs. Later we took turns. Our bladders near bursting with gallons of water drunk straight from the yard tap, we heaved ourselves pain-fully up to achieve ever more gushing results.

'There's someone watching!' May from the garage cried suddenly and pointed to the open lavatory window of Mrs Scott's boarding house, which overlooked the yard.

But whoever it was had disappeared and we carried on regard-less. Until Marlene said, 'Bet you a penny I can chuck something through that lavvy window!'

We all crowded round; May and I contributed a halfpenny each from the handkerchief pockets in our navy-blue knickers. Then Marlene snatched up a short length of pipe left over from one of my magic circle games – and lobbed it right into the lavatory.

Our cheering was silenced by a blood-curdling howl. We scat-tered with hardly a rustle, like leaves in the wind.

'Your lassie keeps bad company,' Mrs Scott complained to my mother that night. 'Someone threw a piece of pipe into my

lavatory and it hit my oldest lodger on the head. He was lucky
not to be killed.'

I was given a row and a clip round the ear, then sent to bed without
the usual mug of cocoa. Pulling the covers over my face, I imagined
being inside the old maroon car which my father had dumped in a
corner of the yard. Imagined launching myself up at its canvas roof
and felt it fold around me like a giant accordion – forming, for the
briefest of moments, a secret space that kept me safe.

~

'Okay, Yoyo, we're off.' Collar, lead, Jenners bag with treats, nappy
bags and glacier mints. Now for the zip-up boots. Bending down
has become a pain, quite literally; I'm getting stiffer these days,
and heavier. On with the new coat for a twirl round the park. My
daughter Janice and I chose it together. The cloth is the colour of
slate with a few flecks of white like unmelted snow; the buttons are
jet black – 'rhombus-shaped', apparently. Pure new Scottish wool.
It'll outlast me by decades. Janice has promised to wear it to my
funeral (summer or winter) and beyond. Such a waste otherwise.

I call the coat my elephant skin: thick, impenetrable, reas-
suring. After David Attenborough's programme about elephants, I
quite fancy myself as one of the ancient matriarchs of the herd,
braying harshly as I thunder-gallop to the rescue of the newborn
calf kidnapped by a rival herd. The way my conscience tells me
I ought to have done with Marlene's children all those years ago.

But I couldn't, could I? Alan wouldn't let me – 'Three of mine
are all we need, Lizzie,' he said. And so Marlene's children were
packed off to their paternal grandparents at Newcastleton. They had
money galore there, I reminded myself, money for good clothes,
good food, good schools . . . If I had stood up to Alan, would it
have made any difference?

'Cold today, Mrs Fairbairn, isn't it? Down, Yoyo, please.' It's Miss
Erskine from a few doors along, returning from her constitutional
around the block.

'Oh, hello.' I coax Yoyo into a sitting position, well away from Miss Chinese Crested as I've dubbed my neighbour. Myself I consider a terrier, a bullterrier – always ready to sink my teeth into things, into people: *snap-snap, snap-snap,* for a short respite from the dullness of my daily existence.

'And how is your leg today?' I indicate the dressing on her shin, which is showing through the stocking.

'Still bruised,' she replies, 'but there's none of that smelly black stuff anymore, thank goodness.' She gives me one of her triangular smiles.

How small she is, how lively even at eighty-five. Her fluffy white hair is impeccably set, rather like a cap, and I picture her ears, vast and flighty, folded from view.

'The antibiotics must be working then,' I say. Poor Miss Chinese Crested with her skin as thin as paper. Anything can make it break: a bump against the furniture, a child knocking into her. Or a playful prod and not-so-playful nip from a badly behaved dog. 'Has the owner of that lurcher been in touch?'

'Oh yes. He called round with a luxury box of Beech's chocolates. Not that I wanted them. Or his apology.' The blood has rushed to her face and she whispers, giggling with embarrassment, 'I tipped the lot into the bin.'

I laugh as I reach into my Jenners bag to offer her a glacier mint. Yoyo swallows his treat whole. We click the mints around our mouths and for a moment suck companionably. Then, blinking her large round eyes, she asks, 'And how are you, Mrs Fairbairn?'

'Not too great, actually,' I hear myself blurt out. 'There's that Swiss girl. She telephoned the other day. Wants to visit me, and I said Monday afternoon. But then she turned up at teatime yesterday. I pretended to be out.' The pavement around my boots is speckled with hardened blobs of chewing gum. 'I couldn't just open the door to her, could I? Not at night?'

Miss Chinese Crested smiles uneasily. 'You did the right thing, Mrs Fairbairn, don't you worry. Better safe than sorry . . . But I must be getting back – it looks like rain.

My face feels a little flushed, despite the cold. I've used my neighbour's own fear of the dark to plead with her. And why am I pleading anyway?

~

Liquorice and Stilton were early starters. They liked straddling each other, hips bucking, tails curved into swishing half-moons. 'Shaggywag', Pete the apprentice called it. As did we, jeering and laughing, shaking them off if they leapt to embrace our legs, muddy-pawed.

One January day I noticed several red splashes in the churned-up snow by the pend. 'Liquorice has cut herself,' I shouted to Marlene, who at that moment was rounding the corner with Stilton. 'She's bleeding!'

We inspected Liquorice's feet, pad by black pad, but found nothing wrong. So we let the dogs romp about while we huddled under a pile of old blankets in the maroon car, making up riddles. I still remember one of Marlene's:

> 'I am thinner than a slice of bread, richer
>   than the richest cake.
> I can't eat or drink, can't spend my money
>   or change my clothes.
> People love me.
> And when I'm needed, they slap me down.'

I can't help thinking of Marlene herself as the Queen of Hearts, juggling with real hearts – and dropping them, one by one. Her widowed mother, who took in lodgers, cleaned for other people and spent her evenings washing glasses at the White Hart, used to tell her daughters, 'Whatever you do, girls, don't marry a poor man. Don't have a life like mine.'

Later that afternoon as my mother stood smoking a cigarette under the pend and tempting Liquorice with titbits, she called out suddenly, 'Whose blood is this in the snow, Lizzie? You didn't let the dogs play together, did you?'

'Why not?' I said. 'They seemed awful keen.'

'Poor darling.' My mother picked Liquorice up and, cuddling her, hissed at me, 'Why didn't you tell me, for God's sake? That stupid, good-for-nothing Marlene!'

My heart froze. Marlene wasn't stupid. She was my friend.

I followed my mother into the house, down the hall, into the sitting room and straight across to the office. The door swung shut in my face.

I waited. Overheard Miss Hunter, the secretary, say in her gentle voice, 'Don't fret, Mrs McLean. She is a tough wee beast.' And, after a rustle-filled pause, 'Here, have some chocolate.' Which my mother refused.

Back in the sitting room, my mother selected a pair of worn-out knickers from the rags pile, cut a hole in their bottom and stuck Liquorice's flailing hindlegs and tail through the openings. 'Pretty girl,' she cooed as she knotted the elastic tight.

Audrey came sauntering in, a pair of silk stockings in one hand, her sewing box in the other. She was humming a Jessie Matthews song, 'Dancing On the Ceiling'. 'Well, well,' she chuckled as she caught sight of Liquorice, 'aren't we fashionable!' The dog escaped behind the sofa and began chewing and clawing at her new underwear.

Mr Ross the vet did something to Liquorice to kill off her puppies if there were any. 'No guarantee,' he said to my mother afterwards with a smile.

I cried.

'She's too young to have a litter, Lizzie.' My mother was cradling Liquorice in her arms. 'See how small her tummy is?'

Nothing happened for a few weeks. Then Liquorice grew fatter. When I got home from school one day, there was no dog, no Mother.

'They're at the vet's, Lizzie dear.' Miss Hunter held out a bar of Fry's Chocolate Cream from her desk drawer. She stroked my hair. 'Everything will be fine. You just go and play with your ball.'

Finally the car pulled into the yard and I ran up to it. 'Liquorice!' I shouted. 'Where's Liquorice, Mum?'

My mother pushed me aside.

'Mum! Where is she?'

My mother's face was almost hidden by the hat jammed down over her brow, but her cheeks were red and puffy. She didn't look at me. Then I saw the short strip of leather with the metal buckle she was twisting in her fingers. I started sobbing, clung to her desperately.

My mother blamed me for the loss. During the next few weeks she'd stand under the pend for minutes at a time, an unlit cigarette between her lips, gazing out across the empty yard.

I for my part blamed Marlene.

My heart felt stone-heavy with grief and guilt. Ignorance is the root of so much harm. So much evil. Perhaps the world would be a better place if people were truly without conscience – as wilful and capricious as Marlene.

3

Spring came wet and mild that year. The grass in the garden shot up, with clusters of ragged weeds like shocks of hair. On my birthday, Uncle Charlie surprised me with three Chinchillas from his farm and Hamish converted a couple of tea chests under the pend. The week after, I asked Marlene round to see the rabbits and come gathering dandelion leaves with me by the river. I couldn't keep away from her any longer; she was so much more fun than the other girls in class, the 'decent' girls who got invited by my parents for picnics and jaunts in the car – as if being born in wedlock proved they'd been conceived there.

Marlene showed up in a glossy new pair of Sunday shoes, probably her first-ever new shoes after years of hand-me-downs. Mrs Gray must have washed hundreds of glasses at the White Hart and cleaned streetfuls of houses to pay for them.

It was a glorious Saturday afternoon. Birds flung themselves into the sky, half-grown lambs ran about the fields bossing the ewes, families of ducks paddled by in wedge formation, and the nearest of the grassy little islands upstream, close to where the Teviot joins the Tweed, shone in the sunlight, emerald-green. Now and then, young couples strolled past holding hands and sweet-talking to each other, blissfully unaware of being tailed by Leering Lenny, a skinny, foxy wee fellow who went around in riding breeches.

I'd brought along an old leather bag from the slater's shop and it was soon bulging with dandelion leaves.

'That's plenty, Marlene,' I called out, patting the stuffed bag. 'Let's head back.'

But she had started to take off her shoes and stockings. 'Don't be a spoilsport, Lizzie. I want to go over to the island. It'll have the juiciest dandelions in the world!'

Of course I gave in. Placed the bag on its side by the water's edge, with our shoes on top, beige lisle stockings tucked inside, neat and tidy.

We were looking for a shallow crossing place when a series of splashes sent the ducks shooting off with loud quacks. I turned – and *there* were our shoes, drifting slowly downstream, the stockings drooping from them like sails at half-mast.

I burst out laughing.

Marlene squawked, 'Oh, my new Sunday shoes! My new shoes!' She flapped her arms. 'Do something, Lizzie! Quick! Get them!'

I couldn't swim. Still can't. But there was no one else around; the courting couples and Leering Lenny had vanished. I knew that the further the shoes travelled, the deeper the river would get and the faster the current, with treacherous whirlpools. Marlene just stood flapping and squawking. I waded in. The icy water clamped itself around my legs. For a moment I pictured the dead cats and dogs that my mother said people threw into the river – funny how she'd never mentioned if folk had actually drowned in it.

'For God's sake, Lizzie, get them!'

I grabbed, snatched, sloshed about – and managed to retrieve three. But shoe number four, one of Marlene's, outsailed me.

'One shoe, I only have the one shoe!' Marlene wailed as we sprinted downstream, past the remains of the bridge swept away by floods long ago. That's when I realised she wasn't supposed to have worn those shoes; Sunday shoes were strictly reserved for Sundays.

Reaching Kelso Bridge, we were in time to see the strange little boat with its waterlogged sail disappear round the bend in the Tweed.

'Why did you let it get away, Lizzie? I can't walk around like this, with one shoe. I'll have to go barefoot now. You too,' she said suddenly. 'You must go barefoot too.'

Before I could protest, she'd wrenched off my left shoe and hurled it down the embankment, missing the water by inches. She smirked as I scrambled after it, grazing my knees, slipping and sliding in the mud. Serves you right, Lizzie, I kept thinking. Why did you set the shoes on *top* of the bag? Stupid, stupid girl!

Next morning Marlene was late for Sunday school. She was wearing her old shoes and although they'd been freshly polished, the scuffmarks showed through. The previous afternoon she'd sneaked indoors unseen, then waited until breakfast to tell her mother that she couldn't find one of her new shoes. Together they'd gone through the rigmarole of hunting for it all over their rented house. They searched underneath chests of drawers, armchairs, dressing tables; they peered into cupboards, groped past chamber pots as they checked under the beds – including those of their lodgers, rough labourers who slept in twos, and that of Marlene's grandmother, who lay quietly dying of a 'growth', the euphemism for cancer. In the end Marlene had confessed that, yes, she had in fact lost her shoe. 'Lizzie put it down the Tweed,' she said to her mother, quite accurately, if not, perhaps, quite truthfully.

~

Not many people in the Meadows today and I don't blame them. Low blotches of cloud, the sun malevolent behind a veil of thin, stringy rain. At least Miss Chinese Crested will have got home dry. In the distance, Jasmine the Dalmatian is taking herself for a run around the park, her policeman master nowhere in sight as usual – 'invisible policing', he calls it.

'Yoyo!'

What a scrounger he is, snuffling round every bench and litter bin for some grimy pizza crust or kebab, trailing way behind so

I have to shout my wizened head off. Should have been stricter when he was a puppy. Maybe it's his terrier nature. Always nosing about, nosing and sniffing, crunching away at bones. He'd make a good ratter. Poor rabbits in those tea chests; short lives they had, despite the dandelion leaves. Ever since, I've hated rats – horrible, slinky, black-eyed creatures. They abseiled down the yard wall one night from the scaffy's midden on the other side, as if the household rubbish carted there daily, seasoned with fresh horse droppings, wasn't tasty enough.

'Yoyo! Here!'

A straggle of university students glance over. Old biddy dawdling her time away in the park, they'll be thinking. So what! I feel like pulling the wires out of their ears, feel like grabbing hold of their sloppy jeans, chopping off the excess cloth and tossing it to Yoyo for chews. That Rachel girl had better be careful or she won't escape my scissors, not in my own home . . . Three more days – what will I do if she turns up on my doorstep tonight?

What on earth does she want from me?

~

Marlene was one for power games all right, even as a child. It was the last Saturday of the summer holidays, not long after my rabbits were killed, and I was in need of all the distraction I could get.

'Marlene!' I shouted from the lane in front of her house. 'Hey Marlene! Fancy playing marbles?' Stilton came trotting round the corner, wagging, then started to prod a half-eaten mouse in the gutter.

The water tap was only a few yards away (the Grays didn't have the luxury of inside plumbing) and I had a quick drink from it. On an impulse, I pushed my thumb into the opening. At first the water sputtered and sprayed my frock, then, all at once, it cascaded up into the sunlight in a shimmer of colours. I had caught a rainbow . . .

'Come on up, Lizzie!' Mrs Gray waved to me from the sitting-room window.

Marlene met me at the door. 'I've got to buy a couple of jotters,' she said in a stage whisper.

'So?' I asked. We were expected to provide our own school things: pencils, rubbers, pens, pen nibs, books.

She didn't reply and we went into the sitting room, a large, rather bare room with a wide bed along the near wall, a kitchen table and chairs by the window, and an armchair and a heavy dresser flanking the fire. Marlene's grandmother was lying quite still, her face to the wall. Dark shadows were creeping from the folds of her blankets. There was a whiff of chamber pot. I held my breath as I followed Marlene over to where her mother was standing on the hearthrug. Mrs Gray greeted me with a smile that crinkled the skin around her eyes, then she resumed staring fixedly at two worn pennies on the fender.

'No, Mother, you *hand* me the money,' Marlene cried all of a sudden. I looked from one to the other and across to the grand-mother, but she hadn't stirred. No one ever made a fuss of her. I wished I could tell her about the rainbow.

Mrs Gray shook her head. 'Take the money, Marlene, or the stationer's will be closed. It's getting late.'

'You *hand* me the money, Mother.'

Mrs Gray shrugged. 'Don't be daft. Take it or leave it.'

'No, I won't. Why can't you *hand* me my money?'

'*Your* money!' Mrs Gray laughed bitterly and walked away, out of the room, her gaze brushing past the bed. It occurred to me that the old woman might as well be dead.

'Please, Mother!'

For a moment Marlene studied me shrewdly. Then she bent down and picked up the coins, avoiding my eyes.

~

Yoyo is still lagging behind, one leg cocked against the playground railings. And there's the Hawk again, striding along at his usual speedy pace. He has a cruel way of walking. Swings his feet up high before stamping them down, ready to trample on anything in his path: pigeons, the reeling bodies of toddlers, small dogs.

Clomp-clomp, clomp-clomp. Past the public tennis courts he comes striding towards me and Yoyo. The young man's face really is like a hawk's, hook-nosed, shaved from behind the ears right up to his temples into a mask of bone sharpness. His head is stiffly angled to one side.

He has a cap on today, a black baseball cap that hides his cropped hair like a shameful secret. The rest of his outfit is unchanged: dark green bomber jacket, black drainpipe jeans, clumpy black boots.

Clomp-clomp, clomp-clomp. The man gives me the heebie-jeebies. And yet I can't help a wince of recognition every time I see him. How appalling that mere recurrence should create a sense of familiarity, of acceptance – like the graffiti-covered litter bin over by the bench, or the scraggly rosebush rooted in the crumbling stonework of the boarded-up parish school to my left.

Clomp-clomp, clomp-clomp. Less than a dozen yards away now and closing in fast. I turn round, find myself shouting, 'Yoyo, dammit, come here!' And notice the elderly shrillness in my voice. The wee bugger keeps sniffing. I force myself to hover on the spot, make a show of waiting. So much for his guard dog qualities.

'Mrs Fairbairn!'

I almost jump out of my skin.

Silly me – it's only Mrs McPherson, statelier than ever in her poncho-style coat, approaching from behind the trees. Skippy, her trim white poodle, is chasing after a tennis ball. My rescue team! I smile as I get out some treats and compose myself for Mrs McPherson's latest dog bulletin from around the Meadows. Last week she told me about her neighbour's terrier puppy and how it knocked over a nearly full glass of sherry, gobbled up the shards and licked the floor clean – with no worse effects than banging into doors and walls, then snoring like a chainsaw until morning.

Here she is now. The Hawk is miles away already and receding rapidly – harmless, to all appearances.

4

I feel raddled today. Barely slept a wink, despite a visitor-free evening and a pre-bed toddy: pains and aches running up and down my spine all night like fingers on piano keys, and my head a hammering discord. Small wonder I wasn't my nice mild self (mild as for meek, inoffensive, loving and demure) when Isobel rang just after breakfast. Definitely more like a combination of malicious, implacable, loutish and dour. Why does she keep telephoning me? We have nothing in common except the past.

Isobel – she of the Burns recitations – was the acceptable face of poverty in my parents' opinion. Always spruce, clean and prissily busy. Always top of the class. Always off doing her homework at the public library, where the reading room stayed open all hours, the heat and light were free, and you could nick monkey nuts from the librarian – not that Isobel would have dared. 'I may be poor, but I'm no thief,' she used to lecture Marlene and me. Her father was a drunk and the whole family lived jam-packed in one room, with a curtain at the far corner to separate off a certain bucket.

Nowadays, Isobel is hyper house-proud. Doesn't even allow dogs into her villa down in Stockbridge – the legacy of her late, civil engineer husband – in case they spread germs across her gleaming worktops. She does bake lovely cakes, though: Dundee cake with the dried fruit steeped generously in sherry, Christmas cake whose icing melts in the mouth. Of course she is lonely. But that's hardly my fault, is it? Has she never wondered why both her children moved beyond the confines of an easy bus trip?

All the same I feel sorry for her – and a little guilty.

'Lizzie, good morning!' she said in that brittle-bright voice of hers. 'Did you sleep well?'

'Indeed I did,' I lied. 'With Yoyo as my personal foot warmer.'

'Regarding your dog, may I suggest –'

'You may not.'

'Still, you wouldn't want to make it a habit. Too unhealthy.'

'What isn't, at our age? Sex, perhaps?'

I couldn't help grinning to myself when she abruptly changed the subject. 'There's a nasty wind today, Lizzie, you'll need to wrap up. That flu jab won't protect you against a cold, you know.'

Marlene and I used to hide when Isobel came to fetch me to go to the library with her. She'd stop near our front door and pluck off her hat, tidy her hair, reposition the hat, then smooth down her skirt, all before calling out my name. 'She'll be bringing a mirror next,' Marlene commented on one occasion, and we giggled so much Isobel had no trouble discovering us behind the pend door. Mostly, though, Marlene and I gave her the slip. Scaled the wall over to the scaffy's midden, nimble as rats.

Adults all liked Isobel. Disapproved of Marlene. There was poverty *and* poverty, it seemed.

~

That Christmas Mrs Robson, our Sunday school teacher, decided to put on a nativity play.

'We'll need lots of shepherds and shepherdesses,' she said, smiling at us encouragingly.

No one volunteered.

'There'll be a couple of real sheep, too. And a real dog.'

A few hands went up and Mrs Robson noted the names in her little red pocket book in which she normally recorded bad behaviour.

'Now for the three kings. They'll get to wear golden crowns.' Some of the older children sniggered and the teacher glared at them. 'So,' she continued, 'which of you boys would like to be a king?'

'King Kong!' cried Tom Reid. More sniggers.

Mrs Robson ignored them. 'Angels next.'

Most of the girls leapt at the glamour of wings, frilly nighties and halos. I was given the part of Gabriel. The idea of a blaring trumpet suited me fine.

Isobel and Marlene held out until the end. Until Mrs Robson announced, 'Last but not least, we shall need a Mary and a Joseph.'

I'd have loved to be Mary – Holy Mary in her flowing blue robes. But I knew I wouldn't have the ghost of a chance. I wasn't pretty enough. Too muckle and gangly altogether.

Out of the corner of my eye I saw Marlene's hand fly up, fingers straining heavenwards. First come, first served, she must have thought. And yes, she'd beaten Isobel to it.

'Not you,' the teacher said reproachfully. Then she paused as if there was a choice. 'Well, Isobel, you will make a glorious Mary.'

Marlene had begun to sob and I stroked her arm, whispering the old mantra that never failed: 'Mrs Robson is a cow. A stupid, stupid cow.'

The teacher was standing in front of us. 'Don't fret, Marlene. I've a better role in mind for you. You shall be Mary Magdalene. After all, your name's a blend of the two: "Mar-y Magda-lene" – "Mar-lene". You see?'

Marlene lifted her wet face and it was obvious she didn't have a clue. Neither did I. How on earth did Mary Magdalene fit into all this? Only Isobel nodded, very faintly.

Lesson over, Marlene and I broke away from Isobel. It was a stormy day and she soon tired of hurrying after us, busting her lungs against the wind and rain to yell, 'I'm sorry, Marlene, but it really isn't my fault!'

We ran into the weather. We let it tear and claw at us, howled along with its hellish incantations and allowed ourselves to be driven off course, bibles clamped to our chests, towards the ruins of a cottage which had lain empty for as long as we could remember.

I still have nightmares about that place sometimes. Its rooms fester in the dark. They smell of death and damnation. Cobwebs cling to the draught from the broken window we've climbed through. Spurts of rain are driven like nails against the walls, the jagged glass pane, the roof. There's a keening in the chimney above a grate choked with small, blackened bones. A heap of stained sacking by the fireplace bears the imprint of a human body. Marlene kicks it, laughing softly as a bottle rolls out. From further down the passage comes a sudden yelp. Then a shout. Then the heavy blows of what must surely be an axe shaking the floorboards. I can see blood running down the grooves. I always wake up in a sweat. Unable to tell the difference anymore between what's real and what isn't, what's past and what's now.

~

Isobel was right, yet again: my hatless head has been wind-chilled to near-freezing. Climbing the four steps to my front door, I feel I've turned into a slab of meat straight from the cold store, sparkling with ice crystals. Yoyo licks his lips and grins up at me through rakish tufts of hair. Time for his half-bar of Milky Way.

We're hardly inside when the telephone rings. The cordless variety is a godsend, the best present I've ever had from gadget-son John.

It's that girl Rachel. Saying she'd been round on Thursday night, but I wasn't in. 'Your dog went berserk, gave me quite a fright.'

I smile down at Yoyo. 'You should have called beforehand,' I reply amiably, shrugging off my coat.

Then she asks can we meet tomorrow instead of Monday, and my heart sinks. Tomorrow already! After a pause she adds, perhaps by way of an apology, 'Because I've got something for you.'

No doubt Marlene would have approved of the girl's tactics. I grimace at myself in the hall mirror, take one-two-three deep breaths to recover my former pretend-briskness.

'You're in luck,' I tell her as I follow Yoyo into the kitchen. 'My daughter Janice usually visits on a Sunday, but she's away somewhere this weekend.' I open the press for a Milky Way.

'It's Advent Sunday,' she states.

'Oh?' I cut the Milky Way in two and drop half into Yoyo's bowl. 'Are you religious?'

'Spiritual,' I answer, not missing a beat. What an odd, point-blank sort of girl! I switch on the kettle. 'Three o'clock sharp,' I say before hanging up. Marlene was always late.

Yoyo has finished and is grumping for more. 'That's it, my boy.' I try to sound adamant, but he jumps up on the chair next to me, twitching his eyebrows so pathetically I slip him the other half.

Doreen the cleaner arrives soon afterwards and I withdraw to the front room. Rocking gently back and forth in my chair, I recall my conversation with Rachel. Then my religious arguments with my husband Alan. He was a Catholic, a widower with three young children who needed a mother. My convictions were of secondary importance to him. But the idea of transubstantiation provoked me. 'Mumbo-jumbo,' I used to say. 'Just like the powders and potions of medicine men, only more dishonest.'

So tell me, Alan, how could a dry, rational person like you, a doctor-of-chemistry-turned-grocer, believe in bread and wine as the body of Christ?

Even now I can see his hand swat me away like a fly, *Into the kitchen, woman, I'm waiting for my tea*, then reach for the *Scotsman* or the tumbler of whisky on the coffee table.

He accused me of literal-mindedness. Not enough heart to encompass faith. *Faith is* revealed *truth, Lizzie, not truth per se.*

'A catholic? A cannibal, more like!' My best exit line.

Doreen's aggressive cleaning routine jolts me out of my thoughts. The hoover crashes into chair legs, the TV trolley, the skirting board. It attacks the sagging bottom of the sofa until Yoyo flees with a growl. Doreen is a Great Dane – big-boned and fleshy, she's hardly less intimidating. I stop rocking. My chair is next.

'Fancy a cup of tea, Mrs Fairbairn?' she shouts above the noise, furrowing her brow as she wipes it with the sleeve of her scabby sweatshirt. She knows full well it'll be me boiling the kettle for her. But I'm glad to escape. And she knows that, too. Still, I'm quite fond of the girl. Her and her crazy tales about her love life. A fortnight ago she told me she'd travelled all the way down to Newcastle in a police car to pick up her unemployed fifty-something boyfriend and his dog, who'd gone missing after yet another row with her and been reported wandering the streets there in the rain, the picture of misery.

~

In many ways I blame Mrs Robson for Marlene's rise and fall. After our flight from the 'cottage of horrors' that stormy Sunday, Marlene had buttonholed her eldest sister Jane in their shared bedroom and, holding out the damp bible, demanded to be shown the passage about Mary Magdalene in the Christmas story. Jane had told her that Mary Magdalene wasn't in it at all.

'She meets Jesus much later, as a young man. He is at a meal and she washes his feet and he forgives her her sins,' was how Marlene put it the next day.

'What sins?' I asked, wondering if it could really be a sin to give someone's feet a wash while they were eating.

Marlene lowered her voice, 'She was a hoor.'

For a moment we stared at each other, solemn and round-eyed. Then I started to giggle nervously.

In the play that Christmas, Marlene was the young (and nameless) Mary Magdalene who saw the star of Bethlehem yet failed to be guided by it. She had to stumble about the stage like a drunk, searching and searching, unable to find her way to the stable. No one, not even Marlene or her mother, seemed to see anything wrong with this. But my heart still bleeds for Marlene when I think of it.

~

That's it for tonight. I hit the off-button and the TV screen goes blank, with a ghostly reflection that's vaguely my shape. As if part of me, part of my life, has been trapped there. Besides *Pet Rescue, Coronation Street* is my only indulgence – the omnibus is perfect for taping: two hours of near-nonstop *Corrie* if you zap through the adverts. Old bats like me need a bit of vicarious living now and again.

'Yoyo, take that bone off my foot!'

My stocking's slick with saliva and blood. Not that it matters; there's no one here to be shocked and the blood isn't mine, after all. My skin's a lot tougher than that of Miss Chinese Crested. What will she be doing just now? Distracting herself with another medieval romance from the library, perhaps? Legs up on the sofa and the stiffness brushed from her hair, eyes wet with tears as she reads about some chivalrous knight and his lady love? I myself prefer thrillers and detective novels – though that new Grisham blockbuster from Janice has far too many characters in it.

Doreen's a great storyteller when she is in the mood. This afternoon, munching her way through a plateful of Jaffa cakes and sipping the tea I'd duly brewed, she was preoccupied. Kept talking about her cleaning job at Barclay Church and her 'finds' there. Once a pair of lacy knickers, stuffed into the bible rack, and just her size, too. Another time a sodden geriatric nappy behind a couple of cushions. Then, last Monday, a letter for 'Our Lord in Heaven', peeking from a wilting flower arrangement on the altar. It was beautifully handwritten, signed and dated, and asked for swift deliverance from 'a living hell', quoting the psalm: 'Hear my prayer, O Lord, and let my cry come onto thee.' Doreen had slipped the sheet into the minister's bible. But then, yesterday, her curiosity had got the better of her and she'd tracked the address down to a bungalow in Morningside.

The elderly woman who'd opened the door to her was well-groomed and happy-looking, 'beaming all over her wrinkles, with white candyfloss hair'. Doreen had apologised, saying she must have got the house number wrong. Just then, a second woman had appeared in the doorway, also beaming, even happier-looking, in dress and features almost identical to the first – except for her hands, which were like claws, the fingers bent sharply into her palms. And that's when Doreen, my brash Great Dane, had become confused and uncertain. She'd turned tail and run.

'Tell me, Mrs Fairbairn, which one was the troubled soul?' she asked. 'Which one?'

It's not that simple to pinpoint despair, my dear, I wanted to say, trust me. Instead I leant over to give Yoyo the last of the Jaffa cakes.

If my purpose on this earth has been to help troubled souls, I've failed dismally. I couldn't save my own husband, never mind Marlene. I can feel her blighted existence begin to weigh on me once more, a weight I thought I'd thrown off all those years ago.

I'm not guilty, I reassure myself. Not guilty.

5

Rachel is one of these pierced young people, with a brutal silver ring in her bottom lip. 'I'm doing research on the Protestant Reformation. For a PhD,' she tells me when she's seated in my front room.

Marlene would have laughed out loud. But no, maybe not. Maybe she'd have preened herself. Started reading up on John Knox or the *Confessions of a Justified Sinner*, spiking her conversation with quotes.

Rachel is giving me the once-over, from sky-blue suit and cream blouse to beige laced shoes. I sniff, and she glances up.

'I've got a cold,' I lie, then realise I'd better say something complimentary. 'PhD? Your grandmother would have been proud of you. Milk and sugar?'

'Just milk, thank you.' Her accent seesaws between Scottish and foreign. Even the way she stirs her tea is different. So vigorous the spoon clangs against the china and the leaves swirl up. 'Marlene?' she continues. 'I doubt it. Not from what my mother told me about her.'

Straightforward bordering on rude. One thing's for sure, the Scots are more polite than the Swiss. Again I feel that prickle of annoyance at her coming here and forcing me to tunnel back into the past until I'm stuck. I have no intention of joining those old biddies living in the never-never land of their youth. I had a rotten adolescence anyway; everybody had a bust except me.

'Well, Catriona is wrong.' I say firmly, then toss Yoyo a Café Noir.

'*Was* wrong. My mother is dead.'

She watches me over the rim of her teacup.

'Oh, I'm so sorry, Rachel. I didn't . . .'

Yoyo is crunching away, a lusty reminder of life.

'That's okay. She died almost six years ago. A skiing accident in the Alps.'

The girl sounds so matter-of-fact it makes me feel flustered. Marlene used to come visiting me with her daughter Catriona sometimes, before things fell apart. 'How terrible for you and your father.'

Rachel nods, bites her lip with the ring in it. I look away.

For a sickening moment an image trembles in my mind, of seawater eyes and milk-teeth framed in gold, dangling from a beret. The winter before Marlene's clandestine marriage, she and I had bumped into Tinker Jeanie in one of the dark closes off the Royal Mile. Without asking, the old woman had grasped our hands and, teeth glinting on their gold chain, examined our palms. 'I ken you better than you ken yourselves,' she said, then whispered to me to 'keep that Marlene lassie safe from what's not yet fated.' There had been a dusting of snow on the ground, over a blade-thin layer of ice.

And now Marlene's daughter is dead too. But Rachel's a survivor. Marlene was obstinate to breaking point. Rachel seems resilient. She's observing me now, and for an instant her eyes flicker with her grandmother's I-don't-give-a-damn look – or is it only the reflection of the candle flame?

We're in the front room. I've given her my rocking chair while I slump on the sofa, cushions behind my back to stop it acting up. Between us on the coffee table is her gift, a wreath of fir sprays with four white candles, one of them burning. When I caught sight of it on opening the door to her, my first thought was, I'm not dead yet, am I? But then she explained it was an Advent wreath. You're supposed to light a candle for each Advent Sunday: one candle today – the 'Prophecy Candle' she called it – a new one next Sunday and so on, up to Christmas.

Rachel smiles behind her teacup. 'So you liked Marlene?' There's a faint tinkle from her lip ring against the porcelain. The girl's a dachshund – down to the wiry brown hair and brandy-coloured eyes – small, alert and intelligent, moving into the attack before you can say Jack Robinson.

'We had fun together.' I take a gulp of my G & T. 'Life was never dull with Marlene, right enough.'

'Which isn't the same thing, though.' She crosses her legs. No flared trousers, more's the pity (my sewing scissors are on the sideboard behind me), just ordinary black corduroys and a blue cardigan with pearly buttons. Surprisingly conservative.

That PhD is a pretext. It's her own history Rachel is after. Catriona wouldn't have been able to piece it all together for her; she was in India during the years of Marlene's decline.

I toss Yoyo another Café Noir, double his usual ration, and his eyes glow with immediate rapture. No wonder I prefer dogs to humans.

Rachel must have sensed my displeasure because she changes tack. 'Actually, the Swiss and the Scots have quite a lot in common.'

I stare at her blankly.

'Mountains and size of population for starters. Thrift. Stubbornness.' She laughs, pauses. 'Calvinism. Here you've got Knox, and where I grew up, near Zurich, we had Zwingli.'

Soon she is lecturing me on the 'Protestant cause', the literal reading of the Christian scriptures and its theological and political implications, and I almost drift off.

All of a sudden she asks, 'What did you mean by "spiritual" that time on the phone? Do you believe in a higher power, Mrs Fairbairn?'

I have another slug of my G & T. 'Certainly not in God. In spirits, yes. Astral bodies, ghosts and poltergeists.' For an instant I'm transported back to my first spiritualists' meeting. Marlene and I attended it for a laugh. In the darkened room, everything seemed more intense: the sound of people's breath, the rustling of clothes, the creaks of chairs and bones, soap scents, the smell of sweat and garlic, perfumes turning rancid. But there'd been no messages for us – not *that* night.

I offer Rachel more tea and biscuits. Yoyo clacks his teeth. I do my best to ignore him; wouldn't want the girl to think me an old softie. Refreshing my drink, I decide to tell her about the last-ever séance I went to, three years after Marlene's death. It was held at a private house in Heriot Row, with a famous medium. None of the other spiritualists knew me and I didn't know any of them.

'We sat in a circle in utter darkness. To my right was an empty chair. Before long the medium began to speak in a quavering voice. It had a message for me: "There is a woman with a longish face seated on that empty chair. She wants you to know that she has met her real father at last. And this time he hasn't sent her away."'

Rachel doesn't say a word. She is staring into the candle flame, quite motionless. Yoyo has abandoned his vigil and now lies snoring under the small bookcase. My eyes snag on the set of Dickens I inherited from my father. Great expectations indeed! Lucky Yoyo, so oblivious of old ghosts, of hauntings and regrets.

I finish my G & T in silence. Why does the girl have to bring it all back? Why?

After Rachel's departure I feel wrecked. And wretched. It's dark outside and I've drawn the rose-embroidered curtains I invested in when Alan died. I could sleep a thousand years and still it wouldn't be enough. My eyelids drag. My head hangs heavy. The weight of my body presses down into the rocking chair, pulls me through the floor, into the earth.

'I'll see you again, Mrs Fairbairn,' she said. *See you again. Again. . . Again. . .* Her words echo around the walled-in memory lanes of my mind.

Something's burning, I can smell it, very close . . . Half-jerking out of my chair, hands shaking, I grab the teapot, throw the rest of the Earl Grey in splatters over the Advent wreath. A quick sizzle and froth – and that's that, thank God. The Prophecy Candle has well and truly gone up in smoke; only its spike and silvery base remain, drenched in a crater of charred pine needles. Yoyo is already licking the soggy carpet, tail wagging. I try to laugh, to smile. I can feel my mouth widening . . . and just manage to stop myself from blubbering like a baby.

My fingers have started scrabbling at a ripple of wax on the table top, but the wax won't come off and I have to scrape at it with my nails, scrape and scrape and scrape. What have I told Rachel? And what have I kept to myself? My mind is a blank. I reach for the Grisham on the sideboard – better to lose myself in that than in the confusions of the past.

Janice telephones shortly before seven and is intrigued to hear about my visitor (I prudently omit the scorched wreath). She remembers Marlene with the annoying accuracy of a child: the holes in her stockings, her prone body drunk on the bedroom floor, her naked prancings around our front room.

At the news of Catriona's fatal skiing accident, she goes quiet. I help myself to a glacier mint from the bowl on the gas fire.

Janice met Catriona a few times in her youth, but always disliked the scrawny wee creature, Lord knows why. I felt sorry for Catriona, tried fattening her up with whatever scraps Alan allowed me to bring home from our grocery business: crumbling or runny bits of cheese, meat off-cuts, broken biscuits, chocolate bars nibbled by the mice that had outwitted the shop cat.

'Let's hope that's the end of it,' Janice says finally.

'The end of what?' My mint makes a smacking noise. 'You're not still jealous of –'

'Those gypsy warnings you used to talk about.'

I almost swallow the mint. 'What . . . gypsy warnings?'

'Oh, Mum! Don't pretend you've forgotten.'

Tinker Jeanie, I think with a shiver and bury my free hand in Yoyo's fur. He raises his head, then, finding there are no treats, flops it down again.

'Anyway,' I wind up, 'Rachel's different. Serious and solid, very bright. Takes after her Swiss father, I expect.'

Janice laughs. 'Good old Mum. Not too keen on her, are you?'

~

Acquainted with the facts of life, Marlene still hadn't put two and two together (or if she had, they must have added up to five), hadn't cottoned on to what had long been common knowledge in town. Then came that fateful March day, a month after her twelfth birthday.

We'd gone primrose picking by the Tweed. It was warm. The sun stroked our backs as we stooped on the riverbank, gathering flowers and leaves in large, fragrant bundles and placing them in our baskets. I'd begun to feel hungry and was ready to go home when Marlene blurted out, 'My sister Jane told me something about your uncle Charlie!'

'What about him?'

'"All balls and no brains," *she* says.' Marlene grinned and sat down on a stone, smoothing her frock over her fat lower legs (she loathed them, called them 'stumps' even then). Star-shadows trembled on her cheeks as she blinked. Baiting me.

I was getting annoyed and ever hotter-feeling. People kept shooting their mouths off about my uncle, doing him down. He'd let me have the chinchilla rabbits and he always brought presents when he visited, real presents – not just chocolates and sweeties that never outlasted the day – things like skipping ropes, necklaces with shiny beads, kid gloves softer than catkins.

'You don't know him, Marlene, so you better shut up.'

'But I know what Jane said. She heard he's made a bairn with the barmaid at the Royal Oak. And that woman isn't even his wife! They aren't even married! "A bloody disgrace," says Jane.' Marlene's upper lip drew back from her teeth and twitched like that of a nasty horse. 'A bugger of a disgrace, if you ask *me*.'

She was much too scathing, much too sneering. I homed in for the kill, furious now. So hot and angry and vengeful. 'Oh, it happened in *your* family, too. It's no secret.'

'What do you mean?' Her eyes had widened and their blueness seemed to blot out the sky.

She clearly hadn't been told. Pulling her basket on to her lap, she plunged her hands into the delicate drifts of flowers and spoon-shaped leaves and, clutching a bunch at random, went through the names of her elder sisters. It was a cruel guessing game.

'Was it Jane?'

'No.'

'Was it Mary?'

'No.'

There was a bruised scent of primrose and sappy green.

'Dolly?'

'No.'

The air was getting clogged with sweetness.

'Bessie?'

'No.'

Marlene's nostrils began to quiver. 'Was it my mother?'

I stared at the crushed flowers in her hands. Shreds of pale gold and dark green stuck to her skin and clotted under her nails like dirt. I didn't nod, didn't say anything, coward that I was.

But she understood all right.

For a second I thought she would burst into tears. And suddenly I felt like sobbing myself. Felt like begging her forgiveness. Wanted to bend down and wash her feet in the river. But the words were out whatever my penance; the breeze had blown them away and there was no calling them back. For the first time in my life I realised that words are weapons – weapons that cut deep and leave wounds. Perhaps that was the moment when Marlene lost her innocence, and her trust in people.

Eventually she replied, 'But my father died three years before I was born, everybody says so.'

To this day, I haven't been able to work out her logic. I managed to mask my snort of derision with a cough and pretended to sniff the primroses in my basket. Their smell almost made me retch. After a long pause, during which I felt her eyes pleading with me, I said, 'Aye. But babies don't stay inside their mothers for years, do they?'

Marlene's mouth opened, and closed. A minute passed. At last she mumbled, 'If it wasn't him, then who *is* my father?'

I shrugged. 'How would *I* know? I wasn't born at the time, either.' I was so callous. So very callous.

Many years later, perhaps in the hope of salving my conscience, I asked Marlene if she had really not known about her illegitimacy, and she said, 'No, it was you who told me. Up on the primrose bank.' Her answer was like a slap in the face. And I deserved it.

~

Why torment myself with all this, for heaven's sake? Now I can't sleep. Even that moss-green Night Nurse doesn't soothe. I'm tempted to blame Rachel. Tempted to trade places with Yoyo and his doggie dreams whining up and down the hall. I wish he did snooze on my bed so I could hold him close. Why can't I stop my thoughts? They're going round my head like a game of Russian roulette.

—Was it really me that betrayed Marlene?

—No, of course not.

—Who was it, then?

—You tell me.

—I am asking you.

And just as I begin to relax and think the gun is empty, I get hit full force all over again.

6

Having trundled round the park, slipping on leaf mulch, yelling 'Yoyo!' every so often, I watch a blackbird settle on an arrow-tip of the Royal Infirmary railings. When it begins to fling out its melancholy notes, they hit me straight in the heart – full force yet again.

Yes, we all corrupt ourselves. We don't need help for that.

After she first met Alan, Marlene said to me, 'He's an ugly bugger.' She was never one for subtleties – unless she played at being the lady: posh accent, ponies for the children, expensive silverware and numbered editions of china (which, without any qualms, she'd throw at visitors if they happened to annoy her). I knew my husband wasn't a looker – prematurely bald, he wore the few leftover strands of his hair draped in complicated meanderings across his skull. But then, I hadn't married him for that.

The blackbird has flitted off like a shadow of heartbreak. I strain to recapture its shape and harmony in the dusky branches above me. And instead glimpse the memory of a face – a face I've tried hard to forget. Why did I ever send my true love away? Dafydd with his clear, bright eyes, his Welsh wit and tailored Scottish tweeds. Dafydd with his mocking grin that undid all my good resolutions. Why did I? Not out of spite, not to punish him? I wasn't that arrogant, surely? Wasn't that stupid?

I still have his letters, a mosaic of coral pink, eggshell blue and oyster white beneath the scented lining paper of my underwear drawer.

Perhaps marrying Alan was the best way out. Thanks to him, I rose from a mere employee-dressmaker to Mrs Fairbairn, co-owner of a grocery shop. No more fittings of satin evening gowns for flirty girls who thought they'd invented love, no more letting out waists for married women leading the good life, no more adjusting busts for shrinking spinsters. And, with his three young, motherless children competing for my affections, there wasn't much left for him – we both knew that. While he dreamt about his late wife, I dreamt about Dafydd. A balance of sorts.

'Yoyo, come on now!' Malingering behind another bin, the little devil.

And here's Skippy with a tennis ball in her mouth. She drops it, wags her tail and grins expectantly.

Mrs McPherson gives me a wave. 'Mild today, isn't it?'

I wave back and smile as I fumble a treat from my Jenners bag. Then I line up the ball to kick it . . . into a nearby tree. But Skippy doesn't mind and darts after it quite happily. Animals, at least, don't judge us.

~

It was the year of the primrose bank that the war started. By then we were already in secondary school, though in different classes: Isobel, naturally, in the A stream (A for 'auntsy ants', as Marlene said), nice and middling me in B (for 'bloody bedbugs' – whatever that was supposed to mean) and Marlene in C (for 'cocky cockroaches').

When the air-raid sirens screeched into action for a test·run after Chamberlain's announcement on 3 September '39, my mother crammed me, Miss Hunter and herself into the understairs cupboard with the tins and jars of preserves, convinced the Germans were at that very moment marching up the road towards our home.

Kelso was soon teeming with troops. The Corn Exchange and

most of the primary schools and church halls were converted into barracks, and we children got bussed to outlying schools for half-days. Officers were billeted in private houses; my parents had to put up two military men, one in my brother's old room, the other in the 'refuge' up in the attic. The countryside around the town was used as training grounds by the regiments: first came the Royal Engineers, then the Royal Marines, then the Polish Mounted Rifles – who were learning to operate British tanks so they could form the Polish Tank Corps – and, finally, the Czechs.

Evacuees and displaced persons started arriving. The former were mostly children from Edinburgh; we took in twins, Tommy and Brian, who for two years followed my mother around like puppies. The displaced persons, from Poland, Germany and Ukraine, were housed in Nissen huts at Springwood Park. They didn't mix much with us locals. But sometimes Marlene and I detoured past the park after school to get a peek at them and listen to their harshly melodic speech.

Our chief pastime, though, was loitering in the streets, watching the soldiers drive by in their army vehicles. The tanks were our favourites. Their caterpillar tracks slid on the cobbles in the rain so we had to jump to safety – there wasn't a lamppost left standing in town after the war – and their thrumming invaded our bodies until our teeth whined with it.

I began to see more of my sister Audrey again. Every Friday evening she'd step off the train from Edinburgh, where she was clerking for a lawyer, to go to the weekend dances at Stempel's with her girlfriends. 'Plenty young servicemen on offer,' she'd say with a wink.

Our brother had been posted abroad. Poor, poor Hamish. It was on what would have been his twenty-third birthday, in February '42, that the telegram boy cycled into our yard: Hamish had been shot to pieces outside Tobruk. For months afterwards I could hear his voice in my head, saying over and over again, *Myself I'd opt to be shot . . . opt to be shot . . .* And I could see his grin as he blew a smoke ring.

~

A few yards from my gate I remember the damaged Advent wreath. 'Sorry, Yoyo. Change of plan.' I swing him round on the lead, but he digs his heels in and I have to drag him, drag him back round all the cars parked with their boots and bonnets jutting out, drag him through loutish groups of pupils from nearby Gillespie's. Boys and girls these days seem so free and easy together. So sexually aware. At their age, I was too inexperienced even to contemplate messing with the soldiers.

Two blocks down, I bribe Yoyo with a biscuit, then grip the large sewing scissors hidden in my bag. The fairy lights on the fir tree just inside the garden fence twinkle invitingly. By the time Yoyo has licked the pavement clean, I have finished. With a bit of luck, daughter Janice won't see anything amiss with my Advent wreath when she calls round later tonight.

~

A year into the war my appendix burst, poisoning my insides, and I became too ill for any hanky-panky, in thought or deed. After endless weeks in the infirmary, I was kept at home for the best part of six months – no classes or games in the yard, no hanging around the streets with Marlene. Instead of fresh air, I got pills. 'Dr. Williams' Pink Pills for Pale People' said the pink letters on the small bottle decorated with a large P.

Because Marlene was hardly ever allowed to visit, it was several months before we met again. From then on I began to send for her in secret, when my parents were away in Edinburgh at some plumbers' warehouse sale or other. She had grown up. Her body had filled out, her blonde curls were darker and her eyes a deeper blue, with more of that I-don't-give-a-damn look. And she had started to smoke: Du Mauriers – probably because of the sophisticated-sounding brand name. One of her mother's officer lodgers (the two-to-a-bed labourers were sleeping elsewhere now and the old grandmother had died in the nick of time, vacating the double bed) had bought her a cigarette holder of amber and wrought silver. 'He's taken a shine to me,' she said, adding, 'Don't frown like that, Lizzie, you look an awful moron. Anyway, he's a daft old fart!' Which reassured me she was still the Marlene of the primrose bank.

My own hormones, meanwhile, made me hate the sight of myself: big yet bustless, hairy, blotchy with pimples. 'Don't chill your suet, Lizzie!' was one of my mother's constant admonishments and she enforced it rigorously. Result: I was always hot. The sweat dribbling down my face turned the spots on my forehead into pustules.

During a medical check-up that spring, I had to free my chest. I duly removed my cardigan, my jumper, my spencer, my liberty bodice and my woollen vest. 'Good God, child!' the doctor exclaimed when I finished. After the examination he requested a 'chat in private' with my mother.

The sweating stopped. But the spots remained.

Until Audrey arrived one Friday evening with a little pot from Napier's the herbalist up in Edinburgh. 'Don't worry, wee sister,' she murmured, gently rubbing some ointment into my face. 'This'll work like a charm.' Despite her obsession with silk stockings, fancy hats and dancing skirts, she had actually noticed my plight. She seemed much nicer than I remembered. I felt so grateful I didn't point out the tide line on her jaws from Laird's Skin Tone Foundation. And then it dawned on me: Audrey was in love!

By now I was fourteen. If I pleaded long enough, my father would occasionally let me accompany him up to Edinburgh, brushing aside my mother's warnings of 'enemy action'. Most recently, in early April and again in early May, German bombs had killed several people in the capital and injured many more. 'Life goes on,' he'd say grimly, then, more softly, 'We'll be back before nightfall, never fret.'

One Saturday morning in mid-June we set off for the city with Marlene stowed away under some blankets in the back of the car. When my father realised he had an extra passenger, he just laughed and waggled a finger – and she and I winked at each other.

Drawing up outside the North British Station Hotel, he told us to meet him at half past four at 'the Horse', the bronze statue in front of Register House. Then he reached into his jacket pocket and handed me three half-crowns. 'Spending money,' he said, with a smile at us both. 'And remember to get your mother something nice, Lizzie.' He pulled away from the kerb tootling the horn.

Marlene and I had the day and the delights of Edinburgh to ourselves. We rushed down Waverley Steps to the public toilets, changed into the old silk stockings I'd coaxed out of Audrey and put on the rouge and lipstick Marlene had liberated from her mother's dressing table. Puckering her painted lips, she simpered, 'Remember to get *me* something nice, Lizzie.' Two of her sisters, Jane and Mary, worked in the office of the Royal British Hotel and they had promised us lunch. *Free* lunch, as Marlene stressed.

It was a windy day, dry and irritable with clouds whipping across the sun and flying around the castle like giant flags. Our skirts and coats flapped as we strolled along Princes Street, arms linked, in a stream of shoppers, soldiers and sailors and what looked like lawyers and bankers, and Marlene lifted her stumpy legs a little higher than usual to flaunt the sheerness of silk on skin. The window displays at Jenners brought us up short. We pressed against the glass, gawked at the pricey elegance of the millinery, the non-Utility summer outfits and footwear, which had 'Not For You' written all over them. The previous week, clothes rationing had been introduced. With a grimace, we tilted back our panama hats. Then, dodging a tram, we ran across the street to the Walter Scott Monument to admire the marble statue of Maida the deerhound, comparing it with the one outside Waverley Lodge in Kelso.

Jane and Mary were more than true to their word, and we each had two full portions of sausages and mash (war-time rations didn't take into account the appetite of adolescent girls). All I recall of that meal, though, are the three ladies at a table next to us, talking incessantly between mouthfuls. Wadded-up on one of their forks was a lettuce leaf that, impossibly, seemed to wriggle. I tried to catch Marlene's attention, but she was listening to something Jane was saying. What should I do? Point out to the lady the caterpillar half-drowned in a dollop of mayonnaise? Alert the sisters, at the risk of being found ungrateful? Abruptly the fork disappeared, then reappeared. Too late. The lettuce was gone.

'Waxworks – admission 3d' announced a battered board on the pavement near the top of Leith Walk. 'Remember my present,' Marlene said, grabbing my elbow. We still had over an hour to kill and I had a bob and a few pennies left in my purse (I'd bought us some chocolate, Edinburgh Rock and cigarettes on the black market, and a peacock-blue scarf for my mother). So I followed Marlene through the pend, across a cobbled yard and into a ramshackle warehouse. We didn't see any other visitors.

They weren't ordinary waxworks. The Chinese torture chamber made my stomach curdle – some of the victims had empty eye sockets, with the bloodied muscles and nerve ends sticking out. But Marlene soon had me touch the gouged-out eyeballs, segments of fingers and toes without nails, even the porridgy brain tissue. The more gruesome the exhibits, the wilder our giggles spiralling down the metal staircase.

The prospect of coming face to face with 'Dr Buck Ruxton's Furniture', however, as advertised on a tatty sign outside one of the rooms, was frightening. Perhaps this was because we knew people who knew people who had known Ruxton's murdered wife and the murdered maid.

Marlene and I didn't walk into the room – we tiptoed in. We stood and stared at the sofa, stood and stared at the chairs, the table, the sideboard, the chest of drawers, the wardrobe, the double bed. The wood surfaces were chipped, marked with cigarette burns, spillages and ingrained dirt, the velvet upholstery had been worn to a greasy sheen and the bed sheets were flaccid and rumpled – as if the unshaven attendant from downstairs had set up home here. Shuddering, I pictured the mutilated heads and body parts floating down the steep gully at Devil's Beef Tub, wrapped in sodden newspaper like dead birds' wings. For a long moment I gazed at the badly scarred and stained table. Then I prodded Marlene and whispered, 'Was this perhaps where he –?

'– chopped them up, you mean?' she said in a loud voice, maybe to give herself courage.

I shuddered again. Hugged myself.

She laughed disdainfully, went straight up to the table, leant forward and sniffed, 'Aye, that smells of blood all right . . . ' Another laugh, a little more strident now. 'Want to bet? We can ask the man afterwards.' She glanced round at me, but I only hugged myself tighter and she turned back to the table. Tracing a finger down a particularly deep groove on one side, she muttered, 'Must be from a knife. A carving knife . . . '

I backed away, towards the door. I'd had enough of Buck Ruxton, enough of the torture and pain on show, enough of the whole ghastly place. Next thing, a large hairy hand closed over my mouth and I was pulled out into the corridor. Marlene was still peering at the table. 'Or an axe, perhaps,' I heard her say. I struggled with my attacker, the unkempt attendant. But he was too strong. Lifted me as if I was a featherweight and carried me to the end of the corridor, slammed me up against the wall and started grinding his groin into my buttocks.

Where the hell was Marlene? My face and body were being pounded against raw brick and mortar. For an instant I had a vision of my old dolls, blinded, disembowelled, amputated. That's when I bit the man. Hard. I tasted tobacco, blood. He cried out and cursed, loosening his grip.

'Marlene, where are you?' I screamed as I dashed past the Buck Ruxton room, down the staircase.

She was out in the cobbled yard by the pend, smoking a Du Maurier, trembling. 'I was going to get help,' she said, 'cross my heart.' She was almost in tears.

7

When I look up, he's right in front of me. The Hawk. Hovering in the street outside the bakery window, ogling the trayfuls of plump sponge cakes, powder-pale doughnuts and dimpled sticky buns. Ogling them with predatory eyes. I think of the man's boots, *clomp-clomp*ing along the park. And Yoyo, tied up beneath the window . . .

Seconds later my packet of coconut-and-raspberry-jam tarts explodes on the shop floor. Someone sniggers, over by the sandwich stand.

'I'm so sorry, Mrs Compton,' I manage to stammer, feeling my cheeks go beetroot-red. I stop myself from rushing to the door to check on Yoyo, and begin to stoop towards the mess I've made, one hand on the counter for support. My legs are suddenly jittery.

'Let me do that, dear,' Mrs Compton says kindly. Then she adds with a laugh, 'If only those eligible young men knew what an effect they have on us women of a certain age, eh?' And, still laughing, she opens a cupboard and produces a small yellow brush and matching dustpan. 'I'll put the pieces in a doggie bag for Yoyo, shall I? I'm sure he won't be averse to the odd bit of fluff.'

I thank her with a rather old-wifie cackle. The Hawk, I'm relieved to see, has vanished. His breath has left a faint blur of condensation on the windowpane, which evaporates as I cast a glance round the other customers. They've all been watching me: the two jowly bloodhounds in jeans and logoed sweatshirts drooling over the sandwiches; the group of sleek-coated, impeccably groomed greyhounds and Afghans ready to streak off to the lecture halls across the park; the elegant Chihuahua leaning on a stick. To hell with them! But I'm quaking inside, and my cheeks are hot to the touch.

On my way home the word 'eligible' won't leave me in peace. I shake my head in time to my swaying steps to get rid of it and narrowly miss banging into a lamppost. Poor Yoyo almost ends up strangled by the lead. The Hawk 'eligible'? The last thing I'll ever need is a man, least of all the Hawk. A dog's quite enough.

~

Marlene left school a few weeks after our trip to Edinburgh, just before the start of the summer holidays. Jane had married a solicitor and Marlene inherited her job at the Royal British Hotel, doing bookkeeping – her other sister, Mary, must have drummed the basics into her as numbers had never been Marlene's forte.

For a while I was all adrift. I felt angry and betrayed. Envious. So envious I bit my pillows at night. But my bust was finally begin-ning to develop, and with it my interest in soldiers.

Isobel Goody-Two-Shoes insisted on developing my intellect instead, and every afternoon throughout that autumn, winter and spring she dragged me off to the library (perhaps my mother was in cahoots with her, trading extra ration coupons for chaperoning services). I never did do any homework there. My peritonitis had destroyed what little ambition I'd once had, and I amused myself by pinching monkey nuts from the librarian, looking at newspapers and magazines, and drawing caricatures of the reading public in true chalk-on-the-yard-wall tradition. Sadly, Pete the plumber-and-slater cartoonist was no longer around to appreciate my doodlings: like my brother Hamish, he had become a dead war hero.

In the summer, Audrey got married to an officer in the Royal

Marines, the wedding being a small, hushed affair due to our recent loss. Soon afterwards my mother suggested I start an apprenticeship with her sister, Auntie Jenny, who owned a classy dressmaker's in Galashiels – a safe distance, in her opinion, from the chivalrous Polish soldiers now stationed in our town. (What she didn't realise was that the Poles had long since reached Gala and that the reason my aunt was so eager to have me live with her was because her former lodger-apprentice had moved out and she couldn't bear to have any 'army folk' billeted in her spinsterish household.) My father intended to keep me in Kelso, hoping I'd attract a prospective son-in-law with a flair for plumbing, to succeed him in the family business. 'She's your daughter, not a piece of bait!' protested my mother. 'I don't want to lose all my bairns to the Forces!' As for me, I didn't much mind one way or another; the idea of planning for the future seemed futile and distasteful, ridiculous even.

My mother won, of course, and I spent over a year in Gala at Charters's Couture Clothes. A miserable year. I roomed with Auntie Jenny above the shop. For lunch, the main meal of the day, I was expected to go to the same café she patronised, though she never once asked me to join her. My weekly funds of three-and-six (four shillings of my wages I had to hand over to my mother) barely covered this expense and, apart from the 3oz sweetie ration, I couldn't afford any extras. Not, that is, until I decided to live solely on bread and soup – which at least got my weight down – and gave up half my lunch hour to sweep the shop floors and pick up the pins (with a magnet) for an additional one-and-six. Every other Friday evening I took the bus home, the fare paid by my father.

Auntie Jenny, who before the war had been in the habit of travel-ling to Paris in order to buy the latest *haute couture* for her more fashion-conscious clients, now stayed put and designed her own collections. She had to comply with the Utility regulations, which resulted in most of her daywear – dresses, suits and jackets – being of a distinctly military colour and style: shorter, straighter and

more severe, with thin seams and shallow hems, no fancy belts or
trimmings, no unnecessary pleats, pockets or buttons, and made of
fabrics that had the mean scratchiness of uniforms. My aunt's real
gift lay in leisure and evening wear: her pre-Utility gowns and the
few 'general' garments free from rationing were worthy of queens.
But people had become thrifty, and her best *créations* rarely left
the showroom. If they did, 'for trial on approval', they were either
returned the following morning or not at all, courtesy of my aunt's
haphazard ticketing system.

I loved the pictures. My father always rounded up my bus fare
to allow for it. The second year of my apprenticeship had just
started when the Apollo re-ran *Gone with the Wind*. Auntie Jenny
was away for a couple of nights so I went to see it – for the sixth
time since its release four years earlier.

I ended up in a seat surrounded by Polish soldiers from the 24th
Lancers. They kept edging closer in the flickering dark, offering
precious sweets I couldn't resist and polite apologies if they happened
to brush against my shoulders, arms or legs . . . As I stood smoking
and joking with them during the first interval, one of Auntie Jenny's
dressmakers, a war widow, appeared and pointedly invited me to
sit with her and her elderly mother.

Afterwards I walked home alone. Walked along the moonlit,
blacked-out streets of the town, murmuring to myself, 'You should
be kissed, and often – and by someone who knows how.' The
trees sighed in accompaniment to Brett's words and from a window
drifted liquid laughter, a man and a woman's.

Back at Auntie Jenny's house, I didn't go up to the flat immediately. I felt hot and restless, wide awake. I couldn't forget the film's
love scenes. Couldn't forget the soldiers' wandering hands, their
intent, smiling eyes. Prowling round the showroom, the stockroom,
the alterations room, carefully avoiding the austerity of wartime
textures, I fondled unsellable flounces and ruffles. I stroked furs
with poor animal faces, traced the tiny, vein-like irregularities
of raw silk. I kissed velvet smoother than skin, feathers more
insubstantial than stardust. Finally I rushed upstairs to fetch my

aunt's wind-up gramophone and the Edith Piaf 78s she'd brought
back from Paris.

Changing took several minutes. The dress had a *décolletage*
and was made of black tulle with pink crepe de Chine underneath.
It was very glitzy and, despite my soup lunches, a very tight fit.
When I tilted the large oval gilt mirror for full effect, someone
glamorous and adorable gazed back at me, her eyes lustrous with
passion. I watched my reflection seize one of the shop manikins
and try out some dance steps. '*Non, je ne regrette rien*,' Piaf
sang in her husky, seductive voice, guiding me across the floor
of an imaginary ball room until I began to glide and spin and
whirl all of my own.

Suddenly the shop bell rang. I was so dizzy I just waltzed over
to the door, unlocked it without thinking, and flung it open.

The air-raid warden gulped. Glanced from the naked manikin in
my arm to my extravagant cleavage, back again to the manikin,
and said hurriedly, 'Sorry, Miss. Lights.' Then scuttled off into the
darkness as if he had witnessed a crime.

I laughed, intoxicated by my own dare-devilry. 'Night-night,' I
called after him. And to the manikin I said, 'Frankly, my dear, I
don't give a damn!'

Having shut and re-locked the door, I adjusted the heavy
curtains on the showroom bay windows. The Piaf *chanson* had
finished, and the gramophone slowing to a halt was like someone
breathing their last.

Now to get the dress off.

I pulled. I strained. I twisted. The fabric stuck to me like glue.
I held in my stomach, pulled again. Tugged. Not an inch. Welded
to my skin. Try as I might, I couldn't slip or cajole, couldn't rip or
swear the blasted thing off. I had to sleep in it.

Next morning, Auntie Jenny's three dressmakers unpicked the
beautiful tulle and crepe de Chine stitch by stitch off my sweating
body. Their needles pricked me every so often, but I did my
damnedest not to wince.

As a punishment, I was relegated to taking out the linings of fur coats – foosty old fur coats that stank to high heaven because they couldn't be washed. I had to tidy up fabric scraps, to thread endless supplies of needles, to sew up loose ends. I had to dust the dingy corners in the alterations room. And, most demeaning of all, after sweeping the floors at night, I had to unsnarl by hand hundreds of threads that had snagged on the nails in the floorboards.

I was saved by a cat. One lunchtime as I was staring out of the steamy café window at the dreich late-autumn mist, spooning up dishwater masquerading as cock-a-leekie, a woman's shrieks pierced the clatter of eating: 'Oh! Oh! Oh!'

Auntie Jenny was seated at her customary table in a niche at the back – and frolicking on her lap was a kitten, a sleek, honey-coloured wee thing that was aiming playful swipes at her silver-and-onyx pendant. My aunt was trying to shoo it off while dabbing a napkin at her throat, where the claws had nicked her skin.

The café owner came running and the whole establishment went quiet. She was a woman with black fuzz down the bridge of her nose. 'I'm terribly sorry, Miss Charters,' she said and grabbed the kitten, dangling it by its hindlegs. 'It's a stray. Creeps in through the yard door. I'll get rid of it.' The animal threw itself to and fro, yowling.

When I went down to the toilets in the basement afterwards, I found the kitten lying at the bottom of the stairs. Its neck had been broken. I knelt on the ground and wept. I wiped the blood from its face with my handkerchief, then stroked the gleaming little body, which felt just like one of my aunt's furs back at the shop, silky soft. I wept harder. Wept for the kitten and wept for myself, my unhappiness welling up inside me in warm, bitter waves.

That evening I couldn't eat any of Auntie Jenny's supper of potato pancakes and boiled eggs (from the hens she kept in her scruffy back yard as a private contribution to the war effort). At breakfast I left my plate untouched and during my lunch hour I stayed in the alterations room, where I had a cup of tea all by myself. For the next few days I barely ate and my aunt grew more and more worried, offering me thick, golden honey on toast, eggs scrambled with real milk, even her chocolate ration – which I rejected with secret regret. Poor Auntie Jenny. She had no idea what was up with me and I never told her.

Home for the fortnightly weekend with my parents, I snuffled a lot and burst into tears at the slightest provocation. By Sunday lunchtime the constant weeping had worn my mother to a frazzle and she promised I wouldn't have to go back. The following weekend my parents drove over to Gala for my clothes and things. They returned with a large silver cardboard box. Swathed in the perfumed tissue paper inside was a lace-trimmed, shimmery blue dress with a matching hat. I wrote my aunt a thank-you letter, but I didn't visit her again until many years later. By then she was old and frail and half-blind, unable to thread her own needle.

~

Perhaps tears would do the trick with Rachel, too, and she'd leave me alone. I could pretend to blubber the instant I hear her voice on the telephone or, failing that, the instant she sets foot in my vestibule. After all, it isn't easy to cope with people in distress. Old people especially. There's something pathetic about our tears – pathetic and vaguely obscene. Tinker Jeanie was an awful sight the last time we met, at Randall's funeral down at Newcastleton. Everybody had been crying, of course, but she was ancient and so close to death herself that her grief seemed wrong somehow, like a mockery.

And yet – why should we OAPs be any different from younger people? Why should we have a 'special wisdom' or be expected to see beyond the fleshliness of existence? And why, indeed, should our 'special wisdom' be proportionate to the years we've piled up? Sometimes I myself feel as silly as when I was a girl, and if I could get away with it, I'd happily stick my tongue out at the world and give the finger to car drivers who consider old ladies and their dogs fair game. In revenge I press every button for the green man I pass on my way, with a flourish and a smirk so blatant they'll all assume I'm in my dotage, poor dear.

Knowing Rachel, though, a sudden gush of tears might not have the desired effect; she'd probably insist on sounding the depths of my apparent despair, in the name of researching Scottish Calvinism – and what would I do then?

My parents didn't blame me for walking out on my apprenticeship; my father, in truth, was rather pleased to have me working in his office. Miss Hunter showed me how to use the typewriter and my index fingers soon managed. Tolerably.

Spring arrived with full-blown skies of blue and marbled white, and I tingled with life. I made up excuses, flimsy, outrageous, anything that would allow me to sneak away. There were always off-duty soldiers hanging about the Square. One of them was a young Pole called Stans, an engineer from Warsaw. Tall, dark and handsome just like the stranger of my dreams, he charmed me with his heel-clicking, bowing and hand-kissing, with his broken English and his Scottish lilt. Together we'd go down to the Tweed and lie in the sun, and he'd ask if he could feel my 'heart'.

When the real kissing started, I had to force myself not to clamp my teeth shut. His tongue in my mouth was like a slug choking me and I did my best to concentrate on the grass blades twitching against my cheeks, on the lazy *slap-slap-slap* of the water and the birds flustering in the cool of the trees, seeking relief from the unseasonable heat.

Then, one day, I glimpsed Leering Lenny in the bushes behind us. I pushed Stans away almost violently and sat up. He grinned, said something very fast in Polish and tried to pull me back down again. But I wrenched myself free.

Frowning, he watched as I straightened my blouse and put on the red-lacquered straw hat. 'Daft lassie, what is the matter, please?' he whispered.

I hesitated. For a moment my eyes skimmed along the river-bank, past the clumps of hazels and stunted willows, up towards the little island where Marlene and I had hoped to gather 'the juiciest dandelions in the world'. And all of a sudden I could see that ghost of a little boat again, being carried downstream – away from me. I felt sad then, my childhood gone forever in that vision of a single Sunday shoe with a drooping lisle stocking for a sail. I jumped to my feet and ran. Ran and ran.

There had been no news from Marlene in months, except for a recent postcard depicting the rear view of a kilted Scotsman in high winds, with a scrawled message on the back: 'Having fun! Lots of generous American and Canadian servicemen up here with stocks of nylons, chocolates, gum and cigarettes . . . What's keeping you, Lizzie?'

I was dying to hear more. Out on an errand for my father one hot May afternoon a couple of weeks before D-Day, I went in search of Mrs Gray. I found her at the steamie and invited her for a cup of coffee.

As we crossed the drying green with its sloping lines of starched white sheets streaming in the breeze, I felt like careering up and down between them, arms outstretched, mouth yelling open, the way I used to with Marlene.

The riverside gardens of the Ravenscraig Hotel were busy. Scattered groups of the Home Guard and soldiers were playing cards, women were resting from their shopping, swapping ration coupons or simply having a blether, and children were chasing each other round the terraced lawns with their borders of red tulips, panting and yapping like mad wee dogs.

I offered Mrs Gray a cigarette – one of my exclusive ones, with pink rose petals for filters.

'Ta, Lizzie. They're pretty.' She smiled at me, holding out a match. Her hand was scoured raw and swollen from the steamie, and she looked tired.

After ordering our coffees plus a brandy for her, I couldn't wait any longer. 'How's Marlene?' I blurted out.

Mrs Gray gave a shrug. 'Oh, she's as grand as she'll ever be.' We smoked in silence for a while. When the waitress had brought our things, Mrs Gray added, 'Had a miscarriage, Mary tells me. She's more trouble than all my other girls put together. Why on earth I went and made her, I don't know.' Shaking her head, she reached for the glass of brandy and poured half into her coffee.

Marlene pregnant! Then un-pregnant! The clouds seemed to whirl in and out of the sky. But the Tweed continued to flow downstream, the swallows dipped and rose above the water, the cattle plodded across the field beyond, the children shouted, Mrs Gray sipped her coffee, and the tulips nodded, red as blood.

8

Janice acted peculiar last night, not at all like her usual placid self.

'How's Murray?' I said after she'd settled on the sofa, vodka in hand.

'Fine.' She patted Yoyo and fed him a peanut.

'And how are my favourite granddaughters?'

'Fine, fine.' She emptied a handful of nuts into her mouth, sluiced them down with the vodka, then spluttered, 'Why are you doing this?'

'Doing what, Janice?'

'Asking me endless questions.'

'But they're your family, for goodness' sake!'

Her mobile phone rang. She pounced on it and went out into the hall. Returning, she gestured towards the wreath. 'And what's that?' As if it hadn't been sitting there all along.

'A wreath.' I could be monosyllabic too.

She snorted. 'I can see that – but why candles? Not some new sort of psychic game, is it?'

The supernatural has never appealed to her. No doubt that's why she chose to become a theatre nurse: you can't get any more intimate with the physical world than in the operating room. Janice loves fixing broken bodies and clams up as soon as there's talk of souls. No astral bodies for her. During an argument once she accused me of 'intercourse with the dead'.

~

Call me superstitious, but I do believe in fortune telling. My parents and I were having supper one stormy October evening when the doorbell chimed. The wind was tearing the leaves off the trees by the fistful and the rainwater had flooded drainpipes and gutters, its gurgle so fierce our cats refused to go outside.

Someone must have given her a lift because she didn't look bedraggled at all. And yet I hardly recognised her at first, dressed up to the nines in a red wool suit, a small brown felt hat with a red ribbon bow, short brown leather gloves and matching outsize bag, and a cream blouse whose nifty little pearl buttons shot a bolt of envy through me before I could curve my lips into a smile. Her lipstick and rouge were the same shade as her suit. The foreign servicemen must be very generous indeed, I couldn't help thinking. Thankfully, her legs (sheathed in real nylons rather than painted with Silktona liquid silk or, more attractive to the neighbourhood pooches, with greasy Oxo gravy) were as thick as ever. She was chewing gum.

'Who is it?' shouted my father from the kitchen. 'Shut the door, Lizzie, there's one hell of a draught.'

I asked Marlene to come in. 'We're having rabbit pie,' I said as I led her through, adding before I could stop myself, 'Humble country fare.'

She blew a bubble and popped it noisily. 'Don't be so stuffy, Lizzie.' Then she pulled off her gloves and boxed me in the ribs to make me giggle.

At the sight of Marlene my parents gaped. I expected them to send her away, out into the rain and wind, like they used to when we were children. Instead they beamed and she beamed back. My father offered her his chair, then went to find another for himself. I trembled with disappointment. No need to defend her – she was welcome. All I could do was sit down and, after she'd removed her hat, admire the glossy, near-natural blonde of her curls as she leant forward to open her bag.

She'd brought us gifts: two packets of Passing Clouds for my mother, cigars for my father, stockings, gossamer-grey, far too elegant, for me (but maybe it wasn't so much the stockings I felt unworthy of).

'Some pie, dear?' My mother hovered with an extra plate and cup.

'Yes, please, Mrs McLean. It smells heavenly.' Marlene smiled up at her.

Heavenly!

'It's from Boyle's down the road,' replied my mother, who never took undue credit.

One of our cats had begun winding itself round Marlene's legs with ingratiating miaows. She drew it up on to her lap, then proposed telling us our fortunes. 'I have the gift, you see. Someone in the city showed me.'

Later in my room she whispered the name to me. I flinched at the mention of it. And wished she'd announced it publicly, *Tinker Jeanie*, in the middle of our kitchen. Because my father would have stomped off to the plumber's shop in a huff and, gifts or no gifts, my mother would have sent her packing there and then – half-full teacup and half-eaten pie notwithstanding – out into the storm. Meanwhile I could have come to Marlene's rescue, her devoted, ever-faithful servant. Yes, that's what I wanted most in those days. I wanted to *serve* her. It gave me a purpose in life.

'You're going on a journey,' Marlene had said to my father in the time-honoured style of fortune telling. She knew, of course, that he frequently drove up to Edinburgh.

To my mother she said, 'You're going towards changes. Big changes.' Yes, I'd seen the signs myself, noticed the denser hair growth on her upper lip and chin, the suddenly moist brow and red face.

And to me she said, 'You're going away. To a white house.' I had shrugged. So what? Our town was full of white houses.

It seemed we were all *going* somewhere – a true travelling family. What we didn't know, though, was that my father would be dead within the week, from a massive brain haemorrhage, that my mother would sell up and flit, and that I would end up at a place in Edinburgh called Ivory House.

~

Another cup of tea, then off to the park. Yoyo's lying across the kitchen doorway like a draught excluder, one eye slanted open against the jamb to monitor me. If the cup clinks too loudly, his head pops up, both eyes wide and shiny.

'Sleep, Yoyo. Sleepy-sleep.'

To be honest I never felt quite as sad when my parents or my husband died as when I lost one of my dogs. I got along with Alan; I loved my parents. But the grief went deepest with the animals. You start to remember all the times you'd been less than understanding with them. Mungo, my first Norfolk terrier pup, used to drive me round the bend. Out we'd go for a walk and I'd tell him to have a pee, stopping at every lamppost, wall, tree, bush, letter box, litter bin. No luck. He wasn't an exhibitionist. Back home he'd make a beeline for the coffee table in the front room . . . The worst was if Alan had already come in from the shop and was sitting with his evening paper and whisky, tapping a foot while I was crouched with deodoriser and sponge, spraying and rubbing the rug instead of chopping the veg and frying the meat for his supper.

The floor needs washed; it looks filthy. Doreen the Great Dane mustn't have bothered the last few times. Probably thought my eyesight was as poor as my deliberately selective hearing. For the past three weeks now she has hoovered around a crumpled-up paper tissue under my bed. Not that I planted it there – I'd never stoop that low, not literally, at any rate. Reminds me of Alan fumbling for his handkerchief under the pillow one night and pulling out a still-slimy bone instead. 'You taught that dog of yours to hide his bone under my pillow,' he whined – as if I could ever have trained Mungo to do such a clever thing. Not the least obstacle would have been the two mattresses piled on Alan's bed as he was too mean to give away the old one.

'And terriers have awful short legs, don't they, Yoyo?'

Here he is now: melting-chocolate eyes, sugar-pink tongue rolled like a wafer between his teeth, front paws on my knees – the picture of innocence. Calculated innocence. For next to my cup lies Mrs Compton's doggie bag with the broken coconut tarts from the morning.

The telephone interrupts our staring contest just as I'm beginning to relent.

It's my daughter Ruth, calling from Bahrain. Rather upset. Janice had left a bossy message on her answering machine. Something like: Why aren't you picking up, Ruthie? School's out and you should be home by now. Where are you?

'Never occurs to Janice I might be going to the gym or the souk after teaching. I rang her back, and she got all high and mighty with me. Why aren't I married yet, do I shirk the responsibility, time to grow up, Ruthie. Always "Ruthie". Though I've told her I hate it. On and on till I hung up. What in God's name is bugging her, Mum?'

With a groan I sink deeper into my chair. Yoyo has slumped into angry-dog position, his backside to me. I haven't the faintest idea what's up with her sister, I admit to Ruth. All Janice would tell me was that she'd been out on a hike with a nurse pal at the weekend, someone who'd recently got divorced. And when I put my gin down and prompted, 'What's wrong, Janice? Are you and Murray okay?' she merely said she was 'knackered'.

I promise Ruth to stay in touch. Then gaze at the potted amaryllis plant on the hearthstone; its three red flowers are so exquisitely waxy-looking and tranquil I wish for a moment I was one of them.

~

Ivory House, in Edinburgh's fashionable West End, was an exclusive establishment. A few months after my father died, my mother and the minister (of all people!) decided that I should embark on a career in 'superior hairdressing' and she paid the vast sum of £59, in advance, for an intensive ten-week training course.

'It'll always keep you in food and clothes, Lizzie, and put a roof over your head,' she said. 'You won't ever have to be dependent on a man. See how it went with your poor father? He just died and left me.' And she began to sniffle.

'Don't greet, Mother. He's still with you in spirit.' I had the sense to swallow the obvious: *And you've got the business; that plumber and slater's guarantees you a lifetime of leisure.* In fact, she would cash it in within the year.

Hairdressing at Ivory House seemed as good, or bad, as dress-making at Charters's. I still had to do the sweeping – after every single customer – but the floor was linoleum, with no nails sticking up.

Ivory House gave itself airs. It sold its famous RETEP combs (Mr Lambert the owner's first name spelled backwards) and its very own brand of creams and lotions for cuticles, hands, eyelids, eyebrows, the neck, bust, stretch marks, thighs, feet, whatever. Not many people knew, apart from us girls signed up for the hairdressing-plus course, that in the mysterious Lambert Laboratories on the top floor stood nothing but a few big jars from a wholesale manufacturing chemist's in Leith, and that the same stuff went into different little pots with different labels. This was one of Jimmy the porter's jobs.

Jimmy Nicoll was a quiet, fat wee man who had killed his own father. For some reason he'd been imprisoned rather than hanged. Maybe because his father had got Jimmy's wife pregnant while Jimmy was doing his patriotic duty, fighting in the Great War.

Ivory House also advertised electrolysis. 'Hair cut or electro-cuted' was Marlene's phrase. Friday afternoons we girls on the course donned clean overalls to meet Madame Lambert up in the Laboratories. She was French, a tall, elegant lady always dressed in black, with high heels and hair piled in coils on her head. Jimmy, in yet another role, served as her guinea pig. He never shaved on Fridays to provide us with plenty of stubble and looked as if he had ringworm, his face covered in circular patches of baldness – living testimony to the effectiveness of electrolysis *à la* Ivory House.

'A *real* murderer?' Marlene exclaimed when I told her about Jimmy. '*Real* evil flesh and blood?'

'He's very nice, actually,' I said. 'If you like them dumpy.'

She gave a shiver, then ran a slow, wet tongue over her lips. 'Evil flesh and blood,' she repeated. Her blue eyes widened. 'Evil flesh and blood, Lizzie! Much better than a roomful of stupid old furniture that could have belonged to anybody!' Too late she clapped a hand over her mouth, darting me a sideways glance. Wondering, perhaps for the first time in four years, whether I'd forgiven her for abandoning me at the waxworks that afternoon.

I lit a cigarette.

'Lizzie, pleeeease. Let's take him out for lunch. And I'll ask him what it was like.'

'What *what* was like?' I heard myself say, rather testily.

'Well,' she paused, 'being in the jail. Killing his own father. Bloody sure I couldn't do a thing like that.' Then she cried, 'Of course I couldn't! My father's already dead. Isn't he, Lizzie?' I flushed with guilt, reminded of the primrose bank again. Flicking ash, Marlene added coolly, 'You can fix a date for lunch and I'll deal with Jimmy. I might even ask how his wife felt after he'd done the deed. Want to bet on it?'

I didn't say anything.

She nodded. 'Okay, *my* treat. Will soup and seafood suit you?'

'No soup,' I told her. 'It makes me think of dead kittens.'

~

I spot Miss Chinese Crested stepping lightly along the pavement up ahead, almost skipping like a girl. She's too close to the kerb and holding her sky-blue umbrella at a dangerous tilt. The slightest gust of wind and she'll be blown straight off, parachuted into the air. God forbid! I'm about to call out a warning when she veers off across the cobbled street. But there's no car in sight and I'm not her chaperone. As I stand looking after her, Yoyo gives a hearty tug and I'm pulled round the corner.

~

Jimmy beamed. 'Lunch! That's mighty generous of you, Miss Lizzie.' He hadn't shaved very carefully that morning and the bald patches on his face shone in the sharp February sunlight.

As arranged with Marlene, I suggested the White Cockade Oyster Bar in Rose Street, where Jimmy and I settled at a table by the window. A few minutes later Marlene came into view, sauntering along, a cigarette in her mouth. She slowed down to adjust her new polka-dot headscarf, then gave a sudden flail of a wave and shouted, 'Why, Lizzie, old girl!' Hamming it up, but Jimmy didn't appear to notice.

'My friend Marlene Gray – Jimmy Nicoll, porter at Ivory House.'

'How do you do?' Jimmy smiled so broadly his double chin wobbled.

Marlene just stared at him. I kick-started her in the shin and she said quickly, 'How do you do? Lizzie's told me about the electrolysis. Must be sore as hell.'

Jimmy shrugged. 'You get used to it after a bit.' He rubbed his jaw and, at the feel of the bristles, grinned apologetically. Then he went back to slurping his mussels.

'And how're you, Lizzie? I haven't seen you in ages.' She was overdoing it as usual. I kicked her again. 'Ou-ll right. I'd better catch that waiter.'

She ordered a bowl of cullen skink for herself, another beer for Jimmy, and tea for 'the ladies'. *Ladies* indeed. I half-choked on a piece of fish.

'It's got a name too, hasn't it? Something-*cide*.' Marlene laid down her soup spoon and looked at Jimmy. She'd managed to bend our chit-chat round to her subject by referring to a murder case she'd allegedly read about in the newspaper 'a few weeks back', in which a young man had killed his mother.

For a moment Jimmy seemed puzzled. Then his face grew red, even his ears, and his scalp went pink under the grey hair. His eyes slid past mine as he hung his head. I could guess his thoughts: So she is one of them too, offering free lunch for a freak show. All at once, without glancing up, he said in a low, weary monotone, 'Yes, I did kill my father – *patricide*'s the word. Yes, I was put in prison. Yes, I did lose the wife. Everyone knows. Isn't that enough for you? What else do you want?' Reaching into his pocket, he brought out some coins, placed them on the table, and was gone.

Marlene gaped.

I sat gazing at the money on the bile-green Formica.

'I'm sorry, Lizzie. I didn't mean to . . .'

There was a fluttering in my belly, like butterfly wings, then gradually the fluttering became a beating, not of wings anymore but of fists battering and battering to be let out.

9

A metallic creak, then a thud on the vestibule floor.

'Fetch mail, Yoyo. Go fetch.'

A bundle of Christmas cards and a silvery padded envelope, a little saliva-stained.

'Good boy.' He crunches up his Fox's mint without the least show of appreciation. Might as well give him a crust of toast again. 'Bad teeth,' the vet remarked last month. 'You don't feed him sweets, Mrs Fairbairn, do you?' Short of lying, what could I say? So I simply smiled and pretended to be hard of hearing.

The photographs on the front-room mantelpiece are beginning to be outnumbered by Christmas cards – what a comfort to know that people still care . . . Nothing from Cousin Peggy, though. I'm getting worried about her – it's two years since I had her card. With any luck, she'll be safely dead rather than sadly forgotten in some nursing home, napkined and nappied, drugged out of her mind. They put down horses, dogs and cats, even rats – so why not us? I for one wouldn't want to linger. I've made a living will, and Janice, I trust, will do the right thing when the time comes.

The padded envelope is postmarked London. Must be a present from John, my eldest. Because I haven't sent away for anything in months. Never again, I swore after the last couple of disasters, though it's hard to resist all those coupons and Aladdin's-cave catalogues. I complained, of course. Returned the two pairs of airmen's trousers, slim fit, navy blue, and finally received the navy-blue skirt designed for the mature lady. My order from House of Health was trickier. The tea tree oil for my toenails arrived fine, cocooned in bubble wrap, but the invoiced gingko (so I won't go gaga) revealed itself as prostate pills. I had a good giggle as I flushed them down the toilet.

I'll save John's present for later. Better try Murray at his office now to find out what's up with Janice. My granddaughters weren't much help when I telephoned last night. 'Mummy's working and Daddy's out,' Donna-of-the-unspoiled-complexion informed me, amidst the chatter of a TV sitcom.

'Your mother is having a bit of a stressful time at the hospital, isn't she?'

'Mhm. Sophie says it's Mummy's midlife crisis and once it's past, she's past it!' Donna tittered while the TV audience laughed uproari-ously. In the background I could hear Sophie-the-sophisticated shout, 'God, you're such a blab, Donna!'

If the girls had their suspicions, they certainly weren't going to confide in a nosy old bag like me. Not yet, at any rate. But children (and dogs) are the barometers of a home: give them a gentle tap and they'll indicate, one way or another, what the weather is like around them. Midlife crisis? I don't think so.

Murray's in a meeting. 'No message, thank you,' I croak in reply to the smooth, clipped tones of his secretary.

Meetings. Conferences. Late lunches. Sometimes I wonder when these high-powered people buckle down to the real work.

Best for last. Yes, the padded envelope is from John. A small, flat radio in blue or rather, as Sophie would have it, *electric* blue. With earphones and batteries. Perfect for carrying around in the pocket of my new-Scottish-wool elephant skin. Who knows, perhaps I'll soon be hopping and bopping along the streets with nothing but music on my mind – the Mad Granny from Marchmont!

'Dear Mum,' the card reads,
'I hope you are well. As we don't do Xmas here, this isn't
a Xmas present. Just one of my gadgets. You might like
it for your walks with Yoyo. The radio's digital, so you'll be
able to get all sorts of other stations besides the usual FM
and AM. The leaflet will tell you. Have fun!
Love from us all, John x
PS. Ann is away interviewing some big shot, but the two
Ks say hello.'

Why can't he call the twins by their names? 'Kilobytes, kelvins,
Köchels, take your pick,' he says. To me, Kit and Kim is simpler.
    Whatever, I'll knit my son an extra pair of socks as a non-
Christmas thank you. That'll be my good deed for the day.
    'Smart thing, this radio, eh Yoyo? Have a sniff.' He licks it tenta-
tively, then sneezes twice. Not tested on animals, it seems . . . I
cackle to myself and he stalks off, looking offended.
    Now where's that booklet? Operating instructions. In with the
batteries and let's have a wee blast. The earphones feel a bit funny,
like outsize cottonbuds, but I can get used to them. Preferable to a
hearing aid any day. BBC World Service, BBC 1 Xtra, BBC 6 Music,
BBC Asian, Sunrise, Heart, Kiss, Kerrang!, Planet Rock . . . Lots
of pop music.
    Suddenly, I picture myself on one of the benches on Bruntsfield
Links, tuned and plugged in, stamping my feet, waiting for Yoyo the
scavenger, stamping my brogued feet, watching the odd pitch-and-
putter on the course, stamping my brogued feet in time to Planet
Rock. And why not? The strong beat is bound to get the circulation
going and the imaginary keek at the drummer's sweaty six-pack
chest won't do me any harm either. Greyhound Girls and Afghans
will stride by and I'll smile and stamp my feet a little harder: just
another batty old biddy.

~

My hairdressing-plus course was into its sixth week when Marlene casually announced one evening that she'd handed in her notice at the Royal British Hotel.

'I want a change. Go up north like Mary. She says Pitlochry's lovely.'

No wonder Marlene was keen to get away – her mother had moved to Edinburgh and they'd been living together for the past few months. Mrs Gray's younger sister, a private nurse and canny spinster, had bought a house in Hatton Place, across from the Sick Kids Hospital, to retire to eventually. For the present, Mrs Gray had charge of it. She took in lodgers again and constantly nagged her daughter for running around with RAF officers and American or Canadian airmen. 'These boys die like flies, lass. Don't end up a poor widow woman like me.'

We were sitting on Marlene's bed, an electric heater roasting our legs and chests, our backs frozen to the wall, smoking and drinking coffee. For a moment I stared at the burn marks on the sugar-pink candlewick spread, then I stubbed out my cigarette in the glass ashtray with its embossed 'Royal' crest (a 'farewell souvenir', according to Marlene) and drained my lukewarm coffee. I slid off the bed. 'Better be off. Work tomorrow.'

She looked at me in silence, nostrils flared, her long face angled upwards like a horse wanting to be patted. 'Well, what do you think?'

'Why not?' I said with a shrug and started towards the door.

'Tell you what, Lizzie. Let's both go to Stella's Agency in George Street for a hotel job. Much more exciting than that dreary hairdressing of yours. You said you could type, didn't you?'

I turned on the threshold. 'Bye, Marlene. You're a lucky girl.'

Walking back to my digs, I wondered why I'd said that. Surely I wasn't jealous of her?

Jealous or not, I wasn't able to sleep that night. Shampoos and greasy, dandruff-speckled scalps, orange sticks and festering toenail cuticles, mops and buckets – I was fed up with the lot of them. And, closer to the truth, ever since that lunch date at the White Cockade Oyster Bar, I'd felt guilty. Not that Jimmy had ever reproached me. He remained helpful, even smiled occasionally, but his former friendliness had glazed over into mere politeness and whenever I practised electrolysis on him now, it felt as if I was torturing a man who'd already had more than his fair share of suffering.

Next day during my lunch break I went to George Street – with Marlene. The Stella woman beamed at us. 'As it happens, I need two office workers at the Highland House Hotel in Inverness. One experienced, one inexperienced. Starting Monday.'

I looked at Marlene and she looked at me. And I knew I was going. To hell with the £59 my mother had paid for my course – I was only young once!

We took the early train up on Saturday and arrived in good time to explore the town and eye up the local talent. It was the end of March and the last snow had melted into the bright crocus colours of spring; bird cries wove in and out of the sky's shot silk.

By now Marlene had told me about her pregnancy and subsequent miscarriage. 'Not the back row, Lizzie,' she'd said one Saturday as we were ushered into the stalls of the Playhouse in Edinburgh. 'It's where danger lurks. Full of lecherous GIs with hard-ons, waiting for a skirt.' I'd stared at her in the dusty, uncertain cinema light – my Marlene-of-the-primrose-bank, gone forever. She began to laugh. 'Believe it or not, but that's exactly what happened to me. I went into the Salon a virgin and came out a woman.' I winced and she gave me a wink before elaborating in a whisper, 'Blood and every-thing all over my stocking tops, Lizzie. It smelt something foul' – like a mother bent on disenchanting her child who happily believes in storks. 'I thanked God and the devil for losing that baby. I'd already made arrangements through a friend of Mary's –'

'I'm glad, too,' I cut in. 'Wouldn't be much fun wheeling a pram about.'

'Prince Charming's just round the corner, anyway.' Marlene showed me her open palm. 'See?'

I sent my mother a postcard: 'I'm in Inverness now. Love,

Lizzie.' A message from a wretchedly ungrateful brat. I still cringe at the memory of it.

We had been at the Highland House Hotel for nearly two weeks, working shifts, though Marlene sometimes helped me with the book-keeping. The job was a lot easier than I'd feared. The manager was rumoured to have friends with clout, from poachers to the provost, which must have been true, judging by the well-stocked bar (despite the war rationing) and the plentiful supply of salmon and venison. Because he was always busy 'liaising', he mostly left us to our own devices.

It was a Friday night, nearly half past eleven, and Marlene and I were closing up the office behind Reception. 'Hang on,' she said suddenly and went back inside. Through the glass partition I saw her stride over to the panel with the room keys and slip one off its hook.

'You're not upgrading your sleeping quarters, are you?' I called out. I started to lift the counter flap into the hallway, but she stopped me and, putting a finger to her lips, pulled me along to the narrow door at the far end of Reception. 'How about a nightcap for the girls?' She grinned as she fitted the key into the lock. 'Don't look so worried, Lizzie, it's after hours. Your reputation is quite safe.'

The blackout curtains had been drawn, and in the darkness the coal fire glowed like an enormous, watchful eye. Then Marlene clicked on the light and it was just an ordinary fire in an ordinary grate once more. We were standing behind the waist-high curve of the polished oak bar, surveying our clientele: tables, stools and banquettes upholstered in wine-red velour and, above the oak panel-ling, a prize salmon in a glass case and several stag heads with vacant stares and antlers that jostled the framed photographs of various hunting, shooting and fishing expeditions. On either side of us, a glittering array of bottles, real and mirrored, stretched to infinity.

'Will a 25-year-old single malt do?' Marlene held up a squat bottle with a peat-coloured liquid.

'I'll have a Martini first,' I said boldly, blowing smoke from a Du Maurier.

She laughed and poured a large measure. 'It's on the house, ma'am. Cheers!'

As I swallowed, I had the distinct impression of being glowered at by the stuffed and mounted exhibits and, even worse, by the photographs: hounds exposed slavering jaws, ready to sink their fangs into my flesh; lines of bloodied grouse and pheasants turned their beaks accusingly; fish thrashed and twisted in the water. A grizzly bear reared up on its hindlegs, darkness leaking from a bullet hole in its chest, its pebbly eyes slitted with pain and rage, its front paws raised for one final, vicious attack.

I blinked at Marlene, but she clearly hadn't noticed a thing. She was smoking and studying the bottom of her empty tumbler. She had just reached for the whisky bottle again when footsteps sounded in the hallway outside.

I hastily switched off the light.

Too late.

'Who's there?' shouted Eddie the night porter. He was in Reception, trying to push open the bar door. In a stupid, panicky fluster we shoved our shoulders against it, giggling like mad, to keep it shut. Then we heard the grating of a key, the key we'd so thoughtlessly left outside.

'Quick,' Marlene flipped up the bar flap, 'the public entrance.'

It was locked, too.

'Eddie, please, open up.' We rattled the handle. 'Please, Eddie!'

'You might as well spend the night in there.'

'We'won't do it again, cross my heart,' Marlene gabbled. 'We didn't mean no harm, honest. Just wanted some fun, that's all.'

'Fun . . .' His voice trailed off.

'Aye.'

Eddie chuckled as he put the key back in the lock. 'All right, you can have your fun.' But he didn't open up. He was speaking with slow deliberation now. 'My wee man would like some fun, too.' He paused. 'A bit of fun so as I'll forget, eh?' Another chuckle.

'What kind of fun?'

'*You* know, lasses like you.'

Marlene offered to give him a kiss instead – while I mimed disgust.

Eddie remained adamant.

We both pleaded with him, appealing to his better nature.

'Your choice, lasses.'

'Bugger off then!' Marlene hissed.

'Dirty bastard,' I added, under my breath.

The key was removed. 'Okay. Have it your way. Night-night, lasses. Sweet dreams.' And off he went along the hallway, whistling 'Auld Lang Syne'.

For a moment we wondered whether to break a window or bang on the door to alert one of the guests. 'Too much hassle,' I said, downing the rest of my Martini. Marlene nodded and poured herself another whisky. 'Aye, let's really have some fun!'

~

The telephone rings, waking Yoyo from his slumber under the bookcase. 'Yes?'

'Lizzie, it's Murray here. My secretary told me you phoned?' My son-in-law does his best to sound posh, but the Western-Isle burr in his voice is stubborn, thank God. How come business executives all strive for the same nondescript accent? Just like their suits, neutral and noncommittal, and their clean-shaven faces, as blank as walls.

'An efficient girl. . .' I hesitate, then, skipping the usual pleasantries, blurt, 'It's to do with Janice and –'

'Janice? Why?'

I feel stupid and old. Seeing ghosts. Conjuring up trouble. 'She popped in on Sunday night and seemed awful tense. A mother can tell.' I laugh nervously. 'Even a stepmother.'

He doesn't say anything.

I blunder on. 'Is everything all right between the two of you? I don't mean to pry. . .'

'I get your drift, Lizzie. Don't you fret, we're fine. Janice has been working a lot lately. Also helping a nurse friend of hers who's had personal problems.'

Why doesn't he just say 'divorced' as Janice did? Is it to spare my feelings? I can't help sensing an effort behind his words. Then he inquires after my health. Then after Yoyo. And am I warm enough; is the central heating working okay. His burr is suddenly much stronger and I take solace from that. Silly old meddler, I chide myself, let sleeping dogs lie.

~

I was never in the same meddling league as Marlene, whether with people, life in general or drink. That night, locked in the bar of the Highland House Hotel, we hadn't had more than a couple of pink gins each before she began to experiment. Tartan Tornado was her most lethal concoction, containing whisky, cherry brandy, rum and God knows what else.

There was a wireless in the bar we'd put on earlier, very low, tuned to a short-wave station with dance music and crackles of static. The interference felt comfortable. It washed over us in a rhythm of its own, making us bend and sway, bend and sway. Marlene acted the gentleman. She birled us round faster and faster, until the drinks in our hands glistened through the air in perfect, slow-motion arcs of colour and, for the briefest of moments, I had the illusion of dancing inside a double rainbow. Then I tripped. My head landed on the hearth rug, my arms half on, half off it, my legs sprawled all over the place – and I couldn't have cared less.

At some point during the night I woke up freezing because the fire had gone out, and I wrapped myself in the rug with its coal-dusty smell. From one of the banquettes nearby I heard Marlene snoring. When I teased her about it later, she denied it so vehemently I almost believed her.

First thing next morning we were sacked, though we were told to stay on for the weekend. I was in the office by half past eleven, with a hangover that made me feel gutted alive, supervising the new girl who had started work the previous day. The manager was out somewhere as usual. Suddenly, through the glass partition, I saw Marlene coming down the stairs, rouged and lipsticked – and dressed in my very own coat with the embroidered collar. She was carrying her suitcase. I barged out of the door, clutched the counter. My head was hammering and I was desperate for some Askit powder. 'Where're you off to with my coat?' She often did that, Marlene, just borrowed things, then kept them unless reminded.

'Away. Damned if I wait till Monday.' Snorting, she leant over the counter for the telephone and dialled the number of the local taxi firm. She whiffed of alcohol, a sourish whiff, despite the perfume she'd slapped on.

'If you're going, I'm going too,' I said. 'Hold on!' And I clattered up to my room, sod the headache and the Askit powder, threw all my things into my suitcase, clattered down again, then waved cheerio to the new girl, who stood open-mouthed, stuttering, 'But . . . but . . . I dinna ken . . .'

'You will, soon,' I cried over my shoulder.

At Inverness Station we bought different tickets. I'd made up my mind to return to Edinburgh and finish my hairdressing course – it was the safest bet. Marlene was only travelling as far as Pitlochry, to 'surprise' her sister Mary. Poor, patient Mary. As the train pulled into Aviemore, Marlene asked me to get her a cup of tea from the platform (no buffet cars back then, or mini-bars). Eager to be of service to her, I rushed out with the money . . . and stopped dead in my tracks when I heard someone shout my name, 'Lizzie McLean! What are *you* doing here?'

~

'Yoyo, no! Paws off my knitting. Here, have a digestive.'

It isn't time for a walk yet. And won't be for quite a while by the louring look of those clouds. Squashing the light out of the day before it's even begun. No wonder they invented Christmas. Helps us drag our loads through the darkness. Like trusting old donkeys, we follow the carrot of hope. Then into Lent and better weather, and out comes the stick of fasting. Not for me, though. I would run. Just as I did, decades ago, at Aviemore Station. Ran like a bat out of hell and jumped straight back on that train.

The ribbing is almost done. Reasonably neat-looking.

I'm about to start on the heel when the knocker clunks. 'That's enough barking, Yoyo. Enough!' The postman's been and it's too early for a visit from Miss Chinese Crested.

'Goodness! What are *you* doing here?' I exclaim as I open the front door, a faithful echo of the Highland House Hotel manager, who must have been 'liaising' that day at Aviemore Station.

'Please, can I come in?' And Rachel brushes past me, her long black coat tails floating like wings through the vestibule.

10

Standing in the hall, hands balled into fists, she says, 'Why is this country so damn bigoted, Mrs Fairbairn?'

'Quiet, Yoyo!' What does the girl mean?

'I'm sorry. How rude of me to come barging in like that. . .'

'Not as rude as Marlene sometimes,' I reply, then laugh down into her baffled face. She really is a mere slip of a lass. In blue jeans today and a mauve top, with the silver ring quivering on her lower lip. She is holding out her hand. 'You're very welcome,' I add. 'It's nice to have company.' Then I notice the badly healed scar in the centre of her palm and hurriedly take her coat. 'I'll make us a cup of tea. Just have a seat in the front room and turn on the gas fire if you find it too chilly. See, Yoyo remembers you.' He is sniffing her fancy multicoloured bootlaces, wagging enthusiastically, and she scoops him up, cradling him like a baby, which he hates, and trying to cuddle him, which he hates still more. He is a male, after all – even if they did rob him of his manhood.

When I set down the tray with the tea things, the gas fire is on, a soothing, susurrating presence. Rachel has lit the new candle I stuck into her Advent wreath after that unfortunate conflagration. In its steady light the fresh sprays of fir gleam conspicuously.

'Now then. Milk, no sugar, isn't it?' I smile at her.

'Thanks, Mrs Fairbairn. I hope I'm not disturbing you.'

I bring out my knitting. 'A few dropped stitches so far, nothing serious.'

She blushes, bends down to pat Yoyo.

Out in the hall, the telephone begins to ring. Might be Janice. Or Murray again, having decided to ditch the manager spiel.

It's Isobel. She says her brittle-bright hello and have I slept well, then catches her breath: 'Guess what's on BBC Scotland a week today, Lizzie?' Pausing long enough for me to say that I haven't the slightest idea, she announces triumphantly, '"A Portrait of the Borders, Past and Present!" Isn't it thrilling? *Our* Kelso on TV!' She's only just got the new *Radio Times* and wanted to let me know 'ASAP'. (Like that time she roused me at five in the morning to tell me Princess Diana was dead.) Perhaps we can watch the programme together? she suggests. She's happy to come up to Marchmont. I promise to make a note of it so I won't forget. Won't forget to pick up a stomach bug, that is, one that's contagious. I couldn't bear to see Isobel. Not now that Rachel has prodded all those memories back to life. Not with Marlene ghosting around my head again.

When I say I've got to go because I have a visitor, Isobel is on the scent like a bloodhound. She sounds jealous and I imagine her face droop more than ever as she replaces the receiver in the silence of her empty house. I hunch my shoulders – as if to carry the burden of her disappointment. And the burden of her loneliness. I really can't bear to see her. It's too much. And now I'll have to return to the front room, to Rachel and her disfigured palms.

While she talks about Calvinism and predestination and John Knox, the girl keeps clenching and unclenching her hands. The violence of the gesture makes me check on Yoyo every so often, sitting sentry-style beside her rocking chair – all he is concerned about are the coconut tarts on our plates.

Having unclenched her hands yet again, Rachel has another bite, then breaks off the raspberry jelly in the middle to plop it into her mouth. Yoyo gazes up at her mournfully.

My knitting needles click. I'm not hungry anymore.

Rachel's tongue probes her lip ring for stray crumbs. 'How lovely to have a taste of jam at this time of day,' she sighs.

'I beg your pardon?'

'I'm glad you don't understand, Mrs Fairbairn. Because if you did, you'd be one of them, too.'

'Them?' I stare at her, then at the knitting in my lap.

'Well, bigotry isn't just what I've tried to explain; it goes much further than religion, race or politics. It can seep into anything. It's prejudice with a capital P, intolerance with a capital I. Like people here telling me how the Swiss are stodgy and boring and circumspect, a nation of umbrella lovers. Or like my two Scottish flatmates jeering every time I have jam for breakfast. Either toast, butter and marmalade, they say, or bread and butter. According to them, jam's only allowed in the afternoon, though not on toast.'

All of a sudden she turns on me, a dachshund in attack mode. 'Why are you nodding?'

I hadn't realised I was and pick up my knitting again. 'Oh, it's nothing. A nervous tic that comes with old age.' A minute ago she was talking about Calvinism and the doctrine of the Elect, and now she's getting all het up about prejudice. Either it's me that's a bit muddled or. . .

What does she want?

'I'm sorry.' She leans down to Yoyo, who's finally given up and lies dozing. 'We all carry our own Calvary within us, don't we? May I call you Lizzie?'

'I prefer Mrs Fairbairn, if you don't mind.' I glance at her hands.

Why is she here?

She doesn't speak for a moment, then says softly, 'I lost my gloves.' Her fingers are combing through Yoyo's ragged coat and her eyes are on me, brandy-golden, not at all like Marlene's.

'I lost my gloves,' she repeats. 'Skiing with my mother six years ago. The wind blew them down a slope that was roped off. Mum said she'd get them for me. She was an excellent skier. . .'

I knit furiously.

'But the snow caved in under her. There was a rumble like from inside the mountain, and a cloud of white. The blue sky shattered. Then nothing. Then pain. The grips of my ski sticks rammed into my flesh.'

'Poor, poor you.' I suppress a shudder. 'How terrible to witness it all. . .' The knitting needles scrape against each other as I fumble with the loops.

Rachel has broken up the rest of her tart and is pushing the crumbs around her plate. Yoyo grumbles, then dozes off again.

With a sudden sly smile, she lifts her hands to show me her palms, puckered skin and all. 'Or perhaps it's cigarette burns,' she murmurs.

I knit as fast as I can.

'From a dare, a silly juvenile dare. If you screamed, you were out. Nothing to do with Christian beliefs.' She has a sip of tea and her lip ring tinkles.

I keep knitting. I mustn't stop or John's socks will never get finished. Never. I am sure she's lying, but I wouldn't want to see the soles of her feet. She isn't that mad, is she?

'Maybe they're not burns either,' she continues, observing me closely. 'Maybe I had a cycling accident as a kid, hurtled downhill and went over the handlebars into a heap of gravel. See here? There's a scar at the corner of my eye.' I pretend to be counting my stitches. 'Yes, I was lucky, wasn't I, Mrs Fairbairn?' Her mish-mash accent is much more pronounced.

'Do you think I'm a daftie?' I glare at her. 'Nothing's ever cut and dried – you don't need a PhD for that. And now, if you please, I'd like you to leave.' Placing my knitting on the sofa cushion beside me, I struggle to the vertical. Yoyo, alerted by my angry voice, jumps up with a yawn, then gunshot-shakes himself awake. He wants his walk: we are two hours behind schedule already.

Rachel seems crestfallen. Good. She is pointing to the Advent wreath. 'One of the reasons why I wanted to come to Scotland during Advent season was to repent and pray and learn to be patient. To be reconciled with my mother in the country of her birth. And to get to know Marlene – through you.' Her brown wire hair has straggled over her face, hiding her eyes. A dachshund in retreat.

'Fine,' I reply. 'But I've had enough for the moment.'

Twenty minutes later I'm on my favourite park bench, wrapped in my elephant skin, watching Yoyo happily scrounge along a mouldy trail of pigeon bread as if it was a buffet dinner. I feel miserable. All that guilt and anger – why did Rachel have to dump it on me? Why should her relationship with Catriona have anything to do with me and Marlene? I wasn't responsible for Marlene's death, or how she led her life. If anyone fashioned her own fortune, it was Marlene, gypsy warnings or not. And a tainted birth can be overcome, can't it?

So. Out with the new digital radio and earphones. Get myself plugged in. Planet Rock. Easy.

The music booms into my head and sets it ringing, sets my whole body vibrating, and rattles my skeleton until the beat jerks my little toe. *Boom, boom, boom.* That drummer must be a strong young lad. Muscles like ropes, not the soft flabbiness of old age. *Boom, boom.* Then I begin to hear cannon shots. Mortars. Anti-aircraft fire. A man's high-pitched voice screams briefly and is drowned out by a wailing guitar, which in turn gets carpet-bombed by a renewed salvo from the drums. *Boom, boom, boom.* The sounds of destruction visited upon the living.

~

The war ended, but I didn't feel like celebrating. With so many million killed and maimed, it didn't seem right. I mourned my brother Hamish's death all over again, glorifying him in my mind.

I had managed to lie my way back into Ivory House – I'd been ill for that fortnight, I told them. After I 'graduated', I no longer had to wash the floors and was at last getting paid for my work.

Mr Lambert the owner fancied himself as something of a dandy. He was short and spare, with a twirled-up moustache and pencil-thin eyebrows that looked as if Madame had used her electrolysis skills on him. His walking stick was an affectation and had an ivory handle to go with the name of the salon. He reminded me of Charlie Chaplin, minus bowler hat and charm. Whenever he tried his flattery on me, offering me a sample pot of Ivory House Cuticle Cream 'for your lovely, almond-shaped nails, Miss McLean' or a free RETEP comb 'to keep your hair as bright as your eyes', I did a curtsey, bowing my head so he wouldn't see me grimace. Still, I was relieved he didn't compliment me on my 'pearly teeth', which were false and a recent birthday present from my mother, who swore by dentures (and had magnanimously forgiven me my Inverness escapade).

It always remained a mystery to me why Madame had married Mr Lambert. She was at least a foot taller than him, not counting her towering hair and high heels, and they hardly ever exchanged a word. When they did, it was invariably in French and sounded rather like hissing and spitting.

Marlene telephoned once, in early summer, to say how jolly Pitlochry was and to inform me that 'Mary the gold digger' had got lucky, having nabbed the owner of a hotel. 'That's where I'm calling from, Lizzie. VIP treatment for the future sis-in-law. Wedding's in August. I just hope Prince Charming, wherever he is, has leapt on his charger. Because it'll be me catching that bridal bouquet, or I'll be damned!'

Snatching, more like, I thought to myself, then said, 'You'd better not tempt fate.'

Mr Lambert, who'd been eavesdropping while fussing with the display of creams, shampoos and perfumes behind the reception desk, clucked and shook his head. Bemoaning his own marriage, maybe.

'Don't be morose, Lizzie,' Marlene snapped. 'You don't want to become an old maid with only a hairdressing bag to keep you company. Go out dancing. Go to the pictures. Have some fun, for God's sake!'

On returning from Pitlochry that September, Marlene brought me a slice of her sister's wedding cake 'for luck' and a soft white angora sweater 'for looks'. It clung to my chest rather nicely and she crooned in a husky Dietrich imitation, 'And now for love, Lizzie!'

She had got herself a job at the North British Station Hotel, working as a switchboard operator and helping out as a chamber maid, and had persuaded her mother to let her stay in Hatton Place again.

The first time she mentioned Randall was obliquely: 'Mother has three new lodgers, students from the Dick Vet and the Art College. Nice dashing fellows.'

It was mid-November and we were standing just inside the door of Ivory House. I glanced at the passers-by. Some of the men were wearing silk cravats and grey top hats, which was what I called dashing.

Marlene's gaze had followed mine and, with one hand, she quickly rearranged a dislodged curl on her forehead. She was dressed in an elegant new fake-fur coat and matching cloche bonnet. I fingered them appraisingly.

'From Binns,' she said. 'Sank all my dosh into it. Marcus the furriers will be next!' She laughed, then continued, 'Anyway, we're all going to the Lyceum on Saturday to see *Rebecca*, and the Art College chap wants a partner. You'd be perfect, Lizzie.'

Odd man out for odd girl out.

I studied my nails. 'Why *Rebecca*?'

'Why not? What's wrong with *Rebecca*?'

They needed filing and polishing. 'Where do we meet?'

'Come over to my mum's. We'll get a cab.'

'A bit extravagant.' I looked up at her.

Marlene grinned. 'Some people don't have to count their pennies. And, Lizzie, better put on your glad rags. We'll be having dinner at the North British afterwards.'

She took off her bonnet and stepped in front of a mirror to inspect her hair. That's when Mr Lambert came prancing up. Raising his thin eyebrows, he said, '*Mademoiselle* wants her lovely curls reset? *S'il vous plaît*. . .' And he motioned towards the cubicles at the back.

Marlene half-smirked, half-smiled at him. 'Another time, *merci, monsieur. Adieu.*' She replaced her bonnet, waved to me, and was gone.

~

With Planet Rock off, the scene around me has an eerie silent-film quality. Bruntsfield Links seem to cringe under the windblown flotsam of cans, crisp packets, soggy paper tissues, sweetie wrappers. The trees move their black branches without a single creak. Greyhounds and Afghans pass by soundlessly, mouths distorted as they laugh, talk, yawn. Pigeons scatter in noiseless flight, chased by Yoyo. It's only when I have my first mint and hear those undignified suckings that I remember I'm still wearing the earphones.

As I amble homewards on the short-cropped grass, I suddenly glimpse Rachel. Black coat tails whipping out behind her, she is running across the bottom of the Links towards Melville Drive, pursued by someone that looks oddly familiar. Drainpipe jeans, puffed-up jacket. The Hawk?

11

Today it's time to light the Second Advent candle. But I won't. I'm feeling mild all right. Have been since Rachel gate-crashed my home on Wednesday: miffed, irritated, lost and defiant.

To hell with the lass and her stories. To hell with my imaginings.

A sharp few tugs and the moon and winter frost are shut away behind embroidered roses. I settle myself into the rocking chair, press the TV remote. There's a brilliance to the screen that hurts my eyes. An eruption of noise that hurts my ears. Snow and ice splintered by sunlight. Shades of blue. And hundreds of thousands of penguins braying like love-sick donkeys. Preening each other round the eyes as if they were kissing.

'The origin of the word *penguin* is disputed,' the documentary narrator is saying. 'Some maintain that it derives from Welsh *pen gwyn*, meaning "white head", others that it comes from Latin *pinguis*, for "fat".'

Welsh. I can't help thinking of Dafydd.

Penguins waving flippers. Pecking. Fighting. Squabbling over the pebbles and stones that make up their nests. Penguins incubating eggs. Chicks squawking and shrieking. Being fed, bill to bill. Penguins living dangerously as they dive through ice holes, past lurking sharks, leopard seals and killer whales to forage for food.

Yoyo seems spellbound. Shaggy head at a quizzical angle, he

stares over at the TV from the shadows of the bookcase. Does he take the funny creatures for humans? Men in evening dress, perhaps?

That outing to the Lyceum and the North British was the beginning of me and Dafydd. He was a third-year student of architecture at the Art College and Heriot-Watt – and the only man to ever make me glow inside. Almost four years we went out together. . .

When I told my mother I'd had to send him packing, but couldn't bear it, just couldn't, she offered me a hot toddy, and I burst out crying. 'There now, lass,' she said eventually. 'Save your tears. At least you'll always be able to provide for yourself.'

Marlene begged to differ. 'You bloody muckle fool! How could you be so stupid? He was a good, solid man; he'd have built you a palace!' She puffed savagely on her cigarette. We were at Fullers' in Princes Street and several ladies at nearby tables were craning their necks.

'I'd have lived in a hovel with him if. . .' I paused. The tearoom's square little windowpanes blinked at me and for a moment I thought it was raining outside. 'He'll be back, Marlene, you'll see.' I put my cup down hard. Then, with what I hoped was a self-assured smile, I bit into the white icing on my walnut cake and added, 'He loves me.' Of course he did. Despite my big body and my by now too-big bust. And he always would. Despite my false teeth. Always. Despite my words of anger.

'Don't speak with your mouth full, Lizzie. Grow up, for heaven's sake. You're a muckle fool.'

I forced myself to laugh in her face.

Dafydd might be dead for all I know. Dead and buried in his best tweeds in some Welsh cemetery under a tombstone that's already gathering moss.

Marlene came round to my digs after our disagreement at Fullers', spouting clichés about star-crossed lovers until I screamed at her. By then, of course, she had moved on, and up, in the world.

The penguin male never abandons his beloved; he stays with

her forever – that's what I used to believe. But the narrator is saying it's a myth: penguins aren't faithful for life.

The sixth time I met Dafydd, he asked me to close my eyes. His fingers felt hot under the collar of my blouse, and then there was something else, something smooth and cool. The necklace was beautiful: large, oval amber beads with gold-plated links.

'This isn't just to ward off sneezes, Lizzie,' he whispered (I'd once told him that amber was supposed to protect from colds), and the smile in his eyes rippled right through me . . .

Do penguins gaze into each other's eyes during courtship? Do they see the reflections of themselves? Of the other penguins in the colony? Of the sky, the ice and snow? Or can they see beyond it all? Can they see into the soul? Can they see the future?

And so I ended up with grocer Alan. The kind of man who begins every book by reading its last page first, calling it an act of liberation. An anxious man, continually trying to avert the unknown. A man taking refuge in the certainty of his faith until that, too, failed him.

Just like I failed him. His previous life seemed fenced off and clearly marked NO TRESPASSING and I stolidly accepted it. The mental breakdown he'd suffered after ICI assigned him to their weapons programme was never discussed. Nor was his decision to quit the chemical industry and join his brother Neil in the family grocery business. Nor even the death of his first wife.

I like the chinstrap penguins best. With the narrow band of black feathers running under their chins, they look as if they're trying to keep black helmets on. Or keep in place a fixed grin – their only defence against a hostile world.

~

Marlene and Randall soon became an item. In secret. Randall was one of Mrs Gray's three 'dashing' student lodgers and in his second year at the Dick Vet School. He had the black hair, dark eyes and cinnamon skin which hint at mixed blood somewhere along the line. Yet, despite his exotic looks, he always reminded me of a well-trained Border collie: quick, obedient, and faithful. He was of good gentleman-farming and race-horse-breeding stock from down Hermitage near Hawick. Too good really for Marlene. Not that this deterred her: 'So his family owns several farms? All the better for me, Lizzie!' Why shouldn't she become county if she gave it her best shot?

Although she'd had her eye on Randall from the start, she never missed an opportunity to tease him about the sort of woman his family expected him to marry. 'A fat-bellied wife you'll have. County-fed and county-bred,' she'd drawl in exaggerated RP and laugh out loud. She was insanely jealous of potential rivals, which, incredibly, seemed to include me. Even when she knew I'd lost my heart to Dafydd, who like Randall boarded at her mother's, she never allowed me into the house if only Randall was home. Instead, usually with a reference to the weather, she made me wait for her on the doorstep: 'After all, it's not raining/sleeting/ snowing too badly and your coat is already damp/wet/covered in sleet/snow. . .'

Mrs Gray had been prudent enough to set up a post-office account for each of her five daughters. After Marlene received hers, on her nineteenth birthday, she smiled at me in triumph. 'Just wait and see, Lizzie.'

Two weeks later, towards the end of February, she invited me round for a cup of tea with her mother and Randall. I had barely greeted everyone and sat down when she stubbed out her half-smoked cigarette and stood up, all business now. 'Wait and see,' she repeated as she went off, shutting the door behind her.

Several minutes passed before the door re-opened. I gawped, hastily stuffed a biscuit into my mouth to stop my giggles. Marlene was dressed in an olive-green tweed jacket, cream-coloured jodh-purs, both tailored to perfection, and reddish riding boots. Whip in hand, she wiggled her hips. She pirouetted. She posed. Lifted each foot to show off the tooled leather. 'Russet-gold.' Right foot. 'Custom-made.' Left foot. She pirouetted again. And again. Then nonchalantly flicked the whip against one of her boots. As if on cue, her mother's Jack Russell rushed over to her and, ears pricked up, sat to heel.

Mrs Gray had grown pale during the performance. 'What the devil. . .?'

Randall gasped. A gasp of amazement, admiration, pure delight. 'I didn't know you could ride, Marlene!'

'Oh yes, of course I can,' she replied loftily, parading around the room in her beautiful boots. 'I had lessons from when I was seven.' She rolled her eyes at her mother and me, defying us to contradict her.

I didn't say anything.

Mrs Gray stared at the teapot, cheeks aflame.

Randall's eyes shone as he addressed Marlene: 'Some of us Dick Vet students have been given permission to exercise the army horses every so often – thanks to my father's connections. Saturdays, usually. Would you care to join us?'

'I'd love to, Randall.' Marlene twirled her whip in what was no doubt a mirror-rehearsed gesture. She strutted around some more, tweaking her lapels, polishing the shiny buttons with a white handkerchief and patting down her jodhpurs. I took another biscuit and studied the paisley rug. I knew Marlene had never sat on a horse in her life.

When I called in on her after the weekend, there was no sign of the jodhpurs, tweed jacket and riding boots.

'How did you get on then?' I asked.

'What do you think?'

'Well, no idea. I wasn't there.'

'You've seen horses before, haven't you?' she said, pouting. 'They pitch and roll like bloody ships. Make you seasick. And this one was no exception. When it was supposed to go into a gallop, it bucked like hell.'

'You fell off.' I tried not to grin.

She didn't answer. Just looked sour.

A few days later she was sporting a navy blue blazer, again

specially tailored to hug her bust, with the insignia KA on the breast pocket.

Tongue-in-cheek, I said, 'And would this be for "Kelso Academy"?' We'd both been at Kelso High School.

'Don't be a fool,' she snapped. 'There's no such place in Kelso, and you know it. The K is for "Kilmarnock". It's a private establishment.'

'Och aye?'

When the door opened and Randall came in, she ran up to him with her most dazzling smile. He smiled back, gazing at her longingly, and his fingers slid down the sleeve of her blazer, to touch her hand. 'Suits you to a T,' he said. And even from a distance it was evident that he'd been leashed up – body and soul.

~

Suits you to a T. That's what Tom McManus from Saunderson's came out with the other morning, glancing up from a slab of pork after slicing off two juicy chops for me. I blushed and mumbled a thank you, then stroked my elephant skin self-consciously. Only to realise that his glance and words hadn't been meant for me. He was complimenting one of those Greyhound Girls. Six foot tall, ash-blonde and porcelain-skinned, she was leaning against the wall to my right in what looked like a discoloured old army greatcoat – though I must admit it did hang on her rather gracefully. To give him his due, Tom did throw in a couple of bones for Yoyo. A pleasant enough fellow, courteous towards the elderly and the infirm, if perhaps a little too flirtatious with the young.

All at once I feel hungry. Might just fry myself the second chop, with some onion on the side. And Yoyo will get a bit, too. My appetite isn't what it used to be; easily satisfied these days, in every respect. What else? Potatoes, rice, pasta? No macaroni ever again, not since the time – pre-shop cat – I saw Neil sorting through the dry goods drawer where we kept it loose, picking and blowing out the mouse dirt.

As I potter around the kitchen, remembering to water the amaryllis, I find myself humming a song. Maybe it's to bolster up my spirits, like whistling in the dark.

But there's no need for that. 'No need, eh, Yoyo? Here's your bone.'

The telephone rings just as I'm dishing out my meal. The frying pan clatters into the sink, a spurt of Bisto hits the windowpane, but my feet refuse to move.

I smile to myself: it's suppertime, right enough.

I switch on the digital radio and turn up the volume. BBC World Service: '. . . just detected another mass grave. It appears that . . .' Not a topic for whetting the appetite. BBC Radio 4: '. . . Lindisfarne. You have sixty seconds. Starting NOW.' That'll do. Nothing like a good laugh to get the digestive juices flowing.

The ringing has stopped. And I resist the urge to dial 1471.

12

When I woke this morning, they seemed all here with me for a moment, caught in the web of my dreams: the three men of my adult life – Dafydd, Alan and Willie.

Poor Alan. Not quite the 'model groceryman' as portrayed in *Law's Grocer's Manual*. Always busy, yes (even wearing the requisite tie), but never cheerful, let alone bulgingly fat with bonhomie. A stickler for correctness, serious, lean and lantern-jawed, that was my Alan. After what he'd been through, his marriage to me and the progress of his children were of no particular interest to him. Life had dwindled to nothing but a tiring round of early alarm-clock wakenings in the cold, two hot cups of tea while shaving, the drive to the wholesalers, then to the shop, a hurried slice of toast and more tea in the stockroom with Neil, then the fixed grin for the customers, lunch at home with no grin, fixed or otherwise; then back to the counter and the grin, frazzled at the edges by closing time and completely worn off once he entered the house; a read through the *Scotsman*, a nip of whisky, then supper, TV and bed.

Meanwhile, I'd mend and wash and cook and clean. I'd weigh out fruit, vegetables and dry goods (except for the macaroni – I usually said we'd run out). I'd ring up totals, chat and smile, and sweep away the mouse poison Alan put down; I couldn't bear to think of the poor wee buggers putrefying alive. In my heart, though, I was far away, invisibly swaying in Dafydd's arms at the Silver Slipper in Morningside, the gold watch he'd given me nestling in the pocket of my shop coat or apron, carefully folded inside a cambric handkerchief.

Willie, of course, was different. Not the least bit interested in me as a woman. But he hailed from Kelso like myself and would tell me stories about Floors Castle, where he'd worked as a landscape gardener before being appointed head gardener at the Astley Ainslie Hospital round the corner from here. He and his best friend Julian, heir to a biscuit empire, were good customers at our shop.

Alan called Willie a pansy behind his back. Yet acted like a jealous wee boy if he found Willie sitting in our front room, sharing a cup of tea with me and swapping childhood memories.

I *loved* Willie. I could laugh with him. Unlike Alan, he didn't weigh my every word on gold scales. But then, weighing things was perhaps the prerogative (a clever word from last Saturday's crossword) of a grocer and doctor of chemistry.

They're both dead now . . . dust to dust, ashes to ashes . . . And maybe Dafydd is, too. Feelings of love, hate or sheer, tired indifference don't matter any longer.

Or do they?

~

Marlene loathed compromises. She'd raise the stakes so the rewards would be all the higher. The rewards − as well as the losses.

One sultry May evening barely three months after her attempts at horse-riding, we were crossing the Meadows, walking in the pink drifts of blossoms from the Japanese cherry trees, when she suddenly kicked up a whole flurry of them and asked would I be free in a couple of days, on Wednesday afternoon.

'Free for what?'

'To go to Chambers Street.'

'The museum?'

'Christ, Lizzie, don't be so thick! No, not the museum. The registry office!'

'Is it really Randall?' I couldn't quite keep the disbelief out of my voice.

'Aye. Who else?' She laughed, kicked up more blossoms like a scattering of wedding confetti.

'Then why Chambers Street?' I persisted. 'Why not the registry office in East Preston Street? Isn't Newington your registration district?'

'Ten out of ten, Lizzie! But East Preston Street is too close to home. Safer to say we're both residents at the North British. One of the perks of working there.'

She laughed again, pleased with herself. Then, stepping into a patch of sunlight, she pulled a small jewellery box from her handbag and with a theatrical flourish clicked it open. There were flashes of white fire.

'My engagement ring!' She slipped it on. 'I won't be able to wear it, though – not till Randall qualifies in three years' time. Same for the wedding ring. Randall says his parents would cut his allowance if they got wind of the marriage . . .' She turned her hand this way and that, gazing at the diamonds longingly.

'It's gorgeous!' My throat felt dry and tight. 'Congratulations!' For a moment my own hand went up to the amber necklace from Dafydd. The gold watch would be next, I reassured myself. Then the engagement ring. Then –

'But don't you go blabbing to anybody, Lizzie. Not even Dafydd. It's a secret. Cross my heart. Remember?'

Still, I wasn't entirely convinced she had snared Randall. Not until I saw the banns displayed in the glass case.

The Saturday after her clandestine marriage I went to meet Marlene at the North British. She was just coming off her shift on the switchboard.

'Hello, Mrs Eliott,' I whispered, then pointed to her unadorned ring finger. 'Must have been one hell of a wedding night!'

'Button it, Lizzie.' She shot a sideways glance at a bald, fat, middle-aged man in a pale green silk shirt and a dove-grey linen suit, seated in the lobby.

She introduced him as 'George'.

George seemed to be a regular at the North British, spending every other weekend there. He was a vet like Randall would be one day, with his own practice in Selkirk, and looked old enough to be Marlene's father. He spoke in a falsetto I instinctively distrusted, but Marlene hung on his every word as he detailed his plans for their evening together: a posh meal at the St Giles' Grill in the High Street, followed by a variety show at the Empire Theatre, then dancing at the Havana in Princes Street.

Before she went off with him, Marlene took me aside and said, 'George is very nice. Wants me to have a good time, that's all. He says I'm "like a breath of spring".'

I grinned. 'Och aye? And he's Father Christmas?'

'Don't be daft, Lizzie. Randall's away down at Hermitage visiting his parents – and I can't go, obviously. So. . .'

'. . .Christmas it is,' I finished for her.

'Don't tell Randall, please, Lizzie. Please?' Her voice was wheedling now and I felt truly sorry for her new husband.

'Lizzie? I'll be able to get your mother another cocker spaniel. Didn't you say she'd just lost hers? George knows someone with a litter.'

When my mother finally heard about the marriage, three-and-a-half years after the fact, she said with feeling, 'If ever a person's tied a millstone round his neck, it's poor Randall. Isobel would have made him a far better wife. That lass knows how to comport herself.' Then she began to stroke the silky black ears of her three-and-a-half-year-old cocker spaniel, and I felt a stab of guilt.

Perhaps my mother wasn't that wrong, after all. Isobel had stayed on in Kelso, was employed as a secretary to a well-respected solicitor and going out with a young geologist 'destined to rise in the world'. Meaning he was a fine, God-fearing man who would one day become a church elder.

~

The phone rings.

'Lizzie! Where were you last night at seven?'

There are all sorts of names for this kind of thing: ESP, telepathy, premonition or, my personal favourite, talk of the devil.

'And good morning to you, too, Isobel. Am I a murder suspect or what?' I cackle as I unwrap a glacier mint.

She gives one of her too-shrill laughs. 'I'm sorry, Lizzie, but why didn't you ring me back? I was waiting.' A pause. 'I was worried about you. How have you been? Any news?'

I pull a face and Yoyo turns his head away with an offended grunt. I know Isobel is dying to hear more about Rachel. 'Not really,' I say. It's true. Not even a cheep from that girl, and no more sightings of her or the Hawk either . . . 'Only Doreen the cleaner missing the screwed-up paper tissue under my bed, for the third time now.'

'What on earth are you talking about, Lizzie?' Her voice see-saws from annoyance to mild concern. Concern for my mental health, that is.

'Oh, nothing.' The Great Dane had been more energetic than usual with my old hoover on Saturday and accidentally ripped out the cable after crash-racing the poor thing round the flat. She was apologetic, of course. Took it over to Wallace's for repair and promised to return it before nightfall, but never did. Maybe her boyfriend has run off to Newcastle again?

'So what about the Borders programme on Wednesday? Shall I come to your house? You did write it down, Lizzie, didn't you?'

I'm racked by a sudden coughing fit. How could I have forgotten? Wheezing a little, I tell her she's very welcome and my sore throat will surely be past the infectious stage by then.

She'll call again, she says, to see if I've improved (here's hoping) and in the meantime to remember and drink at least three cups of camomile tea a day.

Camomile tea!

~

At some point before Christmas that year Marlene said to me, 'Don't you think we should go and visit the poor?'

The poor? What in God's name did she mean? Having graduated from being a Miss Gray of Nowhere to a Mrs Eliott of Good County Stock, she had taken on airs, though no one knew she was married.

'What poor?'

'I'll show you,' Marlene said.

She led me to Hunter Square, behind the Tron, then up and up the stairs inside a tenement which smelt of stale cooking and swarmed with children – boys playing cards, girls with their scraps and rag dolls. On the top landing, the door to the right stood open. Marlene walked in.

There were more children, a shaggy little dog, several kittens, and an odd-looking couple, the man afflicted with some kind of eczema that blotched his face, the woman with a twitch that pulled at her eyelids every few seconds.

On seeing Marlene, they fell over themselves, 'Oh, Mrs Eliott, how are you? And how is Mr Eliott?'

That's when it dawned on me: they were the witnesses Marlene had raked up so the banns could be published without drawing too much attention.

Preening herself, Lady Marlene swanned around the kitchen, which also served as sitting room and bedroom. For an instant I pictured her dressed in gold brocade, a basket on her arm with embroidered cast-offs and sugary dainties for the ragged, emaciated serfs. These people were poor all right. Yet they made us sit down on their least rickety chairs, closest to the fire, spread a fresh tablecloth and offered us tea and homemade pancakes. And we, who had come empty-handed, ate their pancakes, drank their tea, and left.

~

The sun has almost gone, but it's a fine, crisp afternoon, windless, the grass and trees stiff with rime – as if the Meadows were holding their breath. I get out a nappy bag. Dog fouling's become a crime, it seems. Only last month an unmarked van pulled up as Yoyo had a leg cocked against some overhanging greenery near Margiotta's. When we moved on, doors slammed and two dog wardens – their job title advertised on their sweatshirts – began parting the branches with gloved fingers. . .

Up ahead a fire engine is blocking the path and there are several police cars stationed in the field with the rescue heli pad, strobe lights turning the frozen ground a ghostly blue. Laughter is floating in the dusk. Afghans, greyhounds, dog owners and other park-folk rubbernecks have gathered, shuffling and blowing on their hands, waiting. Hoping for some real-life drama, a glimpse of someone else's pain. I spot Mrs McPherson talking with a fireman while Skippy keeps nudging a tennis ball up to her feet. Somebody's waving from the far side of the field and I wave back, just as a scream of sirens announces the ambulance.

'Yoyo, here!'

I feel safer once I'm stepping it out along the privet hedge of the tennis courts, having put some distance between me and that ominous scene.

The faint drone in the air suddenly gets deafening as the helicopter banks overhead, making the bare white treetops sway and bow in grief over the injured stranger landing in their midst. For a moment I see Marlene again, that Sunday evening in September half a lifetime ago, out of her mind with distress. I round the corner of the tennis courts, curiously agitated, and –

'Whoa! Watch out!'

Clumpy black boots. Black drainpipe jeans. Dark green jacket. I avoid the hawkish face.

'Sorry.' I stagger back. 'I'm awful sorry.'

He is bolting down a sub roll with thick flaps of raw-looking meat. I back away further still, imagine bones, fur and feathers disgorged on the grass. Then I see Yoyo trotting towards blind Charlie Blues and his Lab, Alice, on the path opposite and I hobble-rush off without a backward glance.

'Hello, Mr Blues. How are you?' Panting, I let my eyes rest on his peaceful features.

'Who's that?' he croaks, but then he smiles and the wrinkles around his dead eyes deepen. 'Aye, I know the voice. Mrs Fairbairn! Have you seen the helicopter?'

'Oh yes.' I shoo Yoyo away from Alice's rear. 'It's silver, with an orange stripe along the side.' I slip the dogs a treat from my bag and offer Charlie a mint.

'Thank you.' His fingernails are ridged like ancient snowdrifts. 'And the rotors are big, aren't they? Big enough to raze down the trees near the pad.' He pinballs the mint around his mouth as he goes on to describe the new colour he has selected for his front door: 'A bright red. Sort of scarlet-like.'

I admire the man. He hasn't allowed himself to feel betrayed by life. Hasn't given up on the visible world that for him must have shrunk to smells and noises, to the height of kerbstones, the strength of Alice's body jerking on the lead, and the clean, strong sweetness of a single glacier mint.

Rather than traipse round the park in the twilight and risk another encounter with the Hawk, I head over to Melville Drive and what used to be my digs on Gladstone Terrace. No litter here for my scavenger, merely a straight line of frost-webbed maples and garden walls, perfect for leg-cockings.

Dogs see with their nostrils, I read somewhere. They can track footsteps along a pavement, their sensitivity to a certain particle in our sweat – some sort of rancid acid that penetrates shoe soles – millions of times greater than man's. I don't envy them . . .

But what does sight really mean? Eyesight? Seeing the visible? What about second sight or foresight? Isn't that already touching on the invisible, the not yet visible?

The not yet visible. I giggle to myself as I remember one of Marlene's stories. Tiny was a chambermaid at the North British, a big fat girl with a bonnie face, who wanted to be thin. So she started taking slimming pills – 'Sylph' they were called – and she shed maybe a pound a week. Then she returned to her room one evening to find she'd left the box uncovered in the sun and, in place of the pills, a writhing mass of maggots. Tiny remained a big fat girl ever after.

My giggles have grown louder, full of an old woman's careless merriment, and Yoyo regards me dubiously, one leg lifted against the tyre of a shiny yellow sports car.

By the time we reach Marchmont, most of the Christmas lights in the gardens and windows have come on, their sparkle easily outdoing the soft, woolly glow of the streetlamps.

Back home, the mortice is unlocked – I must have forgotten again. But when I swing open the door, Yoyo skitters past me, growling and barking.

Someone's in there.

13

Not burglars; they'd have used a crowbar, surely. I shamble into the house. Yoyo's been barking at the stubby shape of the hoover in the shadows of the hall. So Doreen did remember to fetch it back from Wallace's, trusty Great Dane.

'Hi Mum.' Janice has appeared from the front room. No kissing, no touching: that's us all right. 'Thought I'd let myself in. The hoover was stashed in the garden, with a bin bag over it. You're not getting barmy, are you?' She sounds her normal self, thank God.

I smile. 'Hello, Janice.' A titter is stifled in the room behind her. 'Did you bring the girls?'

'See for yourself.' She steps aside.

Rachel is stooped over the coffee table, lighting two of the Advent candles. The teapot is under the cosy, next to three mugs – one for me, presumably.

'Mrs Fairbairn, hello again. Lucky I met Janice here.' She straightens up and blows out the match.

Lucky for whom? I wonder as I nod a greeting.

'Didn't you see me wave?' she asks. 'In the park? I was hoping to join you and Yoyo, but then I lost you.'

'You still managed to arrive here before me,' I remark drily. 'How about some biscuits to go with your tea? Yoyo, stop that scrabbling. No rancid whiffs on my shoes; I've washed my feet.'

Janice follows me into the kitchen. 'You remind me of a cat
sometimes, Mum: quick of tongue and sharp of claw.'

'One of my previous incarnations, no doubt.' I grin and chuck
half a Milky Way into Yoyo's bowl. 'Before I was promoted to the
much superior level of a dog.'

She frowns.

Butter. Cheese. Biscuit tin. 'Tell me, Janice, why on earth did
you invite Rachel in?'

Her frown deepens. 'Why on earth not? She seems nice enough.'

'*Seems* being the operative word,' I mutter as I smear
Philadelphia cheese on my favourite oatcakes.

Janice lifts down the plates. 'I've brought you the newest Rankin
novel, by the by.'

I pause, knife in hand. 'Now you're talking! Thanks, Janice. I
couldn't really get into that Grisham, too many characters for my
bird brain.'

She laughs, shaking her head, and begins to set out some Café
Noirs and Garibaldis.

Tray. Tonic. Tumblers. I, for one, will be needing a G & T. 'So,
Janice, is your nurse friend coping okay with her divorce?'

Janice wheels round as if she's been bitten.

'Murray mentioned her,' I explain.

For a moment she glares at me in silence, then marches back
out of the kitchen. That's when I notice her hair isn't in the usual
ponytail, braid or chignon. Flecked here and there with grey, it
ripples down her back, loose and quite luxuriant for a woman of
her age.

A few minutes later, leaning back in my rocking chair with a large
G & T, I give Rachel a closer glance – and almost flinch: her face
is covered in scabs, particularly around the nose and cheeks. No
wonder Janice invited her in. She must have felt sorry for the lass.

'What's happened to your lovely skin, Rachel?'

Chomping on several Garibaldis at once, she grimaces. 'I had a
new treatment they advertise over in Lauriston Place, to eliminate
thread veins.'

'Thread veins – you!'

'Depends on the lighting,' she retorts. 'Anyway, if they stay away, it was worth the pain; my eyes watered like hell every time that guy stuck his needle in.'

The girl's a masochist, and no mistake. I haven't told Janice about the scars on her palms, and don't intend to.

Janice wants to know more about the procedure and Rachel mentions disgusting things like microwaves for zapping veins, insulated needles, spurts of sebum and visors with magnifying glasses. I reach for the Rebus book.

Suddenly there's a knock at the front door and Yoyo shoots off barking. Might be Miss Chinese Crested – or Doreen, in hopes of a cuppa.

I pull open the door . . . and recoil so sharply the vestibule floor seems to slide from under me. Yoyo has come to a dead halt, head and hackles raised, snarling.

The Hawk is smiling, which does nothing to soften his features. Before I can shut the door in his face, he exclaims, 'Hello again! Small world indeed! I believe we have a mutual friend, Rachel Keller.' *Friend*! I think as he continues. 'I was supposed to meet her in the Meadows, but missed her. She said she might visit you. Gave me your address.'

Rachel gave the Hawk my address? For a moment I stare at him. Imprinted on my memory is the sight of her running across the Links, away from him, and I feel a vague sense of dread. I want to protect her. Keep her safe. The way I never did with Marlene. 'I'm afraid she isn't here. Goodnight.'

I'm about to shove the door to when Rachel calls out, 'It's all right, Mrs Fairbairn. Hi Geoff.'

Turning, I'm in time to catch the faintest smirk tugging at her lip ring before she resumes her dachshund expression of concentrated vigilance. I close the vestibule door behind me – I refuse to let the Hawk into my house. Dear old Yoyo takes up position in the hall.

'Who is it?' Janice is inspecting the digital radio on the sideboard.

I shrug. 'Some peculiar-looking fellow asking for Rachel. I've seen him around for the past few weeks. Gives me the creeps.' I have a quick, shuddery sip of my G & T.

'Not to worry, Mum, I'm here,' she says absently and presses the on-button. A burst of rock music floods the room. Adjusting the volume, she changes stations to something classical. 'Another gadget from John?'

'Aye, his non-Christmas present.'

She laughs and switches it off. 'Nifty wee thing.'

From the front door comes an unintelligible murmur. I help myself to a Café Noir. Janice has started fiddling with the burning Advent candles, pressing her fingers into the soft wax. With her long hair falling over her face, she reminds me of one of those Art Nouveau nymphets on the postcards of my youth.

'Your hair is beau–'

'Sorry,' Rachel shouts from the hall, 'I have to go. Thanks for the tea, Mrs Fairbairn. Bye!' The door slams. Through the window I watch her and the Hawk pass out the gate, their figures lit up briefly by a streetlamp before they disappear into the darkness.

'What was all that about?' Janice is peeling the wax off her fingers like extra layers of skin.

'You tell me.' Yoyo has settled at my feet and I drop an oatcake as if by accident, Philadelphia-cheese side up.

Wax removed, Janice sits herself bolt upright and I know she is going to talk at last. She slings her hair over her shoulders. 'Murray and I have decided to separate for a while.'

'Oh, Janice!'

More hair-slinging.

'Has that nurse girlfriend put ideas into your head?'

Our eyes lock.

'Actually, Mum, didn't Murray say? That nurse friend is male.'

~

And I see myself again as I was then, at twenty-two, lounging in the sun-warm grass halfway up Arthur's Seat, the gorse a fading blaze of yellow around me, scenting the air with the last traces of vanilla and coconut. Dafydd and I had come here for a celebratory picnic.

It was August and he had just returned from Cardiff, where he'd spent the previous few weeks setting himself up in business now that he was a qualified architect. Always a man with a flair for dress and class, he had called at my lodgings in well-cut tweeds and a flashy red sports car with the top down, 'a second-hand bargain not even a Welshman could refuse'. Smiling proudly, he'd opened the passenger door. I'd smiled back, my head tilted to model the brimless new felt hat with the speckled feather trim, the gold watch (his twenty-first birthday present) glinting on my arm. By evening we'd be engaged – he'd promised me a ring often enough.

Arthur's Seat felt like the top of the world, with Edinburgh small enough to be cupped in my palm: a toy castle on a papier-mâché hill; domino lines of tenements, houses and trees; barges like dolls' shoes sailing down the blue of the Forth towards the open sea.

'So when can I join you in Wales?' I asked lazily, having washed down some cooked chicken with a mouthful of the sherry I'd bought for us.

He didn't reply at once, and the sun began to sear my skin.

'Patience, my love, it'll be a fair bit yet.'

High overhead a seagull screeched and jeered.

Dafydd's eyes looked down into mine and in their silvery green I saw myself reflected in all my pathetic splendour: big arms crushing the flowery skirt over my knees, gold watch polished over-bright, speckled feathers ruffled and askew.

'I need to get established first, Lizzie dear, so . . .' He kissed me.

All I could think was, Now, now's the moment when he'll give me my engagement ring.

He kissed me again, stroking my hair, and I pictured his free hand reaching into his waistcoat pocket and . . .

Instead, his fingers started inching into my blouse and under my brassiere. I held my breath. Then the strain of waiting got too much and I blurted out, 'Dafydd, is this our engagement?'

After a pause he mumbled, 'Something like that, my love.'

His kisses suddenly tasted bitter. Around me the gorse smells had become tainted, like perfume on unwashed skin.

'What do you mean, *something like that*? Haven't you brought me my ring?'

Heavily, his hand tumbled out of my blouse and his eyes clouded over. He turned away.

'I'm sorry, Lizzie. I thought you'd realised. The car cost quite a packet and . . .' his voice trailed off.

How could I have been so dumb? So blind? The money he'd saved up for the ring had been blown on the car. I'd have to wait. God only knew how long I'd have to wait.

I felt anger rip through me. 'A bloody car!' I shouted. 'All for yourself! To show off in, just like your stupid tweeds. You promised, Dafydd. You promised me a ring! And I trusted you. All this time I've been waiting. Treasuring your letters. You *promised*!'

. . .

'Please, Dafydd. You're kidding, aren't you?'

. . .

'Dafydd?'

My hands were shaking as I uncorked the sherry bottle to pour myself a glass. I took a deep gulp. 'All right, have it your way. If that's how you keep your promises . . .' the drink had made my eyes water, '. . . then that's for you, Mr Lying Bastard Colwyn!' And I threw the rest into his face. 'You and your bloody sports car! I've had enough. I'm *finished* with you!'

Shaking all over now, I whimpered, 'Finished. Finished. Finished.'

Dafydd didn't move. Didn't wipe the sherry off his face or clothes. Didn't calm me. Didn't plead with me. Just sat there, completely still, gazing at me steadily, with an uncompromising, cut-heart sternness. His eyes had hardened into silver coins, cold metal, and I could no longer see my reflection in them.

Around us the mountainside with its gorse bushes had blurred into a riverbank of pale yellow primroses. I felt a sudden surge of pain. The words were out and they'd hit their mark. They had wounded. Marlene a decade ago. Now Dafydd. And me – *me* most of all.

Half-scrambling, half-falling down Arthur's Seat, I repeated Scarlett's farewell to Rhett over and over, like a mantra: 'After all, tomorrow is another day. After all tomorrow is . . .'

For weeks and months I jumped at the sound of the telephone, the letterbox, doorbell, knocker. I was convinced that Dafydd would try to win me back, would come to woo me afresh. He'd sell off his car and put a ring on my finger.

At Christmas a card arrived from him. He sincerely regretted our unhappy parting and hoped I had forgiven him. Signed 'with lots of love'.

I wrote back by return to ask *his* forgiveness and to confess that he was the one – and always would be, no matter what.

The months passed. And the years. The gold watch he'd given me became crisscrossed with scratches, and doubts.

14

Last night I dreamt of Marlene's silver cigarette case, which she used to flip open to offer round her Du Mauriers. It was exquisite, with a set of RAF wings engraved on the lid. Inside was an inscription, scratched awkwardly into the silver: 'To Tildy with love from Matt.' A present from a pilot to his sweetheart? Marlene never told me how she'd got hold of it – and I never asked.

In the dream, the RAF wings had grown in size to those of a real aeroplane; the case itself had lengthened, stretched and bulked out, with little windows on the side.

'Want a fag?' I suddenly heard Marlene's voice.

'You can't open –'

With a click the lid sprang up, its sheen filling the sky like a mirror. In the centre hovered two words: The Hawk.

And then I saw Marlene and myself reflected there, her features ravaged by death, mine by life, and what looked like stripped logs of wood, ivory-white and neatly stacked right up to the rim of the case. As I watched, Marlene's face merged into Rachel's and the logs slowly transformed themselves into bodies sheathed in cigarette paper. Red patches began to bloom on the white, like rose petals. Instinctively I knew they were wounds. And all at once I recognised the victims. Just when I opened my mouth to scream, the sun struck the mirror.

I woke up twitching and moaning, my face wet with tears, my head aching. From the bottom of the bed came a grumpy snort, then Yoyo jumped down on the floor and padded off to his lair in the hall. It was four in the morning, the worst time for trying to get back to sleep. After an extra-large dose of Askit powder and a nice hot cup of tea, I was still tossing and turning. As if I myself was a cup and Rachel holding the spoon, stirring up the black tea leaves like so many spirits of darkness from another world.

~

Unlike Dafydd, Randall didn't pass his finals and had to re-attend 1st term before he could re-sit them in December.

'Exams in veterinary studies are a lot harder than those in architecture, Lizzie. For obvious reasons,' Marlene was quick to point out.

I didn't ask what those 'obvious reasons' were. I knew quite well she secretly chafed at Randall's failure, which made him one of the Dick Vet 'Christmas Men' and delayed the official announcement of their marriage by a further five months.

Years later I was to visit them in the Borders, where they lived just outside Newcastleton on the Waverley Route. It was the weekend of their tin wedding. My present of the traditional aluminium pan was only slightly sneered at by Marlene, who opened the door dressed in a brand-new Chanel suit. Rowan Hill House was a mansion with a driveway of rowan trees to 'honour the spiritual' and a modern annexe for Randall's animal clinic. A 'poor woman from the village' was employed to keep the picture windows gleaming, the floors and furniture polished and the Persian rugs brushed. Maybe she, too, had ambitious daughters . . .

For Saturday night, Marlene had invited two of Randall's vet friends over for dinner. Afterwards we all played cards. As usual, Marlene was winning and as usual, she couldn't help rubbing it in. In the middle of the game, she threw down the Queen of Hearts and, with a scornful glance at Randall, exclaimed that her

'Christmas Man' had never been the brightest penny in the purse or he'd have kept his king once the ace was gone. She laughed, lit another cigarette and topped up her whisky. Then, raising her tumbler, she winked at everyone except Randall.

Nobody else laughed or moved, and in the stillness Marlene's gulps sounded painfully loud. Her throat made an irregular clicking noise that reminded me of a clock winding down. When she finally replaced the empty tumbler on its silver coaster, she added without looking at anyone, 'At least you're a good cook, Christmas Man.'

Which, indeed, he was. To welcome me, he'd done a roast leg of lamb marinated overnight in cognac, honey, olive oil (exotic in those days and bought at the chemist's, not the grocer's), garlic and fresh mint.

Now Randall did his best to force a guffaw, but I could hear the disaffection in it, and the sadness. His pet Alsatian wasn't fooled either; he lifted his head from the rug to gaze up at his master, amber eyes near-human.

Meanwhile, the Queen of Hearts remained flat on its back on the shiny mahogany table. I took a long drag on my cigarette. I felt like weeping suddenly and didn't know why. Why should the sight of a stupid playing card make me want to weep?

It was only later, in bed, that Marlene's old riddle came back to me, especially the last line: 'And when I'm needed, they slap me down.' I remembered again our winter afternoon in the maroon car while Stilton had his way with Liquorice. As I lay there wide awake in Rowan Hill House, crying over our lost childhood and who we had become and might still turn into, I hoped the children were safely asleep. Perhaps Angus was dreaming about doing the rounds of the farms or going to the Auction Mart with Randall, and young Catriona was stroking the imaginary mane of the pony Marlene had promised her for her fifth birthday in two months' time, as a companion for her brother's Black Beauty.

After my love affair with Dafydd I decided to leave Ivory House, leave hairdressing altogether and return to being a dressmaker. I knew how to sew, how to fix laddered stockings and take up skirts, didn't I? Not only that, I also knew how to unpick the linings from stinking fur coats and was a competent un-snagger of threads. Surely someone in the business would have a use for me?

I ended up with Phoenix Fashion. A select ladies' and gentlemen's outfitters in Edinburgh's Church Hill, it was owned and run by an elderly couple, a brother and sister. Both were unmarried. Mr Phoenix dealt with the gents, Miss Phoenix with the ladies. New customers frequently mistook them for man and wife, but they didn't seem to mind. They were kindly people, eccentric in an amiable, genteel way. I was taught to take measurements and do fittings of females and, as a rule, never to contradict the customers. Most important of all, I learnt how to flatter their figures: if they were generously proportioned like myself, I'd give their bust a shapely prominence, and if they were on the spindly side, I'd mass some fabric around their waist as a *trompe l'oeil* – one of Dafydd's artsy expressions: he'd have been proud of me.

Marlene visited Phoenix Fashion on a sleety, abrasive day before Hogmanay. She tried on dozens of suits, skirts and evening gowns before eventually choosing a purple-striped taffeta cocktail dress – one of the classiest, and priciest, items in the shop. It had long sleeves, a small stand collar and tiny fabric-covered buttons down the front of the bodice and at the wrists, and a full, long skirt with a deep hem frill. Now that her secret marriage to Randall Eliott, veterinary surgeon MRCVS, had become public, she paraded about town, making up in style for the three-and-a-half years of cloak-and-dagger furtiveness.

'I have to dress for the Mrs Eliott part, my girl,' she said as I knelt beside her in the back room, mouth bristling with pins.

I grimaced and gave a shrug.

She clouted me. 'Hey, you're not supposed to disagree with me, Miss Pincushion. You just nod and smile and be servile.'

I spat the pins at her fat, silk-stockinged calves, which were exposed where I'd adjusted the hemline. Then I got to my feet. 'Up yours,' I whispered, with a grin.

Marlene opened her mouth and neighed softly, and I thought that was it, we were quits, equals as in the old days, when she suddenly called out towards the showroom, 'Miss Phoenix, please, could you assist us for a second?'

'*Assist*? What the hell are you playing at?' In a sudden panic, I went back down on my knees to grope about for the pins.

'You're not scared, are you?'

I looked up at her.

Marlene rolled her eyes.

'Yes, Mrs Eliott?' The hurried steps of Miss Phoenix came pattering along the hallway. 'Marlene, for pity's sake!' I made to get up.

'Stay!' Pointing to the floor, she crossed over to the curtains that screened us from view and, at the very last moment, stuck her head out to say with another neighing laugh, 'I'm so sorry to have troubled you, Miss Phoenix, but the problem seems to have resolved itself.'

After that I never wanted to see Marlene again. Never ever.

Some three weeks later she dropped by my digs as if nothing had happened.

'Hey, Lizzie, fancy accompanying me to the Dick Vet School Ball in February?'

Randall had bought two tickets, she said, but had just been told he'd be needed down at Newcastleton to supervise the building work on the new animal clinic. And as her mother would be away in Pitlochry that week, I could spend the night at Hatton Place – 'with no landlady-hassles'.

I was too gratified not to accept. Marlene's follies were forgiven and forgotten in an instant, yet again.

On the day of the ball, I allowed myself a leisurely bath, paying my landlady extra for a full tub of hot water. I filed and varnished my nails – hands and feet – slathered my skin with creams, painted my face and styled my hair to the exacting standards of Ivory House. And when I slipped on Auntie Jenny's lace-trimmed, shimmery blue dress with its matching hat, I thought I looked a million dollars, almost.

I danced mainly with Frank, a first-year student lodger of Mrs Gray's. He was handsome in a bumptious way and Marlene treated him like a pet brother. She herself had picked up a young man called Roger, who kept stepping on her toes, but made up for it by kissing 'like an expert'.

Around midnight the four of us went to Roger's local, which had a lock-in. It was hot and steamy in there, the usual fug of smoke, sweat and beer, and I drank my brandy too fast. I had just started on my second when Marlene brought out her wedding ring and, blowing a kiss at Roger, put it back on her finger with the words, 'Sorry to disappoint you, old chap. I'm a married woman.'

Roger just stared at her, too polite or perhaps not quite drunk enough to call her a bitch. Then he turned to look at me and I felt like an insect trapped between two panes of glass, buzzing soundlessly inside the bluebottle shimmer of my dress. This had nothing to do with me. Nothing at all. At the door he paused for a moment, shrugging on his overcoat, and glanced once more in our direction. Then he was gone.

The three of us returned to Mrs Gray's, where Marlene made a show of kissing Frank goodnight. Then she plied me with a double whisky. Then another.

Quarter of an hour later, Marlene leading, the two of us entered Frank's room, barefoot and perfumed, in our nightgowns. I was glad that mine reached down to my ankles and all the buttons were securely fastened. I was still a virgin.

His bedside lamp was on and I tried to focus on the pastoral print above his bed, imagined the flock of sheep taking fright and stampeding across the picture, out of the frame – out of the room. I was vaguely aware of Marlene grabbing a book from Frank and holding it up. 'See what this naughty boy is reading, Lizzie?' She laughed and flicked through the pages. 'Listen to this: "Her pink tongue between her lips was like a bud about to burst forth and give pleasure. Lord W. groaned again, for her hand had just brushed his –"'

Frank switched off the lamp.

With a giggle, Marlene pushed me towards the bed. 'Get in or you'll catch cold.' Then she clambered over Frank, who protested he was tired, and settled down between him and the wall.

The bedsprings whirred and twanged under our combined weight. I lay with bated breath, motionless, and concentrated on the wedge of light from the door I'd left ajar, my back to Frank, my arms and legs over the edge of the mattress, ready to bolt . . .

Marlene kept giggling and squirming and telling him off for squashing her against the wall.

'What the hell do you think you're doing?' he demanded. Heat was coming off him in waves, a furnace heat that seemed to vibrate all around us.

When Marlene leant towards me, the bodice of her nightdress gaped open next to Frank's face. 'Lizzie,' she panted, 'I want to trade places with you. This ruffian's invading my space.'

There were more giggles, grunts and wrestling noises and I let myself fall quietly to the floor, intending to creep away and leave the two of them to it.

Instead, I climbed back in.

~

My breakfast tea has gone cold. I sit staring at the crossword in front of me, feeling dopey. The kitchen's too warm. Stuffy. Must get this gas fire checked. Though it would be the easiest, most painless way to die, wouldn't it, just to drift off into never-ending slumber . . .

Yoyo is fast asleep, snuffling and twitching his nose, paws scrabbling against the skirting, tail thumping the floor – hunting phantom squirrels and rabbits, no doubt.

It's a sunny day and in the drying green outside the French windows the McConnells' old-fashioned underwear is swaying in the breeze, capacious underpants, lumpen vests, corsets and brassieres, frilly knickers, socks and stockings all ruining my limited ground-floor view of the trees and the yellow rosebush. Sometimes I wish I still had my son's air rifle.

Wonder how Janice is doing? If only I could help her and Murray . . . I feel sad suddenly, sad and a little sick. People hate being deflected from their own path, even if it's the road to perdition. Even if it brings tears and heartache. And don't I know it! I close my eyes. Just for a minute, I tell myself. Then it will be time to walk Yoyo.

An hour later, pulling on my elephant skin, I wander through to the front room for some mints to replenish my Jenners bag. All at once there's a tap at the window.

No! Not *him*! Not again! I'm *alone*. I gesture with both hands, *Go away*! sucking on a mint and swinging the carrier bag as if to sock him. Then I scuttle off, away from him, down the hall and into the kitchen, towards the French windows. Yoyo follows hard on my heels, yapping like a puppy, thinking it's playtime.

For a moment I rest my head against the coolness of the glass. Beyond the flutter of Mrs McConnell's greyish pinks and creams, the large drying green is mostly laid to lawn, with here and there a few ash trees, butterfly bushes, roses, forsythias, children's swings and slides. The whole wide rectangle is enclosed by several dozen tenements: one of those shared back doors is bound to be open so I can escape out into the street.

Yoyo nudges me with his wet nose and like a thief I sneak back to the front door for the keys. It's locked; the Hawk won't be able to get in. And, pushed to, the French windows will look locked.

'Stop barking, Yoyo, please!'

That dog will be the ruin of me one day, I swear.

He charges out into the green like a crazy cannon ball, runs in circles after his scraggly tail, then chases my neighbours' tabby cat and finally lands up against a tree to lift his leg.

I normally avoid this place. Don't want Yoyo to upset any over-anxious parents. But there are no babies or toddlers about today; the morning's too briskly fresh for their tender complexions.

As I prowl along the blue, red, purple and brown back doors, discreetly rattling the odd handle, I ask myself why on earth I'm doing this. It's awful silly. Undignified. The Hawk is only a young man, after all – not a very prepossessing one, maybe, but still a human being. And an acquaintance of Rachel's (though that's hardly a commendation).

'Yoyo!' A window has opened a floor up and someone chucks out a half-eaten slice of buttered toast. My dog isn't a waste bucket, I'm about to shout, then realise the toast-chucker is Miss Erskine. Her white hair is hidden under a fluffy pink towel, waiting to be coiffured into her Chinese Crested likeness.

She waves. 'Oh, Mrs Fairbairn, I didn't see you so close to the wall. Would you care for a cup of tea?' Before I can answer, she has moved away from the window. 'I'll throw down the back-door key, shall I?'

15

In the end it was Frank who leapt out of bed and rushed from the room, clutching the cord of his pyjama bottoms, his unbuttoned top billowing behind him like a flag of distress. Marlene sniggered and started to bounce on the mattress, higher and higher, the way we used to in the maroon car. But we weren't children anymore and her bouncings made me uncomfortably aware of just how less-than-innocent we had become.

'Please, Marlene,' I said, 'you're letting all the warmth out.'

'We'll soon stoke up a fire again.' She laughed and, after a pause, added, 'Don't be such a bloody prude, Lizzie. He isn't even naked! Surely you've seen a man in jimjams before? Give him a wee thrill, for God's sake! Rub your toes against his legs – it won't get you preggers.'

I tried to imagine tracing my glossy red fingernails down Frank's spine to tickle him. I had no idea that Marlene was already three months pregnant with Angus.

Frank took ages and ages. Marlene, meanwhile, jawed on about selfish enjoyment and how it damaged your brain. When Frank returned, he smelt of soap, the buttons on his pyjama top were closed, and the cord on his bottoms was knotted tight. Marlene wriggled provocatively as he rejoined us under the blanket, but he merely patted us on the shoulder with brotherly hands, saying, 'Would you go to your own beds now so I can sleep?'

~

By the time Yoyo and I get back from the Meadows after visiting Miss Chinese Crested, there's no sign of the Hawk. I unlock the street door with a flourish, smiling to myself. Of course I didn't tell my neighbour why I'd been prowling round the drying green. Our chat was agreeably bland, a bit like the best porridge, neither too salty nor too sweet. We talked about her injured leg – on the mend thanks to 'dear Doctor Ronaldson's healing touch' – the weather and Rachel. 'She sounds a little foreign, perhaps?' was her delicate comment.

Yoyo is sniffing an envelope on the vestibule floor. A Christmas card I've overlooked? From Cousin Peggy, possibly?

Just a smear of mud where the address should be, no stamp. Junk mail. I tear it open. Read it. Then read it again. What the hell is Rachel thinking? I don't want to see her. Not tonight. And certainly not with the Hawk. 'No need for food: we will have eaten.' The gall of it!

But the evening is still hours away – I'm grateful for small mercies these days.

After a plump chicken thigh from Margiotta's I feel better, almost in the mood to do battle with that girl. The new Rebus novel will be perfect for keeping me on edge.

Then I remember Isobel and her TV programme tomorrow. Damn. Damn. Damn.

I punch in the number.

'Stockbridge 2569,' she says, a trill of expectancy in her voice.

'It's only me,' I reply, coughing.

'Lizzie, my goodness, I thought you'd be over that cold by now. Are you taking your camomile tea?'

My humming and hawing gets blasted to kingdom come by a series of squeaks, courtesy of Yoyo attacking his rubber hedgehog.

'Hang on, Isobel.' I bend down painfully. The toy is slimy with saliva and I chuck it out into the hall. 'Fetch, Yoyo!' Then I close the door.

'Peace at last.' I sigh. 'Sorry, Isobel.'

The upshot of the call is that on 'no account' would she want to 'inconvenience' me if I was 'too ill' to play hostess. Which, I suspect, she knows I'm not. That's probably why she offered to bring one of her irresistible Dundee cakes. Pure bribery.

Afterwards I reproach myself for not being more welcoming. For all her Goody-Two-Shoe-ness, Isobel is desperate to be friends. Desperate to share things – food, our childhood memories, even our loneliness. But how can I oblige her when I haven't come to terms with Marlene?

~

Marlene snorted when she heard Isobel was getting married to a geologist church elder. 'Mining for jasper and sapphire in Heaven, he'll be! That's the reward for the faithful, isn't it? To live in the holy city descended from Heaven, New Jerusalem, with its walls of precious stones, gates of pearl and streets of gold?'

But Isobel's husband was too much of a realist to rely on Divine Providence. He opted for the earth's natural resources instead, taking part in the exploration for 'black gold' in the North Sea.

By then, of course, Marlene had long been ensconced in her mansion with the sparkling windows. She'd look out over the shallow curve of the rowan trees along the drive, gaze at their bridal-white starflower clusters in spring, their blood-red berries in summer, their dying leaves in autumn. She'd watch Angus being taught to ride Black Beauty by an aging ex-jockey. She'd stare at her newest set of crystal glasses and the limited-edition Wedgwood in the display cabinet. She'd tell her cleaner to polish the brass doorknobs.

She rang me occasionally to gripe about Randall being 'addicted' to his animal patients, more concerned with their welfare than the wellbeing of his own family. 'Maybe me and the bairns should try bleating, braying, mooing or grunting.'

She began to caution me against marriage. 'It's a bloody health hazard, Lizzie. A trap. Don't fall for it and end up like me – we're birds of a feather, the both of us.'

Thankfully, she couldn't see my face. Perhaps she guessed. Because she usually burst out laughing, a laugh corroded by a hacking smoker's cough.

My mother always said that between my hairdressing and seam-stressing, I wouldn't need a man. She went to meet her Maker when I was twenty-nine, leaving the bulk of her worldly possessions to various church funds. No wonder the minister had been so keen to see me enrolled at Ivory House after my father's death: with me a safe distance away, he could spin his silky web around my mother, the wealthy widow, without risking a snag.

Fairbairn Bros., Grocers, was three doors up from Phoenix Fashion in Church Hill and handy for my shopping. For seven years I had exchanged pleasantries with the Fairbairns while they served me. I'd watched wee John and Janice take their first tottering steps behind the cheese-and-meat counter. I'd commiserated with Mrs Fairbairn over the miscarriages that followed. And then, only weeks after my mother's passing, she died in childbirth.

When Alan asked me out for a drink at Bennets Bar some five months later, I wasn't too surprised. After all, he had to find a replacement mother, quick. I was about to turn thirty and looked matronly enough to qualify for the job. And, to be honest, I'd had it with working for others, even for nice, decent people like the Phoenixes. As a farewell gift, they said to pick any outfit I liked. Dior's comfortable A-Line had just come into fashion, but I chose a dress that accentuated my 'curves'. Made of orchid-pink silk taffeta, it had a wide, off-the-shoulder neckline, small cap sleeves, a fitted bodice with a wrap-over effect above the bust, and a straight, long skirt without a waist seam. My wedding dress.

Like Marlene and Randall eleven years earlier, Alan and I got married in May. Theirs was the best and costliest wedding present of all: a gold cigarette box and matchbox enamelled inside with bluebells. It was clearly meant for me as Alan suffered from asthma and didn't smoke. I'd often complained to Marlene how he kept nagging at me to give up my 'filthy habit'.

Alan promptly felt slighted. 'It's a snobbish gift, a real snub,' he declared, and from then on held a grudge against Marlene and poor, unwitting Randall. If I reminded him of his religious principles, quoting, 'Love thy neighbour,' he retaliated, 'And hate thine enemy,' before stomping from the room or letting his fork and knife clatter into his plate, splashing gravy. We never argued about anything – except transubstantiation, and Marlene.

One afternoon close to Easter, Marlene showed up at the shop with young Angus and Catriona in tow. As soon as Alan spotted them, he called me over. 'I need you here, Lizzie. Don't go gallivanting about with that woman.'

When I started to walk off, he grabbed the sleeve of my shop coat.

'Let go.' I tried to unclasp his fingers.

But he stepped closer and whispered, 'She's poison, believe me.' He'd said the very same thing nearly two years earlier, after being introduced to Marlene at our wedding reception. He was jealous, of course, jealous of our giggles and reckless regression into girlishness – because I hardly ever laughed when I was with him.

I tugged myself free, pulled off my shop coat and hung it up by the storeroom door.

'The apprentice will have to cut the butter and cheeses then.' Alan slammed the macaroni drawer shut.

The girl always made a right hash of it: unable to tell the difference between ounces and quarters, she would leave behind a pile of unsavoury, experimental slabs, crumbly, half-melted and rejected by our customers.

'Fine by me.' I scooped up Ruth from under the teak counter, where she'd been asleep. On my way out, I helped myself to the most expensive item we sold in the shop during Lent (and which I'd been dying to taste): a luxury simnel cake from Ormo's, packaged in a tin of holy purple.

Alan opened his mouth to say something, then quickly turned away towards a couple of customers who had been watching us.

And off we went along Church Hill, down Strathearn Place and Strathearn Road, Marlene, the children and I, giggling about men and their stupid threats, the cake tin sitting like a trophy on the buggy blanket.

When we got in the door, Angus pounced on John's football in the vestibule and began kicking it up and down the hall. Marlene didn't stop him. Not until Mungo yelped.

'Watch it! How often do I have to warn you?' she cried. There was a smack and a short, sharp wail. Then another, louder smack. Then continuous wailing.

The lad could only be silenced with an instant chunk of simnel cake, including one of the apostle marzipan balls, and two glasses of lemonade.

While I put our tea things on a tray, Marlene laid out her gifts on the kitchen table: a small teddy bear for Ruth, some sweets for John and Janice, and a frilly red apron with an appliqué of a Norfolk terrier for me.

'Saw it in a shop window and knew it had your name on it.' Waving aside my thanks, she slipped it over my head and tied the strings. 'Go on, girl, give us a twirl!'

And I did, cake tin in one hand, teapot in the other, all the way to the front room without spilling a drop, to the accompaniment of Mungo's woofs and her laughter.

'Grandad was a footballer, a professional footballer,' we heard Angus shout in the hall as he thunder-crashed the ball off the bathroom door.

Marlene winked at me, 'He'll soon be a better player than the old man, eh?'

I shrugged, then refilled Catriona's lemonade glass. At the meal after Marlene's registry-office wedding I had asked her why she'd told such a daft lie. Her answer: 'He may very well have been, Lizzie – he may even have been a lord.'

'Mm, what yummy cake!' Marlene broke off a lump of marzipan and popped it into Ruth's mouth. 'Thank Christ you jacked in the hairdressing and the sewing, Lizzie!'

That's when I noticed the plumminess of her accent. She'd mastered it to perfection, to go with her county wardrobe of cashmere and family tartan. A shame she hadn't adapted her vocabulary accordingly.

I took a sip of tea. 'Aye, no more danger of you having to lug my hairdressing kit across town. Remember the time I'd left it at your mother's and asked you to bring it? "Wouldn't be seen dead carrying that," you said.'

'Did I really?' Marlene chuckled. 'I'm happy to carry my groceries from Fairbairn Bros., though, *and* to pay good money for them.' She paused, blinked long lashes over blue eyes. 'Any chance of something stronger to join my milk and water?'

As I turned from the sideboard with a small measure of brandy, I glimpsed myself in the mirror above the mantelpiece. My mouth was a thin white line.

'Cheers.' I set the tumbler down in front of her.

Marlene looked from me to the drink and back again. 'Now that's what I call mean-spirited.'

'You've got your children to think of.'

'Which is why my beloved little daughter is getting more cake.' Marlene smiled at Catriona, then placed a large slice on her plate, with one of the crystallised primroses for a treat.

The candied flowers had made me wince on first opening the tin, and I'd almost closed it again at once – closed it not just on the simnel cake, but on the memory of my betrayal of Marlene's trust.

With Catriona temporarily occupied, Marlene downed her brandy in one, then grinned at me. 'Oh, it's empty, Lizzie.' Her grin reminded me of our mischievous years as children and teenagers. Reminded me of our last night at the Highland House Hotel, locked in the bar, and how the contents of our glasses had arced and swooped around us in glittering rainbows.

I poured her some more.

Which Marlene drank down with slow deliberation.

I glanced away. Catriona had begun to play with Ruth and Mungo on the floor.

'Again! Again!' Ruth clapped her podgy hands and tried to do a somersault.

Just then Angus came barging in from the hall. 'I'm hungry, Mum.'

Marlene had whipped her tumbler out of sight. But he knew, and his eyes – dark like his father's – went black for a moment.

I gave him a smile. 'Some more cake for our football star?'

He nodded and wordlessly accepted another piece.

When the football was once more banging off the bathroom door, Marlene brought out her tumbler from under the sofa cushion. 'How about a top-up, Lizzie dear?'

This time I didn't budge.

'Only one. Please.'

. . .

'Half a one then, dammit.'

I leant down to the children. Ruth was covered in dog hairs, bits of marzipan, dried fruit and goo.

There was a tap on my shoulder and I caught a whiff of simnel cake steeped in brandy. 'Come on now, Lizzie, don't be such a Goody-Two-Shoes.'

I dribbled some spittle on a hankie and started to clean up Ruth's face.

'If you let me have a droppie, just a wee droppie, I'll tell you my latest adventure. It's a grand story, cross my heart.' Her plummy accent was gone.

~

Six o'clock. Rachel and the Hawk will be here in a couple of hours. The nerve of it! What should I do? Go over to Janice's in a taxi?

She may not be in, though, and the last thing Murray would want is to have his evening spoilt by the mother of his renegade wife. A trip down to Stockbridge? Could I bear the glow of Isobel's triumph? Her inquisitiveness? Could I bear the smell and taste of her camomile tea? There's always Miss Chinese Crested a few doors along; she'd be pleased to see me. But she's too gentle, too trusting. Too thin-skinned altogether.

So why not Ruth? I did promise to call her, didn't I?

Four rings, and her answering machine clicks on. I wait a few seconds, in case she is in the shower or out on the roof terrace, watering her hibiscus and jasmine plants. She'll know it's me because I never speak. I loathe answering machines.

Nothing. No Ruth. She's probably in bed by now; it's three hours later there and she gets up at the crack of dawn.

That's that then. I've run out of options.

My home is my castle. My home is my castle. For the past half-hour the phrase has been going round and round my head, complete with images: watchtowers, parapets and battlements rosy in the sunset, concealing archers and musketeers; windows bright with the reflections of lochs and bens, their inside sills laden with buckets of boiling pitch whose stink will cling to the curtains forever; drawbridges; iron portcullis as lethal-swift as guillotines.

My mother enjoyed a bit of gruesomeness every now and again. Reports of hangings on the wireless. Ghost stories. And her own, thinly disguised tales of wild men. Some nights, my father brought home his drinking companions, including Red Ray and Mr Ross, the vet. As soon as she heard their hollerings echo around the yard, my mother would gather us together – me, Hamish and Audrey, the cats and, for a few short months, Liquorice – then send us up to the 'refuge' in the attic. In cold weather she'd plunge a shovel into the kitchen stove and, holding the burning coal out in front of her, come rushing after us, carrying the fire like a true goddess of the hearth. 'Never mind those men downstairs,' she'd pant. 'They're welcome to freeze their suet, and good riddance.'

I feel better all of a sudden, more confident; at my age, what else can I do but take comfort from the dead? And I feel mild, as for Marlene, Isobel, Lizzie and Doreen – with a Great Dane among us, who is to worry? And I have Yoyo, of course.

'Here, boy. You're for real, aren't you?' He wags his tail, scrunches up the glacier mint, then, with a low growl, demands another. I am glad. His teeth may be blunted and chipped, but they can still snap to bits anything that gets in their way.

Lurching out of my chair to prepare supper, I remember Willie's first visit here, at the beginning of my marriage. We were sitting reminiscing about our childhood in Kelso, Willie with his legs stretched out under the coffee table, when puppy Mungo scampered in, made straight for the table and peed over Willie's elegant, two-tone shoes. I was mortified. Took them to the kitchen, saddle-soaped them and put them near the gas fire for drying. An hour later, checking on Ruth in her cot, I found a trail of chewed-up leather in the hall . . . Willie wouldn't accept my money. 'I'm a bachelor and you've got three children, a husband and a dog to feed.'

As he left – wearing Alan's old hiking boots (least likely to be missed overnight) – he gave Mungo a pat. 'Well done, wee chappie. You certainly know how to protect your mistress.'

A few smears of butterspread, some cucumber and a generous wedge of goat's cheese from the French *fromagerie* van, and my roll is plump and ready. Yoyo is slobbering up yesterday's spaghetti like a maverick hoover, splattering most of the tomato sauce across the bottom of the French windows. Kettle's boiling, three spoonfuls of tea for extra strength. Tray, plate, saucer, cup, milk jug, napkin. And a Café Noir from the tin – no, two: one's for Yoyo.

Rachel and the Hawk notwithstanding, I shall enjoy my meal and watch this afternoon's recording of *Pet Rescue*.

Next moment the doorbell sounds and Yoyo is up and running, yapping his head off. I must have noddled. The tape has finished and three comedians in chefs' aprons and reindeer hats are chopping vegetables. I press the off-button. Thank God I remembered to draw the night curtains. As I seize the tray, the crockery starts to jump and jig: I am trembling like a schoolchild before an exam.

'Dammit, Yoyo!' His jaw drops in mid-yap and the silence comes as a relief. Slowly, carefully, I carry the rattling tray through to the kitchen before, ever more haltingly, I approach the front door.

16

'Hello, Mrs Fairbairn. Good boy, Yoyo.' Rachel's voice is oddly high-pitched. 'This is Geoff – you've met before.'

I grimace. I can feel my head shake and there's nothing I can do about it. The Hawk doesn't look like the Hawk anymore. Despite the darkness, his face seems fuller and his hair is different, much longer, curlier, though this can't be, hair doesn't grow overnight. He is wearing a tweed coat and some sort of thick black tights. Shoes with silver buckles. And he's holding a sports bag.

'May we come in?'

I realise I've been blocking the doorway and step aside. Must be a wig. But why would he bother?

At least Rachel appears to be the same. Bright little dachshund face, no more scabs, winter coat with flapping tails, corduroys, multicoloured laces.

In the light of the hall, the Hawk's cheeks have a rouged glow. His lips are vermilion and his eyes rimmed with kohl. I gasp. He is grinning, clearly relishing my shock, and I notice his teeth for the first time. They're too small and there are too many of them crammed into his mouth. Do hawks have teeth? When he takes off his coat, I let out another gasp. He is in tights all right, plus a knee-length woollen dress in blues and greens.

His grin is even toothier now. 'Didn't have time to get changed. Soon as the show was over, Rachel dragged me off.'

Drag being the operative word, I think to myself. Isobel will be agog. Maybe the Pubic Triangle in West Port contains more than just lap-dancing clubs . . .

'I can change if you prefer. My clothes are in here.' He points to the sports bag on the floor.

I picture his usual outfit, the clumpy boots and drainpipe jeans, picture the cruel haircut, the tautness of bone.

'N-no, no, it's all right.' I attempt a smile. 'One thing my friendship with Marlene taught me was to be less prejudiced.'

'Actually, Geoff's in a panto.'

I stare. Seconds later I start giggling. Can't help it. And then we're all giggling while Yoyo makes his hedgehog scream.

They've brought a bottle of Australian chardonnay. The Hawk, wig-free now, pours out two glassfuls. I have a G & T.

'Cheers,' Rachel says, clinking the glass to her lip ring. The metallic sound gets me sobered up instantly – not that I've had any of my drink yet. I remember her disfigured hands and glance at them, then at the Hawk's. Has he got scars too, or claws instead? He's reaching down to pet Yoyo, who has sidled up to him.

Why the hell are they here? And why was Rachel's voice so squeaky when they arrived?

I yank Ropey from between my seat cushions; Yoyo is mine.

After a minute of tugging-and-warring, I ask without looking up, 'And how's the thesis going?' – assuming it was a mere pretext. But that's where I am wrong. Rachel embarks on a detailed progress report, with comments on the most recent publications in the field, until I feel so thoroughly Reformed and Calvinised, or should I say Presbyterianised, that I start glugging down the gin. All at once I become aware of the Hawk's eyes. They're fixed on me as if I was a field mouse or a baby bird.

He must have seen me flinch. 'Another drink?' he suggests.

Rachel has stopped in mid-flow. She's watching us.

'No th-thanks,' I stutter and hate myself for doing so. But then

I sit up straight and, with a laugh that's a lot brasher than I really feel, shrug off my fears. 'Well, why not! Just a wee droppie.'

The Hawk is smiling as he uncaps the bottle of Gordon's on the sideboard.

~

Just a wee droppie . . . The story Marlene told me that afternoon before Easter had caused a scandal in the Eliott circle.

The previous autumn she'd been driving over to the house of her in-laws with Catriona in the back and a ten-year-old Laphroaig between her thighs. The whisky was for Eliott senior, to pacify him after she'd scoffed one of his numbered bottles during her last visit.

The day was warm and sunny, windless, with a sky so high and wide it seemed to span the whole world. Marlene had the windows open and steered with one hand, smoking. Her new Bush radio with its carrying handle sat on the passenger seat, tuned to Radio Luxemburg. Elvis Presley was shaking the airwaves, louder, then fainter, then louder again. She kept tootling the horn and flicking the swing-out indicators in time to the beat while Catriona rock 'n' rolled on the back seat, whooping and squealing with delight.

All around them was 'a rampant extravagance', as she put it. Giant beech trees, thick glossy hedges, verges bursting with weeds. Lipstick-red rosehips, brambles so ripe they glistened white. Rainbow flashes of pheasants and songbirds. Picture-book rabbits. Furry and feathered carcasses. Fat sheep, cows with ponderous udders, horses nuzzling each other. Stubble fields of pure gold. Heady smells.

Finally Marlene couldn't bear it any longer. She stopped the car, broke the seal on the malt and had a quick swig. As the dark, peat-smoky taste slid down her throat, she toasted her father-in-law – after all, she'd only drunk part of his bottle, so why not share this one, too? Catriona stared at her until she gave her a KitKat. And off they went again. Tootling and indicator-swinging, rocking 'n' rolling. The whisky level dropping steadily.

Then the lane bent sharply and into view came a couple of berry pickers, mother and child, standing close to the hedge. A basket filled with brambles sat a few yards further along.

'Of course it was an *accident*, Lizzie!' Marlene finished her 'wee droppie' with an exaggerated slurp. 'I didn't *mean* to knock the bloody thing over. But it was *right* in my path.'

The berries had spattered across the lane like fat ink blobs, spraying the hedge and the car. Some of them had even landed inside. Marlene plucked one off the passenger seat and ate it, laughing at the woman who was chasing after the car and shaking a fist at her.

Catriona was staring again so Marlene said, 'I'm your mum and mum's the word, eh, lassie?' Then she brought out another KitKat.

They drove on a little more slowly, singing along to 'Jailhouse Rock'. Quarter of an hour later they heard the police bells. 'Bloody bitch must've called the plods.' Marlene pulled over. Shreds of brambles had dried in purple splashes on the chartreuse-yellow bonnet of her car. As the Wolseley screeched to a halt, she slipped the bottle of Laphroaig under her seat.

A fair-haired young policeman strode up, the spitting image of James Dean.

'Lovely afternoon, isn't it, officer?' Marlene turned down the radio and made a show of rearranging her skirt.

'Could I see your driving licence, please, madam?'

Humming along to 'Don't be Cruel', Marlene reached into the glove compartment, then handed him the papers with a big smile. 'You're not really a policeman, are you?'

He didn't smile back. 'Have you been drinking?'

'No, of course not.' She fluttered her eyelashes. 'Smell my breath.'

When he leant in, she raised her face and kissed him full on the mouth.

'One kiss, Lizzie, and he fined me! Lost my licence for three months.' Marlene looked at me and held out her empty glass.

~

Loud panting next to me. Something damp and cool pushing into my palm: Yoyo's nose.

. 'Good dog,' I say automatically, grateful for his company. My bones ache as if I'd been on the rack; my neck feels stiff and my left leg is all pins and needles. Gingerly I move my head. Dingy grey morning light above the curtains, the rain drumming on the windowpanes – a grim, grim day. I'm about to go back to sleep when I sense something is wrong. I am not in bed . . . and I'm rocking back and forth ever so gently. Rocking in my chair, which is covered with my downie. On the coffee table before me are three empty glasses.

What on earth happened yesterday evening?

There's a growl-and-thud as Yoyo begins to batter Ropey against the furniture. I can remember watching *Pet Rescue* and the poor marmalade tomcat whose tail got squashed in a trap. I also remember the Hawk's pantomime getup and having my second G & T, a rather strong one, proffered by him with an eager gleam in his eyes. And I remember telling Marlene's kissing-the-policeman story.

Everything else is a total blank. I have no memory of being swaddled in the downie nor of Rachel and the Hawk's departure. Did he put a sleeping pill into my drink while mixing it? But why? I keep my money in the bank and own no jewellery of any value except the sentimental kind. I don't even have an engagement ring. And my silver is as tarnished as myself.

I can't telephone Janice – she has other things on her mind. And Ruth, little Ruthie, who wears Dafydd's amber bead necklace for luck, will be teaching; it's mid-morning in Bahrain. I'll try her in the afternoon.

'Yes, Yoyo, nice Ropey. Off into the garden with you, or your bladder'll burst.'

The door of the press behind the rocking chair is slightly ajar and I snib it closed on my way out. Nothing special in there. Just some detective novels and thrillers. And photographs – albums and boxfuls of them. A few are Willie's because there was no one to claim them when he died. His nephews and nieces were more interested in his collection of rare books on horticulture from his days as head gardener, which ended up fetching thousands at auction.

After a generous dose of Askit powder and some breakfast, I decide to ring Isobel. Perhaps the scouring effect of her presence will do me good; the sherry in her Dundee cake certainly will. Mercifully, that Borders programme lasts only an hour, I've checked.

I reach for the telephone, then stop. The press in the front room . . . How could I forget? There's something else I've kept in there – something I ought to have thrown out decades ago.

Wrenching Ropey from Yoyo's mouth, I fling it down the hall, as far as I can.

17

Marlene had always liked North Berwick. A year after her Easter visit, she invited me and the children to spend part of the summer holidays there with her. She'd rented a house near the beach, with a 'perfect view of the Bass Rock' – though God knows the water was icy even at the height of summer. I was flattered that she should ask me rather than one of her sisters. But my own sister, Audrey, was coming over from Malaysia, where her Royal Marine husband was stationed. She planned to pick up her daughter Sheila from boarding school in Kent and stay with us for a fortnight. Audrey and I hadn't seen each other in almost four years, not since our mother's funeral, so I couldn't very well go off with the children, leaving her and my niece behind to keep house for Alan, could I?

Marlene laughed when I told her. 'Course you can't! Bring them, too – it's a barn of a place. It'll just be us women and the bairns. The men can turn up to perform their husbandly duties at the weekends.' Her laughter was scathing now and made me cringe.

Since my one and only visit to Rowan Hill House four years earlier, Marlene's marriage had been getting rockier. Soon it would be on the rocks completely. In April she'd rung me and ranted about Randall associating with farm labourers and 'suchlike'. On one occasion he'd allowed an old farm hand, a bachelor, into their posh downstairs parlour, offering him a brandy because the man had just lost his beloved pet pig. 'Stank like a pigsty himself, Lizzie, and there he was, plonked down on our nice, clean sofa! I *had* to do something. And that Chinese tea service wasn't much use, anyway.' She'd started throwing cup after fragile cup out of the window above, then saucer after saucer. By the time Randall had dashed upstairs, there was only the teapot left, dangling from Marlene's pinkie as she pulled back her arm. He had pounced and saved it.

The second Saturday in North Berwick, Randall slaved the evening away in the kitchen, making a fish pie for us adults. The children had already been fed and put to bed, except for Sheila, who at sixteen was pert, smart and very attractive, with a proper bust and long legs. I noticed how Marlene kept a beady watch on Randall in case he strayed too close to the girl.

We'd all had our fair share of 'wee droppies' when Randall presented his pie at last, the topping of mash a golden sand colour decorated with tiny fish shapes of peas and diced carrot.

'Seems a shame to cut it,' I said, my mouth watering at the tangy smell. Under my chair Mungo gave a grunt.

'A culinary masterpiece!' Audrey smiled at Randall and flicked back a strand of hennaed hair. Her nails were brightest scarlet. Vanity dies hard, I couldn't help thinking.

Randall beamed, looking even more handsome with his dusky skin, wavy black hair and dark eyes.

Marlene took a drag on her cigarette, then blew a long furl of smoke at the ceiling rosette.

'Happy, dearest?' With a little bow, Randall offered up the dish for her inspection. Clever Randall. Playing servant to his mistress while, like a Border collie, herding her towards the fold, towards a night of peace and harmony.

Alan had tilted his chair against the wall, in the pose of someone bored and not hungry in the least. 'Damn shilly-shallying,' he muttered, jiggling his foot. He was tired from the week's work at the shop and, I suspected, a little jealous of the only other man in the house – one whose college education had led to success.

'It'll get cold,' Marlene said and, propping the cigarette against her plate, she reached for a serving spoon. 'Let's eat the bloody thing.'

With a deliberate cough, Alan the asthmatic leant over to squash out her stub in the ashtray. Then he wiped his fingers on a paper napkin.

Sheila licked her lips after a couple of forkfuls. 'This is delicious, Randall. Absolutely scrumptious! What's your secret?' And she thrust her bosom at him.

Randall smiled. 'I'll write out the recipe for you. It's simple.'

Moments later Marlene held up a two-inch fishbone. 'What the hell is *this*?'

Randall flushed. 'I'm sorry, Marlene. I must have missed that one.'

'Bet you knew where it was and gave it to me on purpose.' Marlene's voice was too shrill.

I glanced at the others. Audrey was staring at the dregs in her glass like a fortune teller, Alan continued stuffing himself with pie, and Sheila was busy scrumpling up her napkin.

'Marlene, please calm down. It was you who served us, remember?'

'*Remember. Remember*. How bloody funny. You could have killed me with it, you bastard! Eat it yourself then, and die!' Suddenly her plate was empty and Randall's shirtfront a mess of herb sauce, mash, peas, bits of carrot and fish.

Randall remained motionless. Surely not even he could ignore the insult? I held my breath when he lifted his glass . . . to down the rest of his drink. Then he slipped off his chair. Rounded the table like a sheepdog. Pinned Marlene to her seat with one hand and with the other grabbed the oven dish, dumping what was left of the pie over her head. She shrieked. And I felt myself shrink and shrivel inside. Gentlemanly Randall – reduced to this! For once in his life he had lost it; she'd pushed him too far. But I couldn't find it in me to pity Marlene as she spat and kicked and clawed.

No one spoke. No one tried to stop Randall as he began to work the food into Marlene's hair, methodically rubbing and rubbing until it was ground to a pulp. She finally submitted, with a resigned grimace at us as if to say, Now you can see what I have to put up with – I, the poor, long-suffering wife.

~

Opening the door of the press too hastily, I knock into the shelves and everything comes tumbling down: books, albums, boxes of photographs. Lids fly off in mid-fall. Yoyo's paw has been struck by a corner of *Law's Grocer's Manual* and he limps off in a huff. I kneel down awkwardly. Pictures of different families, different countries, different epochs lie in mixed heaps. Hopeless now to try and sort through things. But who cares, anyway? Who cares? Painfully I straighten up.

'Who cares?' I hear myself shout. 'Once I'm dead – who fucking cares?'

A minute passes in utter silence, and I can feel another headache building up.

Yoyo has slunk up to me, tail between legs, eyes averted, ears and eyebrows drooping in misery. I pat him, kiss his rubbery nose. 'It's all right, my boy. Everything's all right.' My voice sounds quavery, the voice of an old woman.

When he's grinning again from pricked-up ear to ear, I replace the books and shove the photographs back into the boxes, imagining the children one day in the future, perhaps quite soon, sweeping the contents of the shelves into black bin bags without so much as a blink or a second glance. I'm only their stepmother, after all.

But everything is *not* all right. My head is pounding and the something I've been looking for seems to have vanished. It isn't among the photographs. For a moment I wonder if I got rid of it and have simply forgotten – which is nonsense, of course.

White-hot knives of pain have begun to stab into my skull. Tears of pain, rage and hurt stream down my face. I want to howl and scream. How dare Rachel and the Hawk come into my home and betray my trust? How dare they?

Next thing I'm in the bathroom and clutching the stockings that have been soaking in a basin – clutching, tugging and twisting them dry, slapping them back underwater, making them gurgle and bloat. Again and again. Until I haven't a single tear left.

The telephone rings just as I crawl into bed for a late-morning nap, exhausted. I pull the downie over my ears. But I can't sleep.

~

And *there* is Marlene, a year after that holiday in North Berwick, barging in on Randall and his Alsatian while he is watching the news on the television in the downstairs parlour of Rowan Hill House.

Holding a large brandy, she launches her attack point-blank. 'Marigold Montgomery – what a stupid bloody name! The bitch is county, isn't she? A county bitch! A fucking county bitch!'

'Marlene! This is no way to –'

'Keep away from her, Randall, or you'll never see your bairns again.' Marlene's fingers close around the belly of her glass, press, then press harder. The thin crystal breaks with a tinkle of laughter, spraying brandy and blood.

The Alsatian has sprung to his feet, but Randall calls him back. 'For Christ's sake, Marlene! You're drunk!'

Scrunching over the shards on the carefully brushed Chinese rug, she staggers right up to him. Spittle hits his face as she hurls her ultimate abuse at him:

'Go take a dose of Nembutal!'

Then she is upstairs, sobbing, her cut hands under the cold tap. Behind her, the antique silver coffee service (a wedding present from her parents-in-law) melts slowly on the hotplates of her new cooker.

'County bitch! County bitch!'

The water hisses into the sink, rusty red.

~

My head feels sore. At this rate, I'll soon run out of Askit powder.

When I call Isobel at last, she's in a right stushie.

'Frankly, Lizzie, I thought something had happened to you. I rang six times – every half- hour.'

I manage a wan smile as I picture her setting and re-setting the electronic kitchen timer she is so proud of.

'Sorry, Isobel, I was out,' I say. I'm not really telling a lie. I *was* out. Out for the count.

'Surely you didn't walk the dog in this beastly storm?'

As if on cue, a whoosh of wind comes down the chimney, rattling the metal sheet behind the gas fire and making Yoyo grumble under the bookcase.

She misinterprets my silence. 'Dearest Lizzie, if you're not more careful, you'll catch your death one of these days.'

'Won't we all!' My laugh sounds almost natural and I pinch a glacier mint from the bowl.

Stiffly she replies the weather is in fact the reason she'd been trying to contact me. Would I mind terribly if she postponed her visit? Too wild out there, even for a taxi ride. 'I'm sorry, Lizzie. I hope you haven't gone to any trouble on my behalf.'

'No bother,' I say. 'Better not catch your death yet, eh?'

There's a pause. 'You're annoyed with me, aren't you?'

'No, no. It was a joke, Isobel, a silly joke. Sorry.' Truth is, I *am* a bit disappointed. Before dialling her number, I had given the 'for-best' silver cutlery and cake dish a quick polish with the toothpaste – an old trick of my mother's. Isobel insists on decorous eating. No hands-on experience for her, or her children: if she is to be believed, they were born with perfect table manners (unlike little Ruth, who still crammed fistfuls of mash into her mouth at the advanced age of three).

Isobel hasn't said a word.

'Listen,' I prompt her, 'I'll record the programme and we can watch it another day. How's that?'

'Well. . .' she hesitates, 'would you be free this Friday?'

I cough, suddenly remembering my alleged cold. I don't want to appear too eager. In the end we fix on Saturday, three o'clock. 'To allow the elements a few more days to quieten down', as Isobel puts it.

Afterwards I punch the speed dial for Ruth in Bahrain, but it seems the offspring's grapevine works just fine without me.

'Email,' Ruth explains. 'I emailed Janice after you and I spoke. And she emailed me straight back. Found it easier to write about things, I guess. She and Murray have agreed he'll move out for the time being. He's already signed the lease for a two-bedroom flat so the girls can stay with him at weekends.'

No family Christmas, I think to myself. Poor Sophie and Donna.

Ruth mistakes my wee gulp for shock. 'Janice said she'll be in touch with you, Mum. Dinnae get yersel intae a fankle nou.' Her Scots sounds unreal, a Middle-Eastern desert Scots reserved for emergencies.

We soon wind up. Hearing all these details via Bahrain hurts a little. But not too much: I've got Yoyo and my elephant skin.

It's mid-afternoon when I finally venture out into the sleety rain. Underneath the blue tea-cosy-style hat, my headache is undiminished, a relentless, dull throbbing despite powders, pills and willpower.

The last remaining leaves in Bruntsfield Links are mottled with black spots of pestilence. A pigeon lies dead in a drift of rubbish. Yoyo, wedged like a sausage in his red tartan coat, has exposed its muddy, ragged wings and scabby feet, the holes where its eyes should be. Blasts of wind and rain drive me across the wizened grass, stumbling, my back bent and sore again, down towards the children's playground. Seagulls swoop, heckling. Salisbury Crags and Arthur's Seat with its telltale outline of a crouching lion have been washed off the horizon. On good days I sometimes picture the hill coming furiously alive, tossing its giant head to cast off the human fleas crawling all over it.

I follow the trees to the left. Barclay Church rears up like a gothic monster, its outside shielded and fortressed, studded with all kinds of devilish-looking designs, though even they can't always fend off anguish and despair. I haven't forgotten Doreen's stories. The geriatric nappies she found while doing the cleaning in there . . . I hope and pray I shall be spared that sort of indignity. I'd rather die first.

Coming towards me from Glengyle Terrace is the flaxen-haired lass with the stroppy dachshund. She gives me a bedraggled smile.

'Dreich day, isn't it?' I call out and stumble on, head down against the buffetings of the weather, my back straining, my tongue wrapped round a mint for comfort. I feel like an old battleship with a cracked and leaking hull. Yoyo has sneaked past the girl's dog under cover of the trees, and I don't blame him – once bitten, twice shy . . . The dachshund has reminded me of Rachel again. Of Rachel and her quest.

~

Marlene wasn't much good at writing. Suffered from word blindness and always spelt my married name 'Bairfairn' (though perhaps that was simply to annoy Alan). In all the years I knew her, she only ever sent me the picture postcard of the kilted Scotsman's bare posterior, a couple of ivory-coloured cards gilt-embossed with *Many thanks from Mr and Mrs Randall Christopher Eliott*, and one single letter, dated late October 1961. It is this letter that's missing from my press, including several newspaper clippings contained in the same envelope.

A month or so after she crushed her brandy glass and fried the silver coffee service, Marlene had another row with Randall about Marigold Montgomery.

It's a Saturday afternoon. They're in the downstairs parlour again, but this time Marlene is sober. Randall has been sitting in front of the television with the sound turned down, his trusty Alsatian at his feet.

'I can smell that county bitch on you. Get out of my house, you bastard!'

The dog lifts his head.

'Please, Marlene, calm –'

'I *ken*! Now get the fuck out of my house, or your bairns will suffer!'

Randall pats the dog, keeping him down. 'The children are *ours*, Marlene, remem–'

'I'll kill them, I swear I will! And that bitch, too!' The Alsatian snarls, his lips drawn back. 'I'll cut them up and throw them in the river, every bloody piece of them, just like Buck Ruxton did!'

'Let's be sensible, Marlene. We can work something out. You know I shall always look after you and the children.'

'Fuck you!'

More snarls. The dog tries to pull free. 'Please, Marlene. We can work things –'

'Go take a dose of Nembutal!' The door slams shut behind her.

And that's what Randall did. Went and ransacked his surgery's drugs cupboard. Swallowed a large enough quantity, then telephoned his mother to tell her what he had done, collapsing halfway through.

While the Alsatian stood over his master's prone body, licking his face and hands, whimpering, licking and licking, Marlene was busy in the bedroom, ripping up Randall's shirts, ties and spare collars with a kitchen knife, cursing him.

She told me the story so often afterwards it feels as if I'd been there myself – an observer without the power to intervene.

The ambulance arrived too late.

When Catriona got home from the Brownies that day (Angus was away on a camping weekend with the Scouts), the body had already been removed. Randall's parents had contacted the police before driving over to Rowan Hill House and accusing Marlene of murder. Not that the pathologist could find any proof. There was Nembutal in Randall's stomach all right – an overdose that would have killed a horse – but whether it had been administered by

Randall himself or someone else was impossible to determine. And as no one had witnessed the argument, the Procurator Fiscal eventually decided against further action.

Throughout the funeral service, Marlene kept her head bowed. Her face was hidden behind a thick black veil and her arms were around the shoulders of Angus and Catriona. The children's eyes were unblinking, unseeing, empty – the eyes of shellshock victims. Marlene's mother and sisters shared the pew with her, but her parents-in-law, together with their only surviving, unmarried son (their eldest had died in the war), were seated across the aisle. I wondered what Marlene was feeling. Guilt? Relief? Exultation?

It was after the burial that I caught sight of Tinker Jeanie. Like an apparition from another world she looked, as eroded as the tombstones in the old part of the cemetery. She was wearing the same mouldy greatcoat, the same beret with the front teeth on their gold chain. I watched her approach Marlene. Watched her whisper something into her ear. Watched Marlene flinch, then rush off towards a throng of mourners, kissing, hugging and holding on to them as if they could protect her.

Once the reception was in full swing, I buttonholed Marlene. By now she had slipped off her veil. Her make-up was hardly smudged.

'Tinker Jeanie,' I asked, 'what did she want with you?'

Marlene shrugged and, when I repeated my question, said, 'He lay on our bed, cut like a slab of meat, Lizzie. Lengthwise and across his chest and belly, then stitched up again. A rough job.'

I shuddered at the thought. And at her gall. Why on earth had she requested to have poor Randall's corpse returned to Rowan Hill House after the autopsy?

'He reminded me of those Chinese waxworks up in Edinburgh. Remember?' Her voice had grown louder, almost mocking. I could tell she was drunk.

How come I hadn't ditched her long ago?

'But he smelt all chemical,' she continued. 'See, it wasn't really him anymore. Not the Randall I knew. Not the Randall I loved.

That's why it was bearable, Lizzie.' A shadow flitted over her face, and I was glad of it. With one step I pulled her close.

While I was still embracing Marlene, Tinker Jeanie passed behind us. Her ruined face was contorted and wet, her seawater eyes like cracked mirrors. She was pointing to the palm of her hand and mumbling something I couldn't quite catch. Then she was gone.

The story of Randall Eliott's 'suspicious death' was given lavish coverage in the regional press. But Marlene didn't mind. In fact, judging by her letter and the enclosed newspaper clippings, she rather enjoyed her sudden notoriety. Even more so when, a few weeks later, Robin Hall and Jimmie MacGregor immortalised her in one of their topical calypsos on the Cliff Michelmore show, *Tonight*. It was called 'The Merry Young Widow of Newcastleton'.

Marlene had reached her pinnacle.

18

They burst clanking from behind the trees ahead of me, like executioners in the gloom of the afternoon. *My* executioners. For the briefest of moments I recoil. Then walk on. Pretty unusual for them to disport themselves at this time of year, and in this kind of weather. There are two of them, one with an impressive seal's moustache, the other with a curly black beard, both youngish, both kitted out in full armour: helmets, breastplates, backplates, gauntlets, metal-plated legs, halberd and mace. Battle reconstructionists.

I try not to stare too much as they get into position on the squelchy, cropped grass, facing each other, then begin to wield their weapons, a little ponderously, in a series of complicated battle moves that seem to require high winds and horizontal rain. Perhaps they're testing their armour for fatal chinks? Or do they want the odd rust mark for authenticity? I indulge myself for a minute, imagining their wives or girlfriends resplendent in chastity belts, knitting them chain-mail undershirts for Christmas.

'Dammit, man!' There's a violent clash and when I glance back, Warrior Moustache is lying flat on the grass, like a beetle on its back, his mace a few yards away. Warrior Beard laughs metallically before bending down and offering a gauntleted hand. Just as he is about to pull his adversary to his feet, Yoyo cannonballs past in pursuit of some seagulls and, oh no! the man loses his balance and crashes down on his knees.

'Fucking dog! I'll bash its head in!'

Next thing I know, I find myself beside the two would-be warriors, clutching the mace I must have picked up.

'Drop that, Grandma. Hell you think you're doing?' Warrior Moustache struggles to get up, but the turf is too soggy.

The club is flimsier than I expected. Not heavy at all. A wet leaf clings to the shaft. I brush it off. Then, gently lowering the weapon, I tap its tip on the metal-plated shoulder of Warrior Beard, who is still kneeling on the ground. The rain streaming off his helmet makes him look tearful. So, with my mildest – most mischievous, ironic, loose and debonair – old-lady smile, I intone: 'Don't be afraid, dear. That's you knighted now. You may stand.'

'Fuck's sake!'

I throw away the mace.

'Bloody madwoman.'

They both stare up at me, little-boy macho-men.

Not nearly as mad as the pair of you! I say to myself as I go skeltering off, braving another gust of sleet and feeling rather jaunty and light all of a sudden, despite my water-logged elephant skin. As if someone had just freed me of my own armour, whatever that may be.

'Let's go home, Yoyo. Enough fun for one day.' I adjust his tartan coat, which is all askew. Behind us I can hear the two warriors shouting. They're not using very refined language. True to the Middle Ages, right enough.

'Mrs Fairbairn. Hello!' Miss Chinese Crested comes tripping along one of the paths, her sky-blue umbrella, miraculously intact, held at its familiar, dangerous tilt. 'I hope these ruffians haven't attacked you?' She peers at me from under a paisley headscarf.

'On the contrary.' I laugh into her worried face. 'Nice to see you, Miss Erskine.'

Together we walk home through Marchmont, detouring past Margiotta's, where she keeps watch over Yoyo while I get some groceries. She tells me the lurcher's nip on her leg has healed, but the skin cancer is spreading again. 'I'm like a leopard,' she says without self-pity, 'and my spots are deadly.' I almost stop in my tracks, she sounds so unlike herself.

At my gate I invite her in for a cup of tea and a strawberry tart. She hesitates, glances up at the cloud-swollen sky, then declines with many apologies. Dusk makes us old ladies feel vulnerable.

'Another time.' I smile at her and sketch a wave as she departs, leaning into the wind with her umbrella – my dainty Miss Chinese Crested, after all.

Moments later I deeply regret not having persuaded her to come in. Lurking in the half-dark of my kitchen, seated at the table – my spare set of keys and the missing envelope in front of her – is Rachel. The street door had been locked and bolted as usual, and Yoyo didn't bark when we went inside, scampering off down the hall instead, whining and wagging his loo-brush tail. Surely he can't be pleased to see *her*? The girl is a thief. And worse.

'What a wet little dog you are!' Rachel removes Yoyo's tartan coat with a matter-of-factness that leaves me speechless, then she pats him on the head and his pink tongue licks her hand.

I grind my teeth.

'Oh, sorry, Mrs Fairbairn, you're soaked,' she exclaims. 'Let me get you a towel for your hair.'

What the hell is she doing, pretending this is her house and she my hostess? My keeper?

I take a step back, then rally myself. No, I'm not going to give in. For once in my life I am thankful for being big and bulky. With my substantial body parked in the kitchen doorway, Rachel can't squeeze past. The rules are reversed. She is my prisoner now. Standing barely a yard away, she looks pinched and shrunken in that black sweater of hers, a lot smaller than me. And a lot younger, too. I glare at her. Yoyo is making growling noises. Waiting for his Milky Way. Too bad.

'I'm sorry if you're cross with me, Mrs Fairbairn. I took you for a fun-loving old lady. High-spirited. A bit like Mar–'

'Don't you dare use her name to get round me, girl! Let me tell you: I'm not cross – I'm bloody furious. Understand?' I switch on the overhead light.

She nods. Bites her lips. The silver ring trembles. Good.

'I was quite happy to be left alone, Rachel. Never asked you to come here in the first place. Nor your creepy boyfriend.'

'Geoff isn't creepy!' she shouts, before clapping a hand over her mouth. And suddenly, of all things, she bursts out crying. Sobs that make her heave convulsively. Then she turns away from me, sits down again on the kitchen chair, slumped forward now, arms hugging her chest, her face obscured by hanks of hair.

A consummate actress. Just like Marlene when she acted out her scenes for me.

~

It's another Saturday afternoon at Rowan Hill House, a few weeks after Randall's funeral. Again the children are away – safely out of harm's way at their grandparents' a few miles down the road.

Mr Cresswell BVM, a recent graduate of the Dick Vet School in Edinburgh, has just arrived on a Lambretta scooter, its fender boldly decorated with a zigzag and the name 'Silver Flash'. When Marlene meets him at the door, he lowers his eyes and blushes to the roots of his hair. She is lipsticked and mascara-ed, and dressed in blackest mourning – high-heeled shoes, long skirt camouflaging her thick legs, V-neck lambswool cardigan (top button undone), gossamer scarf bunched into her cleavage. Her curls are now strawberry-blonde, rich and glossy.

'Follow me, please, Mr Cresswell.' With a gracious hostess smile, Marlene leads him up the stairs and into the living room, where a log fire is blazing and Randall's Alsatian lies dozing on the hearth rug, scarcely opening his eyes to size up the visitor. She is determined to carry on playing the lady of Rowan Hill House – with the young man's help. All he has to do is rent Randall's animal clinic.

'Let's have a wee drop of something.' Marlene manoeuvres him towards one of the stools at the cane bar in a corner of the room.

Once the man is seated, she begins to ply him with drinks. Since Inverness, she has refined her cocktail skills and now uses grenadine, crème de cassis, fresh fruit juice and champagne, garnishing the swizzle stick with whole cherries and segments of orange, kiwi and pineapple from her red, apple-shaped ice bucket.

'I love cherries,' Mr Cresswell says as he sucks on one. Then he blushes, again. Not *that* innocent, Marlene notes.

She chats to him about Edinburgh. What a shame the trams had been done away with. Hadn't it been appalling to see the streets dug up – here she pauses for a moment – *disembowelled* almost?

He blinks, surprised, before nodding vaguely and draining his glass. He probably prefers the modern omnibuses and superbuses, or his own scooter.

And the traffic congestion in Princes Street and George Street, dreadful!

Again he nods.

She offers him a Russian cigarette from the silver RAF case, then takes one herself. He fumbles with a match, a gallant in the making.

Anyway, does he go to the pictures at all?

Another nod, vigorous this time.

She blows smoke rings. And what does he think of *Breakfast at Tiffany's*?

'Aye, it isn't bad. But the book is better. No Hollywood happiness-ever-after.' He taps off ash, coughs. 'Seems the author wanted Holly to be played by Marilyn Monroe. Drop-dead gorgeous, isn't she? Have you seen her in *The Misfits*?'

Marlene pouts. The young man's first full utterance – glowing with admiration for someone else. She draws on her cigarette, exhales languidly and replies, 'Ah, yes. Such a thrill to watch Clark Gable and Montgomery Clift.'

She gets off her stool, kneels behind the cane bar to select

another bottle, and re-emerges with a Courvoisier and a barely
concealed cleavage. As she pours them both a triple measure,
Cresswell's eyes waver between her face and the shadows under
her loosened scarf.

'Cheers!' She begins to talk animals. Cats, dogs, pigs, cows,
bulls, sheep, donkeys, horses.

He becomes expansive, confident. Sip by sip his voice slurs a
little more and his gaze slides down a little further, his cigarette
quietly smouldering in the ashtray.

At last Marlene brings the conversation round to the children's
ponies. They won't eat their hay and Black Beauty has developed
a limp. 'Overnight, it seems. If you could give them a check-
up . . . tomorrow perhaps? They miss Randall. He was so good with
the animals . . .' When the young man glances up, she indicates
the Alsatian on the hearth rug, grief-stricken to all appearances.
'The dog as well. And I . . .' she bursts into tears, 'I m-miss him
t-t-too.' Yes, she did miss him. And hated him for what he had done.

The vet finishes his drink, then gets to his feet, reeling slightly,
to place a hot hand on her shoulder. 'There, there,' he mumbles.
'There, there, Mrs Eliott.'

In her distress she tugs at her scarf, rocks herself back and
forth, back and forth. The mascara has run down her cheeks and
chin, and, pulling off the scarf altogether, she dabs at the wetness.

'No. Not Mrs Eliott. *Marlene.*' She smiles up at him through her
tears. 'My mother thought I resembled the actress, silly woman.'

'I'm Tony.' His smile is fuzzy.

Marlene is about to raise her lips to his when he removes his
hand from her shoulder and, swaying unsteadily, announces he'll
examine the ponies now. 'And then I must be off.' He doffs an
invisible hat, 'With many thanks, kind lady.'

'Please, Tony, don't go. Not yet.' She bats her eyes at him.
'Please?'

'But . . . what about the ponies?'

'They can wait. I'll make us some coffee. Nice and strong.'
She stands up.

Later that evening as they are lying in bed, Tony wrinkles his nose. 'A queer smell in here,' he says, then goes crimson. 'Sorry, I didn't mean to. . .'

Marlene lights a fresh cigarette. 'Oh, don't worry. That must be Randall.'

'Mr Eliott? But Mr Eliott is dead, isn't he?' Tony sits up, staring at her.

'Dead as a doornail, poor Randall. Just relax, lover boy.' She nudges him with her breasts. 'Go on, have a slice of sponge cake to build up your strength.' And she reaches for the plate on her bedside table.

'No, thanks, I couldn't.'

Puffing away, Marlene looks at him thoughtfully. 'Truth is, they brought Randall home after the autopsy.'

'Oh.' Tony's face has a greenish tinge. With bleak amusement, Marlene watches him survey the bedroom, then fix on the large, carved oak chest against the far wall. His fingers are gripping the sheets, ready to pull them over his face.

'No, he isn't in there. He's buried!' Marlene leaps out of bed, stark naked. 'See?' She throws open the chest – to expose nothing but a stack of linen. 'Happy now?'

As soon as she's back in bed, Tony shows her just how happy he is feeling.

'The sex was great with him,' Marlene told me later. 'And I could be as noisy as I wanted.'

~

It's out of spite that I've repeated the whole story to Rachel. The lass needed taken down a peg. Well, I've certainly achieved that: she's sitting hunched on the kitchen chair, gazing down at her hands folded in her lap. When I get up to boil the kettle, she doesn't budge.

Outside, darkness has fallen. The lamplight has turned the French windows into black mirrors, and for moment I have the sensation of being split in two: part of me here, part of me there. Trapped. Between hate and love. Anger and pity. Between Marlene's world and my own. Between her guilt and mine . . . Yoyo's reflection is clacking its teeth at me reproachfully. That's when I remember the fresh supply of Milky Ways is still in the shopping bag. As I begin to unpack, I feel a little peckish myself, and tired. I make it up to him with a Frankfurter.

At the sound of the kettle clicking off, Rachel says without preamble, 'So Marlene was a number-one bitch is what you're trying to tell me.' She unfolds her hands and inspects her scars as though they might reveal a secret.

I look away. 'Your phrase, not mine.' Then I gesture towards the envelope in front of her. 'You're old enough to decide for yourself. Seems you've read her letter and the clippings anyway.' My headache is back, thrumming away with a vengeance.

At the time I'd been shocked at Marlene's frank scrawls across the embossed notepaper, especially the last few lines. They sounded so harsh, and yet . . . and yet I believed her:

Cross my heart, Lizzie, I never thought for a moment that Randall would do such a stupid thing. All I meant was GO TO HELL YOU BASTARD! How could I know the daft bugger would go and top himself?

'Not a complete bitch then, merely half a one,' Rachel murmurs. 'Just like me, wouldn't you say, Mrs Fairbairn? Like grandmother, like granddaughter?'

I fuss with the strawberry tarts, the dessert plates, the teapot, the cups and saucers, the toothpaste-shined silver cutlery. Then I gulp down a glass of water with some Askit powder, shuddering at the chemical taste.

Her dachshund eyes on me, she says, 'Actually, I'd have loved to have known Marlene. But I'm getting bad vibes here, like you don't really care.'

'*Bad vibes*, for God's sake! All you needed to do was ask. Why didn't you? Why drug me? Steal from me? I could have sent the police after you and the Hawk!'

I don't tell her how I mangled my wet stockings instead, and how I cried. And cried.

'The hawk? What's a hawk got to –'

I shrug. 'Never you mind.'

'Look, I'm really sorry about everything. I wish I could undo what I did. But bad words and deeds seldom go unpunished, as I've had to learn . . .' Her voice has grown hoarse and she turns away.

Thinking of my own misdeeds and rash words, I feel faint all of a sudden. It's nothing, I tell myself, you're hungry, nothing else. I sit down heavily. Some tea and strawberry tart will make all the difference in the world.

What a liar I am.

'Please help yourself.' For once, I help myself first. The strawberries seem a bit on the sour-and-past-it side, but the custard-cream filling is all the sweeter.

Rachel gives me a small smile, then says under her breath, 'Mrs Fairbairn, I want to tell you something. A dream.' She pauses, and my heart sinks. People's dreams are rarely of any interest except to the dreamers themselves. Suppressing a sigh, I gobble up a forkful of tart – a mushy strawberry, alas – and prepare to listen.

'On the eve of my birthday after my mother's death, I dreamt I was a child again, playing in our garden. The dahlias were out in full force, so it must have been summer. I'd tucked my teddy bear into my doll's pram and was wheeling it up and down the terrace. Through the French windows I could see Mum moving about in the kitchen. I left the pram with the teddy bear and went inside.

'"Mum," I said, "I want a hug."

'"Do you need that?"

'"No. But I know this is a dream and you're dead, and I would very much like to be hugged."

'She gave me a hug, and I woke up to my birthday. My dad had bought me a chocolate cake from Sprüngli's. I was twenty years old.'

I sip my tea. It's a nice enough dream, but what on earth does she expect me to say?

Nothing, it would seem, because she carries on without waiting for an answer. 'It was soon after this dream that I met Geoff.'

'Not quite the man of one's dreams, is he?' I mutter as I share the last of my shortcrust with Yoyo. Rachel's glance bounces off me.

After a silence she continues. 'I felt I'd made my peace with my mother and was ready to move on. Of course, like most students in Switzerland, I still lived at home. Not that I saw a lot of my father: he buried himself in his work.'

Again she glances at me. This time I smile. 'Well, do please help yourself.' I point to the tarts. Then I struggle to my feet, trying not to gasp at the sear of pain down my back. 'If you'll excuse me a second.'

It's three minutes past five. The video in the front room is purring away, recording Isobel's programme. Before I return to the kitchen, I step into the vestibule to lock the mortice – better safe than sorry – then visit the bathroom. There are a few drops of dried blood in the bowl. Monthly blood. No wonder Rachel looks a little out of sorts, all pinched and pale.

19

To believe or not to believe her, that is the question. Thursday and Friday have been and gone. I urged Rachel to stay away from the Hawk, but I doubt she'll listen to me.

I for my part did listen to her. Sat through the whole story of how she and the Hawk had met at the English drama club in Zurich, which he'd joined as an amateur actor. 'In the role of a predator?' I almost asked. When she told me he'd been teaching language courses at the university, I pictured him clomping along the streets of Zurich true to form, his briefcase bulging with office stationery and toilet rolls stolen from the department. I wasn't too sorry to hear he'd lost his job due to spending cuts, and that his residence permit hadn't been renewed.

'I fell for him,' Rachel whispered, as though she was confessing to a crime. 'I fell hard, head over heels.'

I smiled against my will, remembering myself and Dafydd.

Unlike me, however, she didn't sit and wait, moping and hoping. She tracked him down. Her excuse being she needed to come to Edinburgh to research that old misogynist John Knox and, as if this wasn't enough, to explore her own roots.

Blighted roots, all right. Not that I breathed a word to Rachel about Tinker Jeanie and her dark warnings. (I wonder what happened to Jeanie's front-teeth amulet after she died? Did it get buried with her? Just like the old knife I've always used to mash up the tinned dog food will one day get buried with me?)

At least the girl apologised for pawing through my photographs and nicking a few. It made me feel a little warmer towards her.

'I can't blame it on Geoff,' she said (and bang went my bulging-briefcase theory). 'The sleeping tablet was my idea, too. He's not a bad guy in that respect.'

In what respect, then? But I didn't probe. Instead I gestured towards the spare set of keys on the table. 'So it was you who pocketed these, was it?'

'No, that was Geoff,' she admitted with a sniff. 'He only took them in case I changed my mind and decided to return the photos before you woke up.' She had a sip of tea, and the tinkling of her lip ring against the porcelain set my teeth on edge.

Why was she so hell-bent on protecting the Hawk? Out of a misguided sense of loyalty? Surely not out of love?

She did look rather peeky, hadn't even tasted her strawberry tart. Then I noticed the bruise on her left temple, badly concealed by makeup, under her wirebrush hair.

'Good God, Rachel, how did that happen?' I reached out a hand, stopping just short of touching her. But her hair had tickled my skin and I felt a sudden surge of sympathy. Another lost soul, I thought to myself, so many, many lost souls. Seeking what? Forgiveness? Salvation? Safety? Never happiness – because happiness is never enough.

She shrugged.

'Did Geoff push you around?'

A shake of her head.

'You fell?' Her earlier words had come back to me: *I fell hard, head over heels.*

She glanced away.

A little later she asked if she could stay the night.

My turn to be silent. I wasn't ready. Just wasn't. What else can I say in my defence?

Her parting remark aimed straight for the heart: 'Bye, Mrs Fairbairn. My mother always spoke of you very fondly.'

Now my guilt is back. And my headache. When Marlene was a down-and-out in a greasy suede jacket that had seen better days, I didn't let her stay either. Nor her children.

Does Rachel want to find sanctuary – or a way under my skin?

~

I didn't see Marlene again until nearly one and a half years after the funeral. Playing the lady of the manor had soon got her into debt, and she'd been forced to sell Rowan Hill House. She now lived with her mother in Hatton Place, where Mrs Gray was still taking in lodgers. Catriona and Ralph junior – as well as their ponies and the dispirited old Alsatian – were in the care of their paternal grandparents and their uncle, who ran the Eliott Stables. Marlene must have been glad to get away from her in-laws' accusations and frostiness – God only knows how the children coped with having their mother slagged off as a 'bitch in heat'. The best of food and clothes and schooling couldn't make up for that kind of emotional abuse.

It was a lovely spring morning and I'd just got back from a walk with Mungo when there was a knock at the door.

'Lizzie, hello!' Marlene was all smiles and excitement. Dropping cigarette ash all over the vestibule floor, she stepped inside to pet Mungo, who yelped with delight. 'There now, that's a good boy.' From her coat pocket she drew a paper bag and dangled it above his nose. 'To keep you occupied while your mistress is out.' He lunged, then scurried off with it.

'Out where?' I eyed her suspiciously.

Behind her, the glass of the vestibule door was ablaze with sunlight.

'Marlene, what do you mean?'

'We'll go into town, spend money, have fun! It's a glory of a day.'

From the kitchen came the sounds of Mungo's teeth grating on bone.

'I can't. I'm supposed to have lunch ready for the family. And it's my afternoon behind the cheese-and-meat counter.'

Marlene stubbed out her cigarette. 'They can rustle up a meal themselves, Lizzie, they're not babies. Hurry up now, don't be such a fussy old wifie!' And, tapping her foot, she began to croon 'Chains' by the Beatles.

That decided it for me. I may have been many things, but in 'chains of love' for Alan I was not.

While Marlene leant smirking against the wall, I called the shop and spoke to the apprentice. 'I'm afraid you'll have to do without me this afternoon. Something's come up . . . Oh no, nothing to worry about. And could you give Mr Fairbairn a message, please? Tell him he'll need to bring home some pork pies, Scotch eggs, ham and coleslaw for his and the children's lunch . . . Yes, do write it down . . . And coleslaw. That's it. Thanks.' I hung up smartly.

The telephone started ringing as I was locking the front door. It would likely be Alan. Too late, I thought, slipping the keys into my coat pocket.

Marlene and I took a bus down to the West End, where we strolled along Princes Street Gardens. The daffodils were out, a whole carpet of them.

Marlene murmured, 'And then my heart with pleasure fills, and dances with the daffodils.' When I raised an eyebrow, she added, 'Wordsworth.'

I nodded to myself. She had obviously put some varnish on her scanty school knowledge after transforming herself into Mrs Randall Eliott. She was still in widow's weeds, though I couldn't help noticing the stylish cut and swing of her clothes. I was wearing what she'd dubbed my 'cabbage green' raincoat.

A breeze rippled the daffodils and in the fierce spring light they shone more brightly than the cars and buses and freshly washed windows of the Princes Street shops.

'Abracadabra!' Marlene had unfastened her handbag and flipped it open in mid-stride. 'Have a look.'

I did. And froze. Inside the bag were wads and wads of money: rolls of twenty-pound notes held together by rubber bands.

'Good grief!' Had she emptied someone's cash register? 'Where did you –?'

'From Randall, of course. It's my inheritance.'

'What are you going to do with it?'

'Going to blow it!' She flared her nostrils and laughed her horsey laugh, then grabbed a roll of the money, her blue eyes suddenly dissolute. For a moment I feared she'd let the notes flutter away like exotic birds. But she didn't remove the rubber bands, just lifted the roll to her mouth, trumpet-style. 'Going to blow it! Going to blow it! Toot-toot, toot-toot!'

It was close to midday and the park getting busy with its usual lunchtime crowd of office workers, shop assistants and tourists, many of whom were staring over at us as they chewed their sandwiches. Only the hippies strumming their guitars or lying about in the grass seemed serenely oblivious, drugged out of their minds, probably.

My smile must have looked a bit sour. 'What about *after*?' The words were out of my mouth before I could stop myself.

'To hell with after!'

I didn't say anything. Two small girls, each clutching a single daffodil, ran past. Their parents were walking up ahead, arms entwined. I couldn't help thinking of Marlene's offspring, twelve-and-eleven-year-old waifs-to-be.

Marlene invited me to lunch at Jenners. Then she bought herself, and me, some 'suitable' new outfits in one of their elegant, thickly carpeted departments. There was nothing I could do, she simply dragged me along, chose a luxurious, blue, silk-crepe dress which I considered much too sleek and trendy for my full figure, and ordered me into a changing room. 'A present from Randall,' she said. Good old Marlene. She did have a generous heart – even later, when the money was no longer hers to give.

~

The doorbell goes as I'm buttering my second slice of toast. Yoyo's ears twitch, but his gaze stays firmly on my plate; he doesn't follow me down the hall.

Doreen! I'd forgotten she was coming early today.

'Morning, Mrs Fairbairn. Sorry I had to leave the hoover outside. You weren't home.' She prances in with the graceful fleshiness of a Great Dane.

I greet her without pointing out that she'd neglected to return it on Saturday afternoon, as promised. Then I wipe my mouth, discreetly. If she spots a crumb, she'll expect some breakfast herself. After my usual instructions, which she'll ignore in her usual slapdash way, I ask her to give the front room a special spit and polish.

'Oh?'

I don't elaborate.

Back in the kitchen I share my toast with Yoyo. We've barely finished when Doreen sticks her head round the door. Her glance lingers appraisingly on my empty plate and the half-full teacup. 'By the way,' she says, 'my partner's found a job as a kennel helper. Silverwitch, out at Auchendinny. Best kennels within miles. They've even allowed him to take his dog and –'

'You'd like a cup of tea, Doreen, wouldn't you?'

'An offer I can't refuse.' She laughs.

I smile and get out another cup.

Quarter of an hour later I push back my chair; the lass is here to work, not to sit and blether. That's when she mentions the two old ladies again, from Morningside. 'Remember the woman with the claw-hands, Mrs Fairbairn?'

I nod, expecting the worst.

'Well, she's alive and kicking. I saw her speaking to the minister yesterday. But her sister, her that had nothing wrong with her, she is dead.'

For a moment I remain silent. 'Poor troubled souls,' I say at last. It sounds like an epitaph.

She glances at me and I glimpse my own uncertainty in her eyes. Or is it fear?

While Doreen rams the hoover round the house, I'm overcome by memories of Alan. On the afternoon of my shopping trip with

Marlene, six-year-old Ruth ran up to me as soon as I entered the house, shouting, 'Mummy, Mummy, where have you been? We had a real picnic for lunch and Daddy said you were playing tru-something. What game were you playing, Mummy?'

'Daddy' was plainly in a rage, though he hid it well. Until the children were outdoors with their friends. Then, adopting a priestly tone, he held forth on how a wife was decreed to be the helpmate and support of her husband – made from his very own rib, after all – not some wild roaming beast intent only on satisfying its own desires.

'Amen,' I said and Mungo echoed me with a bark.

Alan flushed. He had guessed I'd been out with Marlene and I wasn't going to deny it (I'd already put the Jenners parcel out of sight under some woollens in my part of the wardrobe). 'I've told you before, Lizzie, I don't like you associating with that woman. She is bad.'

I thought of Marlene's gorgeous gift and wondered if I'd ever be able to wear it.

'Lizzie? I am waiting.'

Mungo was hovering by my side like a wee foot soldier. 'Marlene is my friend,' I replied, glowering at Alan. 'And you won't stop me from seeing her.'

'This is *my* house, Lizzie. *My* house.'

But even as I stormed off with Mungo at my heels, I sensed that Alan's heart wasn't in the argument. His voice had lost its edge. More than anything, he sounded exhausted.

Increasingly he kept his rage bottled up. At home he rarely spoke. Sat in the front room reading the *Scotsman*, watching TV or just staring into space. At the shop he smiled with a resigned servility: 'Thank you, Mrs Harrower, and you. Goodbye, Mrs Harrower.' Or: 'My apologies, Mrs Smith, the apprentice isn't used to the cheese slicer yet. Would you like to try some of our honey-glazed ham?' And all the while he must have been burning with regret at having traded in his career as a gifted research scientist. Turned inward, his rage slowly consumed him.

The letterbox clanks and Yoyo is off, barking. At least *he* is still alive. That's all I care about.

A Christmas card from my niece Sheila in America. How I wish she lived closer! I'm her only living relative now on her mother's side, assuming Cousin Peggy is no longer with us. My turn next. But not yet. Not yet.

Out in the street there's a wintry nip to the air and I huddle into my elephant skin. The sun seems low already, oyster-pale and shrunken. Electric Christmas lights wink from windows. Yoyo is straining towards the Links, but Margiotta's – with its garish tinsel and baubles – is far enough for me. Time to prepare for Isobel's visit this afternoon.

When we get back, Doreen the Great Dane is standing in the hall in hat and coat, waiting for her pay. Over the months her cleaning routine has become lightning-quick (bet she's missed that scrunched-up hankie under my bed again). 'Once I know the nooks and crannies of a place, I get faster, you see,' she told me a few weeks ago.

And then, after a mushroom omelette and a nap, it's me who is waiting. For Isobel. The video is ready to play, at the touch of a button, the programme about the landscapes and places familiar to us from our childhood. My mother's gold-rimmed tea service and the silver cutlery are set out on the tray, the ivory-coloured linen napkins drooping ever so slightly. The kiwi tartlets from Margiotta's glisten neon-green on the silver cake plate, getting a little more sweaty-looking as the minutes tick by.

Isobel doesn't come.

Finally I pick up the telephone.

Someone croaks something unintelligible.

'Hello? Isobel, is that you?'

There's a long pause. 'Lizzie! Oh my God!' A coughing fit. 'I quite forgot to ring you. I've been ill for the past two days, despite that flu jab.' Another bout of coughing. 'I am so sorry. Will you ever forgive me?'

Afterwards I go and sit in my kitchen chair, feeling guilty as hell. Because it never even occurred to me to wonder why Isobel hadn't put in her usual surveillance calls on Thursday and Friday. I'm a beast, Alan was right, a selfish beast, insensitive to the needs of others.

The amaryllis flowers glare back at me, ferocious red. Beyond the French windows, in the gloaming, the grass of the drying green is whitening with frost.

~

Alan was only fifty-nine when he killed himself. But he'd been dead long before. Maybe if I had listened to him with my heart, listened to his silences, to the empty spaces filled with his anger, maybe I could have prevented it. Maybe if I had reasoned with his doctor to prescribe another course of the drugs Alan needed but refused – and which I had to administer surreptitiously, in his food or drink. And yet, in all honesty, I don't think I could have saved him. Call it cowardice, call it lack of backbone. Or lack of love. True love, the kind that stays and grows and doesn't end with death. Like the love he had for his first wife, to whom no doubt he believed he would return.

That night, Janice was here, too. Still unmarried in her late twenties, she was living with us temporarily while working at the Royal Infirmary across the Meadows. Alan had been restless all evening. Around midnight he got up again and I heard him run a bath.

When I awoke at dawn, there were no creakings or snoring noises from his side of the bedroom. And I *knew*. Just *knew*.

The police came and went. No counselling in those days. They simply took away my husband-of-twenty-years, wet and dripping in a black body bag that resembled a large bin liner. They hadn't bothered to drain the bloodied water. It was me who did that – and who found the old-fashioned razor lying at the bottom. Janice rinsed off the bath. Perfect professional that she was, she cleaned and scoured everything, then threw away the razor. Then she cried.

We both did.

Yes, Janice was there for me as I sat weeping over a life that could have been. . . She was there for me even as my tears began to flow faster, thinner, hardly tasting of salt anymore, and I realised it was no longer Alan I was weeping over.

I stopped smoking soon afterwards, like a spiteful child that has suddenly no one left to be spiteful to. Marlene and Randall's gold cigarette box and matchbox were relegated to my dressing table, for storing hairpins and lipsticks.

~

When the telephone rings, I feel all choked up. I don't want to talk. And yet, what if it's Janice? I mustn't fail her, too.

The line is dead by the time I pick up. 1471 produces one of those interminable mobile numbers, and so I press 3.

'Hello?' A man's voice. The Hawk's.

'Sorry, wrong number,' I babble.

'Oh, it's Mrs Fairbairn, isn't it?' he says before I can disconnect. 'This is Geoff. Listen, I need a quick word with the elusive Rachel. She's had her mobile switched off for the past three days. Be a dear and put her on for me.'

'I'm not a dear, and definitely not yours,' I snap.

'Whatever. Would you mind fetching her now, please?'

I'm about to hang up when it hits me: he has no idea where Rachel is – and neither have I.

'She's not here,' I answer, a little too shrilly. Because if what he says is true and he hasn't spoken with her *for the last three days*, that would make it since Wednesday.

'Well, please tell her to get in touch once she's cooled off, would you? Cheers.'

'Rachel's *not* here,' I repeat, with extra emphasis.

'Thanks again, Mrs Fairbairn. She'll recover. Trust me.'

'Are you deaf?' I shout. 'Rachel isn't with me! I don't know where she is!' I cut the call. I'm shaking; my pulse is racing, and I can feel another headache flaring up.

Yoyo, startled out of his sleep, has twisted into angry-dog position. I give him a few haphazard nudges with my foot and he grunts irritably.

Perhaps Rachel has gone back to Switzerland? But no, I feel certain she's still here. Most likely lying low, holed up somewhere. Biding her time.

What did the Hawk do to her? Or, more to the point, what didn't I do for her?

20

Janice is in, thank God. I ask about my granddaughters' Christmas wishes (a tutu, leggings and whatnot for future-ballerina Donna, half an iPod – or more, if I can afford it – for Sophie-the-techno-geek). Then I jump in at the deep end.

'No,' Janice replies, 'Murray isn't *around*, Mother.'

'For the time being, you mean.'

'That's what we'll have to find out.'

Crunching up a mint, I tell myself to back off. I'm about as subtle as a bull in a china shop – or an ancient elephant matriarch galumphing to the rescue of a calf.

'Janice, if I can be of any help, please let me know, will you? If you want to talk or . . . or something . . . My voice cracks. I'm pleading with her. What on earth am I trying to prove? That I care? But I don't care enough, do I? Rachel seems to have disappeared and Isobel is poorly – and I never even noticed. Never even spared a thought for either of them. All at once I find myself sobbing, the sobs disturbingly similar to the cackle of a bird.

'Now, Mum, don't distress yourself. I'm fine. Murray and I are still friends. Better this than staying together and making everyone's life a misery. I'll drop round tomorrow afternoon, shall I? Usual time?'

Yoyo is staring over at me as if he can see into my soul. I turn my head away. Force myself to calm down, then say in a near-steady voice that I'm glad she is okay and look forward to her visit. And to give my love to the girls.

How old I'm feeling suddenly. How old and worn-out.

Between mouthfuls of kiwi tartlet washed down with scalding tea, I reassure myself that the evening will still turn out well. Ensconced in my rocking chair, a glass of sherry at my elbow, I'll watch the tape of today's *Coronation Street* omnibus and perhaps an old episode of *Animal Hospital* while Yoyo lies peacefully snoring under the bookcase.

But Yoyo refuses to snore. He whimpers instead and cries in his sleep. His stomach gurgles every so often. Must have tucked into a rotted pigeon again or a mouldy pizza carton. Wouldn't be the first time. Only this morning I caught him eating earth from my amaryllis pot. I shuffle over and bend down to stroke his ears; so soft they are, much softer than the rest of him. Straightening up, I knock into the corner of the bookcase and collapse full-length on the floor, pain in my head and my back, blood on my tongue, the *Collected Works of Charles Dickens* scattered around me. Yoyo has fled.

So much for a quietly shared evening.

After another dose of Askit powder, I treat myself to a stiff gin. Well, why the hell not? It isn't too late to learn from Marlene, is it?

~

The year of our shopping spree at Jenners I hardly ever saw Marlene. She was always off somewhere: descending on Jane in the New Town; driving up to Pitlochry in her posh new car 'for a bit of fun' at Mary's hotel; travelling to London to stay with Dolly and trail around Harrods; or flying to California, where Bessie the dancer, her youngest sister, had married a college professor. 'Just imagine, Lizzie, I was in America when John F. Kennedy was assassinated!' she boasted afterwards.

The following spring she rented a house in North Berwick and bullied the Eliotts into letting her have Angus and Catriona back. I went to see her on a glorious day during the summer holidays, taking Ruth and Mungo with me. John and Janice were helping out at the shop. Alan had bribed them with extra pocket money so they wouldn't be 'corrupted' by Marlene.

The beach at North Berwick was teeming with people. Marlene and I lounged behind a windbreak on a genuine Persian rug she had bought for the house, smoking and drinking champagne to christen her most recent acquisition, an ornate silver cooler, while the children ran about in howling hordes and demanded money for ice cream and lemonade. Later Catriona showed Ruth how to build a sandcastle, which Mungo duly peed on. When Angus finally returned from a game of water ball, numb and blue with cold, he shivered so much he spilled half the Bovril I'd poured him from my thermos.

'That's bloody Scotland for you, Lizzie.' Marlene chucked the empty champagne bottle into the sand and gestured towards her son's privates, shrunk by the icy water to a sorry little bump under his swimming trunks. 'No wonder I prefer San Francisco.'

I ignored her blatant leer and refilled Angus's mug.

My second and last visit to North Berwick was on Halloween. A dreich, drizzly Saturday. I'd served in the shop all morning, then made lunch for the family before setting off with Ruth and Mungo to spend the night at Marlene's – despite Alan's silent fury.

No one was waiting for us when we got off the train at North Berwick, and we trudged over to the house. But there was no car in the drive. And no one answered the door. I knew that Angus and Catriona had been invited to a Halloween party. Maybe Marlene had gone along with them?

Told you so. Alan's voice.

'Let's get out of this weather.' Smiling at Ruth, I pushed open the door.

The hall felt damp and chilly, and there was a smell. A smell I recognised. For a terrible moment I was back in my nightmare of the derelict cottage, where Marlene and I had sheltered that time after Sunday school. Again I could hear the spurts of rain driven like nails against the broken window, could see the small, blackened bones in the grate and the stained sacking with its imprint of a human body. . .

'Mummy?' Ruth tugged at my sleeve.

I rubbed my eyes, then gently touched her on the head and shouted, 'Hello, Marlene! It's Lizzie and Ruth!'

No reply. Only the *drip-drip-drip* of a leaking tap.

Ruth said hopefully, 'Perhaps Auntie Marlene is playing hide and seek.'

'Marlene! For God's sake, where are you?'

Mungo's nose twitched. Then he barked and scampered off upstairs, followed by Ruth.

Had Marlene nipped out to the shops? But I'd told her I would bring the food. My bag was bulging with a plump, cooked chicken, a Tupperware-load of boiled tatties, some crusty rolls and a fruit trifle.

'Mummy, Mummy, quick!' Ruth called from the first-floor landing.

Marlene was in her bedroom. Sprawled face down on the Persian rug and reeking of gin. At least she hadn't been sick. Mungo was licking her feet.

'Is Auntie Marlene dead?' Ruth edged closer, then jerked away again.

'Dead drunk, more like. Shoo now, shoo!'

Once Ruth was settled in front of the television with Mungo and a bowl of trifle, watching *Grandstand*, I went back upstairs. I turned Marlene over, then threw some water on her.

She groaned and her eyes rolled like those of a frightened horse. 'L-l-lizzie. G-good . . . to . . . see . . .' She gave me a lopsided grin.

As I began to dry her hair with a towel that whiffed of sweat and mildew, I thought of her mother, cleaning and washing for other people so that her daughters would one day have an easier life.

'Ouch, Lizzie, you're hurting me.'

'Sorry.' For just an instant, my hands had seemed to belong to someone else.

Nearly two hours later I went to fetch Angus and Catriona. I'd managed to manoeuvre Marlene between the flabby sheets of her bed with a Humpty-Dumpty hot-water bottle, had put on a coal fire in her room and downstairs, had cooked a large pot of chicken-and-tattie broth for everyone and poured all the gin, rum and whisky I could find down the sink.

Catriona only glanced at me, then quietly got her coat and the tumshie lantern she'd made for the guising. But Angus didn't want to leave and I had to drag him away. I was startled at the change in the children since the summer: their complexion was sallow, unhealthy, and Catriona in particular looked much thinner, almost scrawny.

I fed them both some broth and trifle and told them to keep an eye on Marlene. At thirteen and fourteen, they were old enough to be her guardians. 'Give her more food and tea when she wakes up. No "wee droppie", mind.' There really wasn't anything else I could do. And Alan would be pleased to see me back a day early.

Hugging Catriona goodbye, I felt how bony and fragile she was, and for a split-second I hesitated. But then she broke free, and that was that. Angus clipped on Mungo's lead and Ruth opened the door.

'Wait!' Catriona suddenly rushed off down the hall. When she reappeared, she was holding out her tumshie lantern: 'For you, Ruth.'

The face she had carved wasn't a happy one, I realised. Its grin was lopsided like Marlene's and there were tiny, tear-shaped holes down both cheeks.

Ruth crowed her thanks, delighted beyond words, but Catriona had already vanished inside.

If we got back to Edinburgh in time, Ruth would be able to go guising with her friends. I felt relieved as we hurried off towards the station, away from Marlene and her drunken stupor.

~

Selfish, selfish me!

I stop myself from reaching for the bottle of Gordon's and grab the telephone instead. Not quite eight yet. Isobel should be a little better by now.

'Stockbridge 2569.' Still sounding croaky.

'It's me. How are you?'

'Oh, Lizzie, I'm so glad!' She clears her throat.

I smile. 'Well, what are −?'

'Listen,' she interrupts before I can add *friends for.* 'I haven't forgotten about your Dundee cake.' A bout of coughing. 'It's sitting in a tin on my kitchen table, and I'll get it to you as soon as I can.'

All she is worried about is her damn cake (lovely though it will be) when stupid me was hoping she'd appreciate my attempts at solicitude! Spluttering with angry laughter, I say rather loudly, 'You're doing okay, then? Camomile tea in the pot, broth on the hob, heating on, electric blanket at its maximum?'

'Eh?' She coughs again. 'I'm sorry, Lizzie, but I'd better go back to bed. My telephone isn't cordless, alas.' A subtle hint that I am being inconsiderate: she is cold, maybe in her bare feet, standing in her hallway.

Can I never get anything right, goddammit?

And where the hell is Rachel? What is *she* trying to prove?

21

Sunday morning and the light of day reveals why Yoyo nuzzled me out of my post-*Coronation-Street* snooze last night: there's a nasty-looking puddle in the front garden, neon bright, and he has just produced another.

'No more scavenging, my boy.'

He peers up at me, then begins to lick his bum.

While I cook him some watery porridge – the best remedy for tummy trouble – I'm reminded of Marlene again, propped up in that fusty bed of hers, spooning my get-well broth. I grimace to myself. Lizzie the would-be nurse. Always would-be, it seems: would-be mother, would-be wife. Would-be friend.

~

After a fortnight of no news I tried calling Marlene in North Berwick. The number was unobtainable.

When I went to see Mrs Gray in Hatton Place, she waved me inside. 'Hello, Lizzie. You're here about my Marlene, aren't you?'

I nodded, feeling ashamed.

'Why on earth did I go and make her?' Mrs Gray shook her head and limped off into the kitchen. I remembered her using the phrase once before, two decades earlier, in the riverside gardens of the

Ravenscraig Hotel in Kelso. If I shut my eyes, I could feel the breezy sunshine of that afternoon even now, could see the soldiers, the swallows, the romping children. Could see the tulips, red as blood. That had been the moment when my life cracked apart, into childhood and adulthood – two halves forever separate.

'Tea? Brandy? Both?' Mrs Gray smiled at me. Her eyes had the faded milkiness of old age, though she wasn't yet seventy.

Marlene and her children had been evicted from the house in North Berwick after she refused to pay the rent for the last quarter. The landlord had accused her of letting the property go to rack and ruin. Apparently the mattresses were so soiled they had to be dumped.

'Where is she now?' I lifted the dinky Wedgwood milk jug (obviously one of Marlene's presents).

Mrs Gray sighed. 'Down in London. Dolly telephoned the other night. Quite upset she was, too. Told me that Marlene and the kids had parked themselves on her doorstep with a pile of bags, demanding a roof over their heads. Dolly gave them some money and a meal. She has a family of her own, after all, and no room to spare.' With a helpless shrug, Mrs Gray fell silent, then had more brandy.

Later, her spinster sister appeared. Having retired from her job as a private nurse a few months previously, she'd got rid of the lodgers and now spent all her time 'faffing about the house', according to Mrs Gray. She seemed nice enough to me, large and bosomy, with a wig of blonde curls.

'Couldn't Marlene have moved in here?' I indicated the spacious surroundings.

The sister paused in mid-sip and shot Mrs Gray a sharp glance – *One of your allies, is she?* – then she clattered her teacup down on its saucer and stalked out of the room, her soft, fat face set in uncompromising folds.

When Mrs Gray led me to the door shortly afterwards, her limp was more pronounced and the tears in her eyes made them look almost colourless.

~

'Yoyo boy, what's up? You want out?'

Standing on the front steps, I suck a mint and watch him squat, then squat again, dotting the garden with yellow puddles – so much for porridge as a miracle cure.

On with the coat and the zip-up boots, lock the door and brace yourself for the wind. At least the rain is holding off.

A taxi has rolled to a halt outside the hedge, brakes squeaking like unoiled hinges. Doors slam, then my gate is flung open and here's Rachel, coat tails flapping, with a rucksack, a suitcase and a Tesco bag-for-life.

It's a test, I can't help thinking, I am being tested. Not by God, though – but by ghosts, spirits, poltergeists. Shouldn't be surprised if Marlene herself was behind it all, foisting her family on me just for the thrill of watching my reaction.

'Rachel! Where have you been?' I give her what I hope is a warm smile and retreat back up the steps. 'The Haw– I mean Geoff has been desperate to get in touch with you.'

'Hello, Mrs Fairbairn.' Rachel has swung her rucksack off her shoulders and onto the gravel path, next to her suitcase and the plastic bag. 'And hello you.' She kneels to cuddle Yoyo, who has hobbled over to her like a sick wee man on two sticks, feeling sorry for himself.

Rachel doesn't seem to notice he is out of sorts and gazes up at me. Dachshund-small, hair unbrushed. Pale. Unsmiling.

'Please, can I come in?'

'Of course you can.' As if on cue, the pounding starts up again in my head.

Once she has plonked her luggage down in the hall, I wait for her to explain herself.

We face each other, dressed in our coats, hers black, mine grey, uncertain contestants in an unknown game, with Marlene as the invisible arbiter. I'm aware of the ache in my head, and of Yoyo whining in the garden.

'I'll have to take him for a walk,' I say abruptly. 'Help yourself to tea and biscuits.' Then I turn and stumble out the door, crashing it shut before I can change my mind.

Maybe Rachel is en route to the airport and just wanted to call in for a quick goodbye?

The door opens behind me. 'Would you like me to chum you, Mrs Fairbairn?'

A *long* goodbye then. I flick Rachel a half-smile. 'No need for both of us to get cold, thanks. Back in a jiffy.' And, screened by the hedge, I twitch the lead rather more roughly than necessary to tow Yoyo down the windswept street.

What will Janice say this afternoon? Rachel seems determined to camp out with me. And the time for excuses is well and truly past.

~

Almost forty years ago Marlene and her children travelled the length and breadth of the country in search of a home. Sent on their way by Dolly, they roamed the streets of London until they ran out of money, then thumbed a series of lifts back to Scotland and up to Mary's hotel in Pitlochry, outstayed their welcome, and finally arrived in Edinburgh, passing from Jane's house in the New Town to Hatton Place in the Southside. Mrs Gray had managed to persuade her sister to put them up over Christmas and Hogmanay – 'as any bloody Christian should and she's my bloody aunt' was Marlene's grateful comment.

Marlene found temporary work as a late-night receptionist in Newington and during the day would often pop in to see me. I felt sorry for her children. Angus struck me as far too self-contained and submissive for a teenager; he no longer battered John's football around our hall, but politely asked if he could use his record player. Catriona had become a right scarecrow, much scrawnier than she'd been on Halloween – and whatever titbits I fed her, whether toasted cheese or plain old Cadbury's, she never thrived, poor thing. I'd always had my doubts about her paternal origins, and her hapless runt-of-the-litter looks seemed only to confirm them.

By mid-January the aunt had had enough of Marlene and her frequent 'wee droppies'. Angus and Catriona were returned to their Eliott grandparents in the Borders and Marlene removed herself to lodgings in Hope Park Terrace, at the edge of the Meadows.

'I am sure it's all for the best,' Mrs Gray said to me. But I thought I could detect a note of regret in her voice, if not guilt. Though maybe that was how *I* felt. Still, what could I have done? I had three children of my own (or as good as), in addition to Alan.

~

The wind is vicious today, like a bad man. It slices through my elephant skin, my skirt and stockings; it funnels up my legs to grab at the soft flesh of my thighs; it whips my face and tears at my hair – at least it might kill off my headache. Must remember to take a blood-pressure pill when I get home. Home to Rachel . . .

Yoyo is squatting again. I reciprocate his doleful look as I bend down with yet another nappy bag. If he doesn't improve, we'll have to go to the Dick Vet's tomorrow.

And here comes Miss Chinese Crested. Wrapped in a fur jacket and her paisley headscarf and clutching a large hymn book, probably her parents', she smiles a serene hello. The church service must have been truly uplifting.

I smile back, trying to conceal the stained nappy bag dangling from my fingertips.

'Good morning, Miss Erskine. A ghastly day, isn't it?' Her scarf flutters in the wind and I gabble on. 'Would you like to join Janice and me for a cup of tea this afternoon? Say around two?'

Miss Chinese Crested beams. She has no relatives and Sundays must be difficult for her. 'Oh, thank you, Mrs Fairbairn, you're so kind.' Tiny veins are embossed on the papery mauve of her eyelids. 'Two o'clock would be lovely.'

As Yoyo and I trundle on towards Bruntsfield Links, an inner voice keeps pace with me. Coward, it says. You're a coward, Lizzie. Inviting your neighbour along so you'll be able to hide behind the role of hostess: no Rachel-problems, no Janice-crisis. The easy way out.

'No, Lizzie, you're not a coward,' Willie used to tell me after Alan's death. 'It was very brave of you to marry him and bring up his children.' Then, swivelling round in his leather armchair, he would offer me his box of Bendicks Bittermints.

'And really brave to warm myself like a cuckoo in someone else's nest.' I'd pick one of the mints, peel off the silver foil and, chocolate melting in my mouth, outstare him.

The castle looks bleak today, like a cut-out, isolated and bare. It's just the lack of leaves, I remind myself, in winter everything looks and feels bleak. Despite the weather there are quite a few people about: stragglers from Barclay Church – among them my upstairs neighbours, the ancient McConnells – as well as dog walkers, Christmas shoppers and groups of hooded teenagers, still fresh and footloose, off to enjoy themselves in town. The wind is clogged with the dark, yeasty smell from the brewery. Perhaps the beer brewed on a Sunday is more potent?

Over in the Meadows, I can see the man with the halo of white hair chasing after the retriever puppy that's replaced its grey-muzzled predecessor. I adored that old dog and how it used to lift its head to grin benignly at every passer-by.

Yoyo seems perkier all of sudden. Loo-brush tail spinning, he is busy sniffing a tree, his nose inching sideways as if he were reading a book. And who knows, maybe he is.

Cheer up, Lizzie, I tell myself, there's hope yet, even in the deepest bleakness of winter.

~

Within days of moving to Hope Park Terrace, Marlene rang our doorbell. It was just after nine in the morning and the children were at school, so I invited her in. She was impeccably dressed:

ivory blouse, tartan wrap-around skirt, tan suede jacket. Since the start of her working life, her fashion maxim had always been 'no cheap shit'. Meaning she'd buy one blouse instead of two, and that single blouse would cost double as much as the two put together.

'Hey, Lizzie, I've got a new job,' she said with a flourish of her cigarette. 'At the Three Tuns in Hanover Street, serving in the kiosk. Great wee place. Oh, and can I have a bath? My landlady's bloody stingy with the hot water.'

She was sober, thank God. Maybe it was the stresses and strains of single parenthood that had driven her to drink before. And now, with Angus and Catriona off her hands, she would be able to start afresh.

Dream on, Lizzie, I told myself an hour later. Having finished her bath, Marlene was in the front room with the wireless on, twirling like a dervish to 'I Feel Fine' and clutching a near-empty tumbler of whisky. She was stark naked.

'Please, Marlene, put something on.'

'That's me drying off the natural way. Natural is in, didn't you know?' She giggled and drained the rest of her whisky.

'Natural is okay with me. It's the neighbours I'm worried about. All they'll see is a naked woman and they'll think it's me.'

'Well, to hell with them.' She scowled, slammed the tumbler down on the sideboard. Then she laughed and held out her arms. 'Come on, Lizzie, dance with me! Remember the fun we had up at the Highland House Hotel?'

I backed away. The sixties were in full swing and I, at not yet thirty-eight, was behaving like an old maid.

If the neighbours ever wondered what went on at the Fairbairns' on the mornings the curtains remained drawn until noon, they never said. By the time Alan returned for lunch, Marlene was always safely out of the house and stationed in her kiosk at the Three Tuns. And the children had been sworn to secrecy.

Then came that Saturday morning in early March. Marlene had just reached the drying-off stage and Ruth was frolicking about with her when someone started hammering on the street door, yelling. It didn't sound like either John or Janice, who had both gone out earlier.

'Switch off the wireless and get dressed!' I hissed at Marlene as I hurried past the front room, my apron dusted with flour from making a cake. I seized Ruth and banged the door shut. Mungo had raced ahead in a frenzy of barking.

'For mercy's sake, Lizzie, open up!' Neil's voice.

Alan, waxy pale, was leaning heavily on his brother.

'Alan . . .'

'Daddy, Daddy! What's wrong with your hand? Auntie Mar–'

'Hush, Ruth, your father isn't well. Go and put the kettle on, there's a good girl!'

I stared at Alan's left hand, swathed in a bandage, with a gap where his ring finger used to be. 'What –?'

'An accident with the new meat slicer.' Neil was lugging Alan towards the front room. 'The doctor gave him a shot of morphine. He needs to lie down.'

'Not in there.' I pictured Marlene, scantily clad and merry as a roundabout, courtesy of our Famous Grouse. 'The bedroom. It's much quieter.'

Down the hall they lumbered, Neil half-dragging, half-carrying his younger brother.

I thanked my lucky stars that Ruth's blabbing had gone unnoticed, just like the closed curtains, the reek of cigarette smoke, the loud music.

If only!

Alan questioned me as soon as he woke in the afternoon. A few paltry lies later I confessed. 'She is my friend,' I kept repeating, as if to convince myself that I was helping Marlene out of friendship, not pity. 'She is my friend.'

He studied me for a long moment, then said, 'You have to learn to say "no", Lizzie. Life is a matter of choices. Moral choices. The road to hell is plastered with "yes".'

My gaze dropped from his bald head with its few greying strands to his good hand, which seemed to be caressing the bandage over his wound. And suddenly I flared up, 'So you said "no" to the doctor, too, when he wanted to sew your finger back on?'

I was being facetious, of course; I needed to lash out to regain my dignity.

But he nodded. 'What's the loss of a limb compared to the loss of a life?'

Afterwards, in the kitchen, I sat sobbing. Had Alan cut off his ring finger deliberately, in memory of his first wife?

'Mummy, don't cry.' Ruth had slipped in with Mungo. She placed him on my lap, then snuggled up to me. 'Daddy says he'll be better in a twinkle. He won't die, you know. I've asked him.'

~

If I had my time again, I swear I would walk out on Alan, taking the children with me – would walk off into the sunset, into the dark and flinty cold of a Scottish night. It might have saved him. Might have saved us both. In the end I was no better than Marlene. I, too, waited out my husband.

The children and I have never talked about my relationship with their father. But I can't forget what Janice said last night: *Murray and I are still friends. Better this than staying together and making everyone's life a misery.*

Surely our marriage couldn't have been that bad?

God, my head is sore.

'Let's go home, Yoyo. Home!'

How much does Rachel really know about me? Does she know I denied Marlene a bed because I didn't have the gumption to stand up to Alan? Is this payback time for the dead?

22

Miss Chinese Crested has barely handed me her luxury box of Thornton's chocolates when Rachel butts in to say she prefers Lindt's Lindor Truffles: 'They're the best, no contest.' My neighbour's eyes stray to the girl's lip ring, but her smile never wavers as she goes on to greet Janice, whose ponytail is tied with a bright red ribbon today, then stoops to pat Yoyo. Old biddies are better than best, I think to myself. We've got style, and staunchness.

Now that we are all settled around the coffee table, Rachel lights the first two Advent candles and, holding the match to the third, tells us, 'This is the Shepherds' Candle, for the sharing of Christ.'

I see Janice bite her lips and have a quick sip of her vodka-and-orange. In her opinion, religion as well as spiritualism ought to be avoided 'like the plague'.

Miss Chinese Crested replaces her cup with dainty precision, then inquires what the other candles stand for and are Advent wreaths common in Switzerland?

Rachel nods approvingly and begins to point: 'The Prophecy Candle – to announce the period of waiting. The Bethlehem Candle – it reminds us of the preparations for receiving the Christ child. The Shepherds' Candle. And next Sunday the Angels' Candle of love and the final coming.' She pauses. 'My father taught me how to make a wreath when I was a child, but most people buy them at the florist's.'

'A delightful custom,' declares Miss Chinese Crested.

Janice raises her eyebrows at me. I smile blandly and reach for the bowls of Twiglets and dry-roasted peanuts. 'Nibbles, anyone?'

Rachel had supplied them, together with a duo-pack of Café Noirs and a bottle of vintage port. 'A wee surprise,' she'd said when Yoyo and I returned from our walk. I'd swallowed my remark about goods that probably fell off the back of a lorry. Rachel isn't Marlene, after all.

During a lull in the conversation, I bring up geriatric check-ups. 'A bit of a nuisance, to be honest.' I glance over at Janice, who is frowning. 'Not so much the physical examination, but all those silly "and where do you live and where are you now?" type of questions. We're not morons just because we're over seventy, are we?'

Rachel titters and starts to play with a button on her cardigan, violet today, not blue. At least she isn't showing off her scars.

Silence all round.

Abruptly Janice gets to her feet. Yoyo leaps up at once and pads to the door. 'He wants out,' she says.

Which leaves the three of us. I top up my gin, then crunch on more peanuts.

'And what made you visit Scotland at such an inclement time of year, Rachel?' asks Miss Chinese Crested.

For the next few minutes, we're given a potted history of Rachel's PhD, mercifully without lengthy asides on predestination. No mention of the Hawk. My neighbour offers to lend some books on Knox and the Reformation, inherited from her father, a minister's son.

The door opens. 'Yoyo's been sick,' Janice calls into the room.

I put my glass down and follow her out into the front garden, towards a slick of yellow bile. A sudden gust of wind sprays us with rain. Yoyo is over by the hedge, sniffing and rooting about, and I huddle next to him on the grass. 'Poor boy.' His nose feels warm to the touch, dryish; his eyes seem glazed.

Janice has crouched down beside me.

'Diarrhoea, and now this,' I say in a low voice. 'I hope it's nothing serious.'

'Nothing the vet won't be able to cure, trust me.' She squeezes my arm reassuringly, her belief in medicine as unflappable as it is foolish. 'Mum, you are taking your blood-pressure pills, aren't you?'

Stroking Yoyo's rough tufts, I tell her not to worry about me. 'How are Sophie-the-wise and Donna-of-the-unspoiled-complexion?'

She giggles. 'They're okay. Murray's entertaining them today: first a film, then a pizza.'

For some reason we're both speaking in whispers. Not that there's anyone about; the weather is too wild.

Yoyo has begun to push his nose into the earth, licking it. I pull him away. 'And . . . how is your new nurse friend?' I can't bring myself to say 'boyfriend'.

'He's fine.' A swish of her ponytail. '*We* are fine.'

'You know, Janice, I admire you.'

She blinks. Perhaps she's wondering if I've gone senile in a few easy steps down the garden path.

'Yes,' I continue, 'I really do. If I'd been as brave as you, things might have been different for your father. . .' I falter to a halt. A scatter of rain hits me in the face and Yoyo tries to wriggle free.

'You did your best, Mum. Don't torture yourself.' She hesitates, about to add something, but then simply pats my arm. 'Come on now, we're getting soaked.' And she helps me up.

Yoyo shakes himself without his usual panache and stands for a moment arching his back. As he trots off indoors, he leaves a daisy chain of wet paw prints on the hall carpet and I almost wish it could remain there forever, an indelible pattern of life.

Back in the front room, Janice busies herself with her ponytail, twisting it into a chignon. She has always been a neat sort of girl and even as a child liked to tidy away her belongings, thoughts and feelings into their assigned spaces.

Miss Chinese Crested excuses herself soon after I've pressed a couple of Café Noirs on her. I couldn't very well pass around her box of Belgian chocolates, risking another comment from Rachel, could I?

As I put the kettle on for a fresh brew of tea, I spot Yoyo tucking into the soil of my amaryllis again.

'Hey, stop that! Stop it!'

I've just hauled the plant on top of the dresser when Janice and Rachel appear.

'He's been eating the earth,' I explain, turning away to smooth out the snout-sized craters. I don't want them to see my wet eyes.

'There's something wrong with him all right, Mum.'

I try not to sniffle. 'I'll be phoning the Dick Vet's first thing tomorrow.'

Rachel's gone off in search of Yoyo. She comes back carrying him in her arms, singing to him in what I suppose is Swiss German. For a fleeting moment it's like a *déjà vu* of Marlene the morning she finally showed up again, a good three weeks after Alan's accident with the meat slicer.

'Now for more tea,' I say with a briskness I don't feel, then shoo everyone through to the front room.

Yoyo will get better in no time, I tell myself; he's only seven – forty-nine in human years – a lot younger than me.

~

Marlene rang our doorbell, holding out a bagful of presents: crisps, peanuts and some fudge for the children, a bottle of brandy and a packet of Bristol Tipped for me.

I laughed angrily. 'Do you think I can be bribed?'

'Don't be daft, Lizzie. It's a wee thank you for all your kindness and hospitality. I'll be gone this minute, don't worry. I won't blacken your reputation or darken your door again.'

There were shiny patches on the cuffs and collar of her suede jacket, and grease stains down the front, no doubt from the odd mutton pie. She half-knelt to fondle Mungo, then seemed to change her mind and quickly picked him up, cradling him in her arms. Her face looked ravaged, with circles of exhaustion around the eyes and deep crow's-feet outlined in indigo where the mascara had run, perhaps from the drizzly rain. As if she could read my thoughts, she started to croon: 'Aye, Mungo boy, I'm just a dirty old down-

and-out now: no more husband or bairns, no more house or car, no more lodgings. Goodbye, my pet.' She set him down gently, kissed his nose, then made for the gate with a 'cheerio, Lizzie'.

Rushing after her, I grabbed her by the arm and marched her into the house. 'You've lost your lodgings? Haven't you got somewhere to stay?'

She shrugged, glanced at me sideways, a speculative gleam in her eyes. 'This bag of goodies for you is all I took away with me. Bitch of a landlady is welcome to my underclothes.' She sniggered, and I found myself sniggering along with her.

When Marlene sat down on the sofa, I suddenly noticed how her body had filled out. Could she be pregnant? Then I glimpsed the three different hemlines peeking from under her tartan wrap-around skirt, and the four blouse collars nestling one inside the other like a set of Chinese boxes.

I knew a few people who let out rooms and I promised to try and get her fixed up. Her mother, said Marlene, would lend her the money for a week's rent in advance. But could she borrow a hairbrush and a comb from me? Also a wee towel, a couple of bed sheets? Maybe some cutlery, a mug and a plate? 'Thanks, Lizzie, you're a pal.'

A fortnight later, once she was sure her gifts had been happily consumed, Marlene told me she sometimes helped herself to cigarettes, snacks and bottles, even petty cash, from the kiosk at the Three Tuns. 'And I don't care two hoots if I get the sack.'

23

Funny that Janice didn't seem curious about Rachel being here. Well, *I* am. And now that the lass is alone with me, I intend to find out. I sit her down in my rocking chair, draw the rose-embroidered night curtains, turn up the gas fire, pour more tea. Yoyo whimpers when I lift him up on the sofa next to me and I soothe him with my fingertips. Then I stare at Rachel's wee dachshund face – the bruise on her temple has healed and is almost invisible – stare at her over the rim of my teacup the way she did, so disconcertingly, on her first visit here. And it works.

She gulps down several mouthfuls of tea before clearing her throat. 'Since you were wondering, I spent the last three nights at the youth hostel up in Bruntsfield. Because of Geoff and . . . and . . . But it's my own fault really; I handled things wrong from the start. Made them happen by letting them happen, and then it was too late. So I followed him to Scotland. Shouldn't have. Shouldn't have told him either. Stupid. He flipped, I flipped. We fought. I fell down some stairs. And that was that, problem sorted itself overnight. Then I came here and . . . and . . .'

'And I sent you away,' I finish for her.

We are both quiet for a minute.

Remembering the drops of blood in the toilet bowl, I bury my hands in Yoyo's fur. I have never been pregnant – perhaps my body knew that I didn't want a child by Alan.

Rachel is so skinny, I wouldn't have guessed. And now there's nothing to guess anymore. And no reason for her to hold on to the Hawk.

I say how sorry I am.

She nods, and her wirebrush hair casts a shadow across her face.

Yoyo's paws twitch against my leg as he lies uneasily asleep. After a short silence I suggest she should get Geoff done for physical abuse.

Looking away into the candlelight (she'd replaced the candles with Swiss efficiency once the flames got to within an inch of the tinder-dry greenery), she says primly, 'This is a time for repentance. Repentance, prayer and patience – not revenge.'

'Pious nonsense, and you know it; you're a bright girl!'

I watch her flush. Her fingers scrabble for a mint in the bowl.

As she peels off the wrapper, I splutter, 'So that's what you want from me, is it? Repentance? Even if I did send you away at first, I've given you shelter now, haven't I?' Though maybe the two are one and the same – maybe I'm letting her stay in Marlene's stead, four decades too late, to salve my conscience.

The mint clicks against Rachel's teeth, then her lip ring.

I can feel a faint throbbing under my skull, like a threat. 'Plus you've made me muck about in my past, made me feel dirty, guilty and confused. If that isn't revenge by the bucket-load . . .'

Rachel keeps clicking the mint around her mouth and my irritation grows. Mild old Lizzie: mad, irate, livid, deadly.

'You don't understand, Mrs Fairbairn,' she says at last, calmly sucking on her sweet. 'It's not to do with you at all. It's to do with Marlene. My mother. Myself. Not *you*. But you and I are the only ones left.'

I am stunned. Marlene's story is *my* story, isn't it? It always was. She always, always came back to me. Like a ball bouncing back, off a hard surface. *Bounce. Bounce.* Just like the ball game we used to play in my father's yard. *Bounce. Bounce. Bounce.* I was the hands that would catch her, and the world was the wall.

There's a film over my eyes that blurs everything.

'I'm sorry, Mrs Fairbairn. I didn't mean to hurt you. Sorry.' Suddenly Rachel's by my side, stroking my shoulder, holding out something white – a tissue. Yoyo lifts his nose off the sofa with a weary sigh.

'Predestination,' I whisper, as if I've just solved a difficult cryptic crossword clue. Then I reach for the tissue, wipe my face, smile.

Rachel has moved away a step, her brows knitted in concentration. 'No,' she replies. 'No. Remember that time we were talking about bigotry and prejudice? Well, predestination is an extension of the same idea, sanctified by religion. But it's not what I believe in.'

My head is splitting despite the blood-pressure pills. I need a rest. For an instant I picture Marlene somewhere up in the heavenly spheres or wherever it is that spirits disport themselves, giggling and pulling our strings, strumming on them as if on a cosmic guitar. And I realise with a jolt that Rachel can't be trusted, that what she's said may not be the truth, or at least not the whole truth.

~

After nearly two years at the Three Tuns, Marlene was sacked. Not for stealing from the kiosk – they never found out about that, as she informed me gleefully – but for arriving chronically late, having spent her nights haunting the pubs in Tollcross. She'd been barred from several of them after impersonating Marlene Dietrich in *The Blue Angel* with a maudlin rendering of 'Falling in Love Again' while showing off her stocking tops to young men half her age. By now she was thirty-nine, though she looked closer to fifty, her features honed to the bone – 'a horse face all right,' my mother would have said if she'd still been around – thanks to the pickling and drying effects of too much alcohol and too many cigarettes.

Some mornings she'd turn up on our doorstep (once Alan was

away at the shop), announcing, 'I've been in the cells again. How about a bath, Lizzie, to wash off the grime of crime?'

Then, one summer's day, she told me how she'd met a very nice man in the pub the previous night, a gentleman of the old school in his early fifties. 'Well spoken, well dressed, well groomed and very well behaved, no hanky-panky. And with a well-padded wallet.'

I shook my head, fearing the worst.

'Said he was waiting for a friend. But the friend didn't show up. Then, after we had a wee droppie, he let slip he was heir to a biscuit empire. A bloody biscuit empire, Lizzie! He'd have made one hell of a catch if . . .'

'If what?' I prompted, thinking of Willie's friend Julian. Heirs to biscuit empires were pretty thin on the ground, especially the non-groping kind, and I would have bet my life that Marlene had opened some extra buttons on her blouse. 'Was he married?'

'Wouldn't have made the blindest bit of difference to me,' Marlene smirked. 'Because he said he had a car, and I felt like a spin. "Why waste such a balmy evening when we could be going places?" says I. Had to fairly winkle him out of his seat, mind. His friend was supposed to appear any minute . . . However, off we went, down to Portobello for a quick tipple here and there, then on to Musselburgh and beyond, into the sticks. Soon, he let me do the driving. He was plastered.'

She eyed me with her I-don't-give-a-damn look. 'I need something to wet my whistle, Lizzie.'

'No.' I stamped my foot, waking Mungo, who grunted and curled up into angry-dog position.

'End of story, eh?'

I clenched my teeth.

Marlene reached down to pat him. 'Bye, bye, Mungo boy.' Then she snapped her handbag shut and stood up, lighting another cigarette as she sauntered out of the room.

I held out as far as the front door. I'd rather not have heard the rest, but I had to know for Willie's sake.

Plastered herself, Marlene's steering skills had landed them upside-down in a field. Miraculously, neither she, the man, nor the cows grazing nearby were injured. As she had no intention of admitting to the police that it had been her at the wheel, she simply climbed out of the window, abandoning her companion to his fate, and staggered away to a stretch of road from where the overturned car couldn't be seen. She forced a lift from the very first vehicle that came into view – a farm truck with a couple on their way to the Royal Infirmary. The woman was in labour, and Marlene's dishevelled state and loud hiccoughs went unnoticed.

Although I'd poured her a drink, I refused Marlene her bath. This time she wasn't going to wash off her sins so easily, and definitely not in our tub.

If Willie had guessed the identity of his friend's temptress, he didn't let on when I visited him on a pretext the following day. With a deadpan expression, he told me what had happened, describing Marlene as 'an extremely persuasive lady just past her prime'.

'How terrible. What an awful person,' I said, and glanced away. 'Thank God Julian wasn't harmed.'

'Indeed. Apart from several memorable bruises. No doubt the experience will teach him not to trust females wanting a good time.'

I smiled uncertainly, then nibbled at a bittermint.

'The car will need repaired, of course,' Willie continued. 'But money isn't an issue for Julian, and he doesn't want to pursue the case. After all, he was as much to blame as the lady.'

I breathed a sigh of relief. But I didn't tell Marlene that she was off the hook. Not immediately. Let her writhe and wriggle a little, perhaps it would make her mend her ways.

It always remained a mystery to me how she managed to retain her inflated self-belief even in the grimmest of circumstances and, more often than not, emerged triumphant.

One winter's morning several months after the incident with Willie's friend, I accompanied her to the Ministry of Labour for Women in Rose Street. As usual she was dressed to the nines: ivory blouse, olive tweed skirt, black stockings and dark brown wool coat (the latter a Christmas gift from well-heeled sister Jane).

When it was Marlene's turn at the counter, she spoke in her posh voice and was asked to fill in a form. Sniffing with annoyance, she flicked a nonexistent speck of lint off her lapel, then went over to one of the desks, where she began to tap her pencil on the wooden surface: *tap-tap, tap-tap, tap-tap.*

I was sitting waiting, and her antics were getting on my nerves.

Finally the woman behind the counter called over, 'Mind my pencil, please.'

'Your pencil, your pencil, your stupid pencil,' Marlene snorted, losing her posh voice. She glared in the clerk's direction. 'What's a pencil? I was married to a surgeon. And my friend over there, she is married to a doctor.'

People stared.

I tried to make myself as small as I could. No easy feat if you're five foot eight, with a generous waistline . . .

When we got back outside, it had started snowing, a thick, dusky whirling and swirling of white all around us. I tilted up my face and felt giddy and light-headed just looking. Marlene stuck out her tongue to lick at the flakes, and laughed. 'You're a right sourpuss, Lizzie. I wasn't lying: folk with a PhD *are* doctors and vets *are* surgeons.' Then she poked me in the ribs and ran off.

We ended up playing tig all along Rose Street, giggling through the falling snow, swerving around people, shopping bags, prams, bicycles and delivery vans.

~

There's a knock at my bedroom door and someone lilts, 'Dinner's ready!'

Dinner? Where am I? The numbers on my radio clock glow red in the dark: 20.15. I'm not playing tig with Marlene, that's for sure.

'Mrs Fairbairn, are you okay?' Nurse Rachel is all I need.

'Yes, yes.' I scramble off the bed, feeling grumpy already and spoiling for a fight. Then I remember Yoyo's sickness and diarrhoea and it's like someone punching a hole into me. I shuffle to the door, a deflated, decrepit old biddy.

Rachel confesses with a bright smile that she's raided my fridge-freezer for our meal. The kitchen table is set for two, complete with pallid side salads, frying pan and saucepan. Yoyo looks miserable, lying with his rear end pointing towards the dog bowl and some tinned tripe, his favourite. At my approach, his tail beats a half-hearted tattoo on the lino, but he doesn't bother to get up.

The telephone rings when I'm halfway through my plate of *rösti* and savoury chicken-and-leek fricassee – Rachel is a surprisingly good cook. And a good maid: she's fetched the receiver for me.

'Lizzie, dear, that doctor stepped inside from the rain without as much as wiping his shoes on the mat.' Judging by her opening gambit, Isobel is well on the road to recovery.

I tut-tut and have another forkful of the delicious golden potato crust. Isobel is seized by a prolonged coughing fit before telling me she'll postpone her hoovering until the antibiotics have taken effect. 'It's simply a very bad cold which mustn't get into my bronchial tubes. No unnecessary outings, doctor's orders. And you'd better be careful, too, Lizzie. You're always out without a hat and that's just plain daft at your age!'

I swallow hard. Change the topic to Yoyo, then Rachel, who has polished off her food like a starving dachshund, yet rejects my untouched salad when I push it towards her magnanimously.

'That's good for you,' she mouths, pushing it back.

I wrinkle my nose. Then I ask Isobel if she'd like me to visit her, and my elbow jostles the salad dish, splattering the table top with oily shreds of limp iceberg lettuce. Rachel glowers at me as I mime an apology.

Isobel won't hear of it. 'You've got enough worries of your own at the moment, what with Yoyo unwell and your duties as a hostess' (making it sound as if I had to babysit Rachel). Eventually we agree she'll come over by taxi, with the Dundee cake, next Sunday. 'And please don't watch the Borders programme beforehand, Lizzie.' I just stop myself from admitting that I'd forgotten all about it.

Rachel has started to fiddle with my electric-blue radio. I finish eating, dab my lips with a paper napkin, then clean up the greasy mess of salad leaves, depositing them one by one at the edge of my plate. 'That was very tasty, Rachel, thank you.' I lean back in my chair. 'Though in my opinion iceberg lettuce is best fried or steamed.'

She ignores me. And rightly so. Churlishness shouldn't be encouraged. Except that in this case it does serve a purpose. If Rachel doesn't want me, she can have Marlene. Undiluted.

'Just a wee lesson,' I tell her. 'Because this is how your grand-mother would have behaved: she detested salad. As do I.' Folding my arms over my chest, I wait for her response.

There is none.

I say quietly, 'You can have it if you like.'

'What?' She whips her wirebrush hair out of her face.

I laugh. 'Not the salad. The digital radio, of course.'

A pause. 'But it's yours.'

'So? I'm giving it to you – as a peace offering. Another lesson: don't argue when you're given something, particularly something you fancy.'

Rachel's eyes have narrowed; the hair at her neck seems to bristle.

'Marlene wouldn't have hesitated.'

Seconds later the radio bursts into a jazzy saxophone solo. 'Well . . . thanks, Mrs Fairbairn.'

I can almost hear Marlene applauding from the beyond. I smile. 'Too gimmicky for me, anyway.' We Scots aren't much good at being thanked or praised, let alone praising or thanking.

I glance down at Yoyo. He hasn't stirred. He is panting with his mouth wide open and his tongue lolling sideways in a piteous grin.

~

Half past midnight. Yoyo is in here with me, in case he wants out or is sick again. Rachel has installed herself in the back room where

Alan and I used to sleep – 'until further notice', as I warned her, just so she doesn't think she can stay forever, which is precisely what Marlene would have done if Alan had died earlier: she'd have dumped herself on me for all eternity.

Rachel is an odd kind of girl. At some point during the evening she suddenly blurted out, 'Mrs Fairbairn, why are you angry with me?'

'What?' I jabbed my pen at the Sunday-paper crossword.

She was gazing at me, her face thrust slightly forward, nostrils quivering, one finger twiddling that horrible lip ring of hers. Then she repeated, 'Why are you angry with me, Mrs Fairbairn?'

'I hadn't realised,' I said, with a glance towards the radio in her lap. I felt cornered, and a little annoyed. 10 down: *burning bright, I can end aroma.* Twelve letters.

'But it's coming off you in waves. Waves of fury.'

I could see her reflected in the TV screen, a fuzzy figure rocking back and forth, back and forth, and I saw myself, immobile on the sofa – both of us separate, forlorn.

'I'm angry with you because –'

That's when I got confused. Was it because she and the Hawk had drugged me? Because she'd stolen Marlene's letter, taken my keys, entered my flat on the sly? Because she was playing games with me? Or was it because she was trying to appropriate Marlene? *My* Marlene?

I had always resented Marlene for living life to the full. To its heights and depths. Like one of those surfers on TV, riding the crests and troughs, hugging the sharp glass-clearness of the water, plunging down, down, down, to the gritty, bruising sand of the ocean floor, getting snared by seaweed and tentacles, chased by luminescent, spiky-toothed monsters.

But I couldn't very well tell Rachel that I resented her dead grandmother, could I? So I simply shrugged and read out the clue for 10 down. That silenced her.

Had Marlene ever been truly unhappy? The way I have felt time and time again? Hollowed out like a reed with the wind whistling through?

I'm jerked awake by sounds of retching and gagging. Light on, emergency newspaper. But the damage is done. Yoyo is bent over as if to inspect the small puddle of bile on the carpet.

It is going to be a long night.

24

Quarter past nine and not a squeak from the back bedroom. I leave a note for Rachel to let her know we're off to the Dick Vet's in Summerhall Square. Yoyo doesn't protest when I lift him into my wicker shopping trolley, then wheel him along the streets like an invalid in a bath chair.

After a group of veterinary students have asked me all sorts of questions and prodded Yoyo to their hearts' content – allegedly for training purposes – making him wince and cry, they confer with the supervising vet and finally agree on an injection. No food for a day, but plenty of water. And better not let him off the lead just now.

The flat is empty on our return. My mail's stacked on the hall table, next to a yellow sticker: 'At the library for research. R.' Suits me. Yoyo has already flopped down by the kitchen door and I put the kettle on. Open the letters. More Christmas cards, none from Cousin Peggy.

Big fat drops of rain mixed with sleet have begun to spatter the French windows, blurring the drying green into a jungly underwater world. The wind has picked up again. It's howling in the chimney and rattling the back of the gas fire like the metal bars of a cage. I am glad to be out of the weather. Glad to be home.

~

'*Home, home, home*! Why are you always saying that? Are you trying to rub it in?' The word became an obsession with Marlene after she had to sell Rowan Hill House; one mention of it, and she'd flare up like a sparkler.

It was the end of August, a few days before Angus's eighteenth birthday, and Marlene and her mother were on their way back from a pub in Tollcross, one of the few places that hadn't banned her yet. They were walking through the Meadows, Mrs Gray limping along with a stick.

'Mother started it,' Marlene claimed afterwards. 'She provoked me something hellish.'

According to her, Mrs Gray had ranted on about how certain women shouldn't be allowed to have children and how certain children shouldn't be allowed near their mothers. On and on about drunkenness, the squandering of money, ungratefulness, then winding up with the 'champagne-cooler incident'.

A couple of weeks earlier I'd found Marlene's expensive silver cooler, dented beyond repair, on the pavement outside her aunt's in Hatton Place. Through a jagged hole in the lounge window had come loud shouting.

'Not my fault if it broke your bloody window; you could have caught it, silly woman.'

'You're missing the point, Marlene.'

'Missing the *point*, huh.'

'You were threatening me in my own house! One more time and –'

'Pardon me, but is this a threat?'

I'd interrupted the exchange by yelling Marlene's name.

And now, returning from Tollcross, Mrs Gray had raised the subject with her daughter. Marlene was quick to counter:

'I said I'd pay for the damage, goddammit. First thing tomorrow I'll traipse down to the Ministry in Rose Street. I'll tell the stuck-up cow there I need money so my wealthy aunt can get her window fixed.'

Mrs Gray's reply wasn't deemed fit for my ears. 'Old bitch hit below the belt, Lizzie,' was all Marlene would say. I suspect her mother had called her a home wrecker.

Marlene had put a leg out and hooked Mrs Gray's stick, knocking her off balance, then she'd fled the scene, leaving the old lady splayed on the ground.

She'd made straight for our house. Alan was still at the shop, but I could hear him all the same, smug and self-righteous: *Told you so. She is a criminal at heart and you're an accessory after the fact.*

'My mother started it, Lizzie,' Marlene kept saying. 'Why the hell did she have to bring up that ancient bloody business? I said I'd pay –'

'What you did was unforgivable. Quite revolting.'

'Come on, Lizzie. Give us a bit of sympathy. . .'

Meanwhile, a lecturer from the university had helped Mrs Gray – a little wobbly but otherwise unhurt – to her feet and accompanied her home across the park. Mrs Gray had telephoned the police, reporting she'd been assaulted by her daughter, Mrs Marlene Eliott, who was most likely hiding out at the Fairbairns in Marchmont.

Marlene didn't seem in the least alarmed by the arrival of the police at our door. She strode into the back bedroom, grabbed my silver-plated brush, comb and mirror set and asked, 'Can I have a loan of these, Lizzie?'

I'd learnt by now that lending her anything, fluffy towels, sheets, cups, plates, knives, spoons etc., meant you could kiss it goodbye. She just took things, used them, then lost interest. 'I like travelling light,' she once said.

Before the court hearing, Marlene was held at Saughton Prison. During her time there, she spoke only in her posh voice and managed to get up everybody's nose.

I was in the public gallery the day she was summoned before the judge. She stood very erect, but seemed dazed, drugged perhaps, as the doctor who'd examined her pleaded: 'This is not a prison case, Your Honour. This is a hospital case.'

Marlene was transferred to the recently opened Andrew Duncan Clinic at the Royal Edinburgh Hospital in Morningside.

'I'd rather have stayed in prison,' she told me when I visited her later. 'Prison doesn't fuck with your mind.'

'Surely things can't be that bad in here?' I indicated the large windows bright with sunlight, the thriving plants, the art on the walls, her non-institutional clothes. 'Isn't it all based on modern methods?'

'*Modern methods*!' She spat out the words in disgust. 'Confrontational enough to make you question your own toilet habits.'

The next time I saw Marlene was on a windblown, sun-etched morning towards the end of October. I'd left the street door open for a blast of fresh air while I was doing the washing-up when Mungo started barking.

And there she was, coming up the front steps into the vestibule, a broad grin on her face. 'Hi, Lizzie! Guess what?' She brandished a cheque for twenty-odd pounds, in her name.

'They let you out early for good behaviour?'

She laughed, shook her head, then hunkered down to sweet-talk Mungo into licking her nose. I was relieved to see her looking so cheerful and provided with such ample funds – the clinic certainly wasn't stingy with its patients.

'They had enough of you?'

She straightened up and laughed again, a little more harshly now. Smoothing back her rather untidy hair, she said, 'Getting warmer: *I* had enough of *them*.'

A sudden gust of wind tore handfuls of birch leaves from the tree next door and tossed them skitter-dancing through the air.

'Lizzie darling, how about a wee favour?'

Mungo had managed to tug his lead off the hall table and was slapping it against my shin.

I knew my answer before she'd even told me what she wanted.

For some reason – maybe Marlene had bullied him into it – the doctor at the Andrew Duncan Clinic had shown her the personalised monthly cheque from the government they'd just received for her clothing, toiletries and small, private expenses. Minutes later Marlene was heading up Morningside Road, cheque in pocket. The doctor had been distracted by a telephone call and an 'accidental' spillage of tea – strong and sugary, the way Marlene liked it – over the papers on his desk.

By the time the clinic got in touch with me, Marlene had been and gone.

'You really disappoint me, Lizzie,' she'd said as she departed, in a low tone vibrating with pity for my non-cooperative attitude, a tactic no doubt employed by the staff at the clinic. 'All I asked of you was to come to the post office with me so I could cash the cheque. No big deal. You were going to walk Mungo anyway.'

Later that evening Marlene returned to the clinic – minus the cheque, which had been cashed before noon in the New Town, with the help of her sister Jane, who clearly hadn't bothered to consult her solicitor husband. Marlene had splashed out on a pair of amethyst earrings ('Amethysts are my birthstones, Lizzie, they bring me luck'), an expensive haircut, several packets of cigarettes, a few 'wee droppies' and a box of chocolates for Jane. Challenged by the doctor after her re-admission, she produced a respectably long receipt from Jenners, to prove she'd spent the money on sensible items of underwear like woollen vests and warm knickers, support bras and thick stockings. The receipt was one of Jane's, dated the previous week.

~

Rachel doesn't turn up for lunch. I treat myself to a slice of quiche Lorraine and a few pages of the Rebus novel. Then, thrilled by the dangers of undercover police work, I decide to investigate the back bedroom – to check the girl hasn't made away with the furniture, as I joke to myself.

For a moment I wonder if it's the same room. The bed, salmon-pink quilt smoothed out perfectly, is now positioned under the window, while the small wardrobe, the dressing table and stool are squashed up along the near wall. The pictures have disap-peared: Ruth's watercolour of Mungo and the still life with roses from Willie. The only 'ornaments' are four white candles, three of them used, set out on the sill, and a portable computer on the dressing table. But what about Rachel's rucksack and suitcase?

She hasn't done a moonlight flit, has she? I tiptoe inside. Just as I reach the wardrobe, Yoyo gives a feeble bark.

Miss Chinese Crested, bright and eager despite the high winds messing with her scarf, is standing on my doorstep. She is on her way back from the dermatology department, having had her 'newest leopard spots' tested. 'I'll be in for the rest of the afternoon,' she announces. 'No need for Rachel to telephone before she comes round to fetch my father's books. They're all laid out on the dinner table so she can take her pick.' My neighbour smiles with pleasure, and her brown eyes protrude a little more.

'Actually, I've no idea where the lass has got to,' I reply without thinking. 'She is a bit of a free spirit, you know, and might be gallivanting about in all sorts of places. Reminds me of her dear grandmother, may she rest in peace.'

'Oh!'

All eagerness has drained from my neighbour's face, leaving behind an expression of blanched anxiety about the welfare of her dusty tomes.

Bitch, I scourge myself, bloody bitch. How can you be so heartless? Aloud I say, 'Don't you worry, Miss Erskine. I'm sure Rachel will cherish your heirlooms.'

My offer of a cup of tea is decorously declined.

As soon as the door is closed, I scuttle into the front room, over to the press, and start sifting through the boxes of photographs. Ever since Rachel told me about her miscarriage, I've had a niggling feeling of unease. And now, speaking with Miss Chinese Crested, something has suddenly clicked. . .

I find the picture under a pile of albums. It's a studio portrait of Marlene at nineteen, taken a month or so before her secret marriage. Eyes wide and misty, she is posing against a pseudo-Greek pillar, a cigarette smouldering in the amber-and-silver holder between her fingers. She is aiming for soulful sensuousness, but it's obvious she's breathing in hard to pinch up her nostrils and push out her bosom. She is wickedly, shamelessly alive.

On the back of the photograph, in smudged and faded black ink, is the date of her death: thirty years ago last Wednesday – just as I feared. A coincidence, I tell myself. It has to be. Sheer coincidence.

But as I snib the press shut, I feel a shiver down my spine . . . My head is aching again. Damn blood-pressure pills must be placebos.

When Rachel finally arrives back, after six, I ask her to give Miss Erskine a call. 'To reassure her about things.'

'Why? What's there to *reassure*?' The girl looks at me dubiously, chewing her lip ring.

'Well . . . she may have been expecting you this afternoon, I suppose.' I blush, quickly open a cupboard at random and begin to rummage around inside, shifting tins and jars until I hear her go away.

Supper is a casserole with fresh meat from Saunderson's.

Tom McManus had smiled when I ordered two pounds of prime Angus beef, inquiring, 'Having yourself some visitors, Mrs Fairbairn?' There were no lanky ash-blonde Greyhound Girls about so I nodded and said, 'A lovely young friend, yes.' It was only later, hurrying home across the slippery Links in the horizontal sleet, that I wondered about my choice of phrase. 'What a sad biddy you are, lying to impress the butcher,' I whispered to myself as I stamped the mud off my boots on the pavement. A crow had flapped past, *caw-caw-caw*ing in mockery.

No salad or lettuce tonight, steamed or fried. But Rachel seems happy enough with the stewed onions, leeks, neeps, carrots and tatties alongside the meat. She is bolting down her food like Yoyo used to. Now nothing will tempt him, poor boy, not even a Milky Way. Since our trip to the vet's this morning, all he has done is sleep – apart from managing a dribbly piddle in the front garden. His squeaky hedgehog and Ropey lie bleakly abandoned.

'By the by, Mrs Fairbairn, I've put the paintings in my room on top of the wardrobe.'

Rachel is watching me. Sly little dachshund, she won't catch me out that easily. Her plate is empty and, with a shrug, I lift the casserole lid. 'Help yourself to more.'

'Thanks. It's really good!' she says, as though amazed I can cook.

And that's when I come out with what's been nagging me: 'You know, Rachel, I don't trust you.'

'Don't *trust* me? But it *is* good, honestly. Finger-licking good, isn't that what they say?' She starts to suck on her fingers, one after the other.

'Stop that Marlene act!'

She goes rigid, thumb plugged in her mouth like a baby's dummy.

It's not to do with you at all. It's to do with Marlene. My mother. Myself. Not you. *But you and I are the only ones left.* Rachel's words have got stuck in my mind, and they're beginning to grind me to pieces. She is staying with me out of necessity, nothing more. Just like Alan did.

Our meal is finished in silence. Then, blinking at me furtively from under the straggles of her hair, she gets up to clear the table.

We are behaving like a bickering old couple, trying to win a game that isn't worth winning. I shake my head. And am rewarded with Rachel *stomp-stomp*ing over to the sink.

Yoyo has dragged himself to his water bowl for a few listless sips. He stares at me, glassy-eyed, then arches his back in that odd new way he has, like a cat, before lowering himself gingerly to the floor, where he lies for an instant with his front end down and his rear in the air.

What would I ever do without him? It doesn't bear thinking about . . . I'm much too slow and sore these days to fuss with another puppy. If I were superstitious, I'd blame Rachel for Yoyo's sickness. She is a visitation all right.

Here she is now, armed with the soggy dishcloth. I snatch it away from her and she retreats a step, hunching her shoulders. But I'm quite sane, as she is about to find out.

'You know, lass, I've done my homework.' I pause for a moment, then smack the cloth down on the table, an unlikely gauntlet. 'If

I'm not mistaken, Marlene died thirty years ago to the day last Wednesday. Isn't that when you claim you had your *miscarriage*?'

Rachel has gone white. She steadies herself against the table. 'I. . .I. . .yes. . . but I didn't know. . .' Her voice, too, has lost all colour and I have to cup my ear to hear her. 'I did have a miscarriage, Mrs Fairbairn. Last Wednesday. And that's the truth.' She sits down. Fixes me with a mournful gaze. 'Whatever you may think, I would never have harmed that baby. Never ever.'

I look away with an inward shudder. The dishcloth has made a small puddle on the table and I want to grab it, wring it dry. Want to squeeze every last drop of water from it. Instead, I force myself to look back at her. Maybe this is our chance: hers and mine.

'I am sorry, Rachel,' I mumble, gesturing vaguely. 'Really sorry . . .' My heart is beating too fast.

She continues to gaze at me with those unflinching dachshund eyes and all at once I see in them the reflection of an old woman at the end of her life, at the end of her tether, confused and frightened, lashing out. Trying to make sense of it all before it is too late.

'Please call me Lizzie.' Tentatively, I reach for her hand, take it in mine. Press it. Press the ragged ridges of her scar against my palm. She doesn't respond. Doesn't pull away either. After a while I begin to feel the throb of her blood: strong, impetuous, and warm. Human.

'Another Marlene tale, perhaps?' I say, to keep her from moving. To keep hold of her hand.

Rachel smiles, very faintly. And then the telephone starts to ring, with a cold, mechanical insistence. She gets up to pass me the receiver.

'Yes?'

'It's *him*,' I mouth in her direction. '*Geoff.*'

She frowns and puts a finger to her lips.

No, I haven't heard from her, I tell the Hawk. And yes, naturally I'll contact him. I pretend to write down his number. Cut the connection.

One single telephone call was all it took to destroy the magic.

Never before had I held a grown woman's hand in my own like this. And I know I never will again – not in this life, at any rate. But I shall never forget the intimacy of that touch.

'I'll do the washing-up, Lizzie,' Rachel volunteers. My name in her mouth sounds distinctly and delightfully foreign. A new name almost.

When I lift Yoyo on to my lap, he lets out a yelp, then starts panting. His dull eyes don't seem to see me, or to see anything.

The telephone again. It's Janice, 'to check on our little patient'. I tell her about the injection, grumble that Yoyo isn't any better, still apathetic and clearly in pain.

'Give it some time, Mum. He is a dog, remember?'

'What do you mean, a *dog*?'

'Just that they're tough wee creatures. You take it easy now. If you like, I'll drive over with the girls tomorrow evening after work.'

'There's no need, Janice. Rachel is here.'

A gasp of surprise.

Out of the corner of my eye I watch Rachel set down a rinsed glass, then turn to face me.

'She isn't staying, is she?'

I smile to myself.

'Mum?' Getting louder and petulant, like a child. 'Mum, you never said!'

I smile over at Rachel before answering Janice in my mildest – meek, innocuous, loving and demure – old-lady voice, 'Well, you never asked, my dear. But I'm glad to have her company, for auld lang syne.'

I wink at Rachel. And she winks back.

Then I promise Janice to keep her posted. The girls send their love, she says, and lots of get-well-soon kisses for Yoyo.

25

What with the wretched weather and Yoyo's delicate stomach, I take him on a short stroll down Lovers' Loan. I do my best to ignore Grange Cemetery to my right, with its stone angels, Celtic crosses, tombs and family vaults said to house the homeless drunks – though there's no sign of any humans, dead or alive, this afternoon. The high, narrow walls of the lane and the overarching trees act as a rain- and windbreak, more or less, and except for some scraggly weeds, leaf mulch and sweetie wrappers, my scavenger won't find any rubbish here.

The Grange is a genteel part of town, clean, discreet and rather inert. Not the kind of place you'd ever associate with Marlene . . .

~

After her cheque-cashing-and-spending escapade, Marlene wasn't released from the Andrew Duncan Clinic until early the following year. For me the months in between were a blur of shop work, house work, dog walking and girl-minding – Ruth had started to bring home whole gaggles of school friends and they'd shriek and giggle and flitter-skitter around the flat, jingling their hippy bangles and flicking their too-long hair as they played John's old pop records at full volume. So I persuaded myself that I simply didn't have time to visit Marlene.

'No time to visit, oh yeah?' Marlene mimicked me when I finally went to see her at the snob address in Dick Place, where she now kept house for Dr Stevenson, an unmarried lady doctor whose job at St Andrews House, in administration, had first brought Marlene's case to her attention.

I gave a shrug, then had another bite of scone and strawberry jam.

'*I* know,' Marlene said. 'You were afraid it was contagious, weren't you? Frankly, Lizzie, you could do with a dose of madness. Just think of that buggered old rut you're in.'

'Marlene, please.' I licked some crumbs off my lips.

'Please what?' She puffed rapidly on her cigarette. 'Please help me?' Puff. 'Please teach me a bit of aggro?' Puff, puff. 'Or what?' She glared at me through the smoke.

We were sitting in the sunlit Victorian conservatory at the back of Dr Stevenson's house, which had a splendid view of Observatory Hill. Above us, the sky was a transparent eggshell blue, and as brittle. In the garden, the crocuses made a gaudy splash among the browns and greens. Birds were singing and getting into a fluster as Mungo nosed around the trees and shrubs, cocking a leg at regular intervals. Dr Stevenson's Westie would have a busy evening reclaiming his territory when he and his mistress returned from the office.

Marlene was still glaring at me. Her scarlet lipstick seemed very bright suddenly, like fresh blood.

'Sorry for being a coward,' I said.

'Easy way out.' She slammed down her teacup and for a moment I feared for the fragile china. 'Try again, Lizzie. You'll need to dig a little deeper.' She stubbed out her cigarette and leant back, crossing her legs.

'For Christ's sake, Marlene, cut the therapy talk!' I threw my own cigarette into the ashtray, not bothering to put it out, then palmed a digestive biscuit for Mungo and strode over to the conservatory door. 'I'm off.'

To my surprise Marlene didn't stop me, and I was soon marching along the empty, wall-lined street and up Lovers' Loan, a reluctant Mungo in tow.

That was decades ago, of course. But the memory has a strange poignancy today as I walk down the loan with a different dog, a dog that's ill, while the days are drawing in, and the month, the year. I'm not a pessimist. Just Scottish.

'If they ever open you up, Lizzie, they'll find a tartan inside,' Marlene said afterwards, once we had made up again. 'With you, it's always "not bad" instead of "good", and everything is under lock and key, especially your emotions. You're never truly happy unless you feel miserable.' She spoke with the conviction, and the superiority, of the therapeutically converted.

Dr Stevenson was a kind lady, not too exacting. All she asked of Marlene was to look after the house and do the cooking for the two of them and, occasionally, for a few guests. If she went on holiday or away for the weekend, Marlene was allowed to stay behind by herself.

But neither the peace and quiet of her new situation nor her weekly trips to the clinic for invigorating group sessions could prevent Marlene from sliding slowly, inexorably, back into her old ways.

One glorious September morning she turned up to fetch me for coffee at 'my residence', as she had taken to calling Dr Stevenson's house. When we arrived there, I noticed that she'd left all the windows wide open and the doors unlocked – indeed, the conservatory door was swung right back on its hinges, with a highly polished metal cobbler's last pushed up against it – inviting every Tom, Dick and Harry, every snooper, opportunist burglar and scoundrel to step inside. I said something to that effect, but Marlene just laughed. 'Dearest Lizzie, we're in the Grange here, not in Marchmont!'

That was only the beginning.

~

'Mrs Bairfairn! Mrs Bairfairn!' Ricocheting off the walls of Lovers' Loan, the cry sounds unearthly, like Marlene's spirit playing cat and mouse with me. . . We are on our way back up, Yoyo and I, near the sharp double bend at the top of the Carlton Cricket Ground.

I'm not going barmy, am I? An old bammer is so much worse than a young one: shocking, ridiculous, beyond hope. Just like an old cry baby or an old drunk.

But now I can hear the familiar *clomp-clomp-clomp* behind me. 'Mrs Fairbairn!'

This time I am in no doubt about the voice and I hobble off – an uphill struggle – after Yoyo, who has already disappeared around the corner. I feel wet and dismal.

If I shout loud enough, will my shouts penetrate the solid sandstone walls, the dense growth of trees and shrubs on either side? Will they rouse the retired gents of the neighbourhood dozing through the wintry dreichness of the afternoon? Rouse them to come limping to my rescue, armed with walking sticks?

I have almost reached the second bend when the Hawk catches up. I am wheezing with exertion, but I won't slow down, dammit, I just won't.

'. . . coincidence!'

Has he been following us? Another few yards and I've rounded the corner. . . only to be confronted by a phalanx of schoolboys bearing down on me. Yoyo has stopped by a lamppost. I clip him on the lead, gulp for air surreptitiously as I wipe the sleety rain off my face.

'Trying to win a race, eh?' The Hawk is grinning. No cap. With his short-cropped hair, skull-sharp features and bulky jacket he reminds me less of a hawk today than a vulture.

'Trying to get out of the weather, more like.'

The schoolboys pass us with jeers and stares and curious glances. For once in my life, I'm grateful to see them.

Then I set off, stumbling after Yoyo. It's easy for the Hawk to keep pace.

'I like your dog's red tartan. A political statement?'

I grit my teeth. When I'd fastened the coat around Yoyo's belly earlier, he had flinched.

'Any word from Rachel?' The Hawk's nonchalance is false, I'm sure of it. He must be feeling guilty about her miscarriage.

'Nothing,' I say quickly. Too quickly? He is observing me, head angled sideways – a bird of prey before the kill. Suddenly I become aware of Yoyo. He has stopped again and – oh no! no! no! – is squatting. The sound is awful, like a blocked pipe being cleared. The nappy bags will be useless.

To hell with the Hawk!

'Listen, young man, my dog is ill and that's all I'm worried about right now.'

At the guard rails that separate the Loan from the street, I hang back deliberately, reeling Yoyo in like a fish.

'Well, cheers then.' The Hawk turns left, thank God. 'Sorry about your dog.' His glance towards Yoyo is anything but sympathetic.

At the Dick Vet's, Yoyo has to endure more poking while I'm interrogated about the past twenty-four hours in every sordid detail, as if I'd committed a crime. They want to keep him in for further testing. Overnight. He'll be transferred to the Hospital for Small Animals at Easter Bush.

'We'll be in touch with you tomorrow morning, Mrs Fairbairn. He'll be fine. Out at the Bush, they have all the state of the art equipment.'

How I hate that phrase: state of the art!

Back home, alone with the tartan coat and its doggie smell as it dries over the radiator, I pour myself a stiff G & T.

Isobel rings. She is feeling 'a trifle' better and has started to give her house 'a much-needed spruce-up' so it will be 'agreeable' for her family at Christmas. And how am I? Still catering for my young guest? The girl must be, well, less difficult than her grandmother? Or isn't she? And how is 'my dear little Yoyo'?

Afterwards, slumped in my chair, rocking back and forth between the Advent wreath on the coffee table and the merry-joyful-festive Christmas cards on the mantelpiece – no holly this year, nor any tinsel – I wish I could drink myself into a stupor. Wish I could just sit and sip and sip, then sleep, insensible as a stone at the bottom of a well.

And what's stopping you, old girl? Come on, loosen up, let yourself go a bit!

Marlene is right. Now that Yoyo's welfare is out of my hands, what else is there to do?

But it doesn't work. One glass, two glasses. Three. Instead of sinking down into the well, I am kept afloat by memories.

~

Early one frosty afternoon in mid-February, Marlene showed up at our flat, drunk to the gills. As bad luck would have it, I'd done the morning shift at the shop and was home for the day. Slurring a greeting, she lurched past me down the hall, dropped her bag and fell out of her shoes, then collapsed on the bedroom floor. And there she lay, snoring faintly, dead to the world.

With a lot of shoving, I managed to heave her up on to my bed, pulled off her coat and covered her with a quilt. She merely groaned.

At some point, Ruth returned from school with one of her bangle-jingling girlfriends. After two hours, when nothing, not even the booming pop music from Ruth's room, could revive Marlene, I rang Dr Stevenson at St Andrews House. She made an emergency call to Marlene's GP while I got rid of Ruth and her hippy friend.

Then the doctor came, went into our bedroom and said, 'Mrs Eliott, Mrs Eliott, this is Dr Gibson.'

. . .

'Mrs Eliott, can you hear me? This is your doctor. Dr Gibson.'

. . .

'Now, Mrs Eliott, I will have to put you back into hospital.'

At this, the previously comatose Marlene sat up as if struck by lightning. 'No . . . No . . . hospital . . . Don't want to go . . . hospital! No!'

'All right, all right. Please calm down.'

'Your wife . . . What about . . . your wife?' For some peculiar reason, Marlene had taken an aversion to Mrs Gibson without, as far as I knew, ever setting eyes on her.

. . .

'I could be your stepmother . . . so I could.' Marlene had always maintained that Dr Gibson's father, also a doctor and an amiable old gentleman, had been 'sweet' on her. 'Could be your step-mother . . . oh aye!' she repeated, simpering drunkenly.

'Please lie down again, Mrs Eliott. I'll need to have a think.'

The doctor followed me into the kitchen.

At that moment, Alan arrived. He was livid: hadn't he expressly forbidden me to let Marlene into the house? And here she was, sozzled out of her mind, in *his* bedroom! Damned if he wouldn't get the police!

Shortly afterwards a squad car screeched to a halt in front of our gate. But the bird had flown; only the shoes, coat and bag remained.

It was dark and freezing as I stepped outside; a dusting of snow glistened on the cobbles. Marlene would catch her death in this weather. I rushed from tenement to tenement. Climbed stairwell after stairwell. Down one side of the street, then up the other. Until I reached the corner building. And that's where I found her at last, on the top landing, crouched like an animal at bay, shivering, her stocking soles in tatters, her toes mottled blue with cold.

'Good grief, Marlene, let's get you to a café to warm you up!'

Like the trusting child she had once been – before the primrose bank – she allowed herself to be led down the stairs and along the icy pavement. Maybe the alcohol in her bloodstream had anaesthetised her against pain, both past and present.

I chose a table near the window, then ordered hot soup and tea for her.

We hardly spoke. I had no intention of risking another of her incoherent outbursts. The only thing she said, unprompted, was: 'Mary Magdalene . . . You remember the nativity play at Sunday school, Lizzie?' Startled, I nodded. And wondered whether she, too, was picturing the little girl blundering about the stage, forever in search of the stable.

When I saw the tail lights of the squad car go past the window and vanish into the night, down towards the Meadows, I nipped home for Marlene's coat, shoes and bag and to telephone Dr Stevenson, who had just got back from work.

Ten minutes later the café door dinged and in she walked, tall and grey-haired, still in her elegant office clothes, cradling a furry white bundle in her arms.

'Look who I've brought you,' she said as she placed the Westie in Marlene's lap.

And, for the briefest of moments, it was like seeing the puppy Stilton again, that first time Marlene and I had met. The clash of the two images seemed to make reality crack apart and I had to blink back tears. Meanwhile, I heard Dr Stevenson murmur, 'And I've got a hot water bottle all ready and waiting in your bed.'

~

'My turn for the cooking tonight,' Rachel had announced before leaving for the library this morning. 'Is fish okay?' She'd come back with two magnificent rainbow trout, planning to do them *au bleu* so their flesh would be light enough for Yoyo.

But Yoyo isn't here.

It's a sad, silent meal. At least I've had the sense to ask Janice to postpone her visit. I couldn't have coped with her and the girls acting all subdued for my sake.

Out of politeness I force the food down. Can't help glancing over at the dog bowls every so often. Suddenly, there's the unmistakable *clickety-click* of paws on the kitchen floor and I sit up straight, begin to smile . . . then stop as more rain patters against the windowpanes. I stare down at the table, not wanting Rachel to see my face, stare at the tangled-up fish skeletons on the platter, at their grim, death-gasp mouths, their fins that will never swim anywhere again. As I blink and blink, their boiled eyes seem to grow larger, rounder. Accusatory.

Yoyo is in the most capable of hands, surely. The vets at Easter

Bush will do their very best to make him well again. Won't they?

I push my plate away.

If only I'd had more faith in the medical profession when Alan needed it. If only I'd pleaded with his GP to continue the course of treatment despite Alan's refusal; I could have put the drugs in his tea, after all. Had I, in my heart of hearts, actually hoped he would do away with himself?

Why is Rachel gawking at me?

She opens her mouth, giggles nervously and says, 'Oh no, Lizzie, you're not like that. As for Marlene . . .'

I really must be going barmy, blabbing out my innermost thoughts. As I lift my glass, some of the water spills on to the table. I take a sip, then carefully set the glass down. 'Marlene did not kill your grandfather, Rachel. It was suicide. You read the newspaper clippings, remember?'

What I don't tell her is how mercilessly Marlene used to goad Randall. *Go take a dose of Nembutal!* was one of her favourite phrases whenever they quarrelled.

Rachel has raised her hands. But she doesn't speak. Isn't looking at me either. She is looking at her palms, at the scars that disfigure them like stigmata.

'Rachel?'

She swallows, clears her throat. 'These scars . . . I wasn't lying to you that first time, Lizzie. They were made by the grips of my ski sticks – while I watched my mother get killed in that avalanche.' She lowers her head. 'If I hadn't lost my gloves, she'd never have skied down that slope. She died because of me, don't you see? And my baby dying on the anniversary of Marlene's death . . . it must be a punishment. My baby had to die to close the circle. A child for a child.' She starts crying. Tears are streaming down her face, dripping off her chin. She doesn't wipe them away.

'An eye for an eye – that's old testament stuff, Rachel! You don't believe in such nonsense, do you?' Ignoring my back, I propel myself out of my chair and stand over her. 'Now listen to

me. Life is hard enough as it is. Don't go making it even harder
for yourself.' I glare down at her.

She keeps crying. Sobbing now. A stubborn, rhythmic sort of
sobbing.

I want to give her a good shake, but then, without warning,
I find myself clasping her in my arms, hugging and rocking her
awkwardly. Rocking and hugging until at last she calms down.

'Still,' she says, 'what happened *was* my punishment, Lizzie,
and I have to learn to accept it.'

We gaze at each other for a long time.

'But now the circle is closed and you can move on.'

To myself I add that, to start with, she ought to ditch religion.
I don't mention seeing the Hawk. She is better off without him.

My headache has got worse, a pulsing kind of knocking, like
the clanging of Maxwell's silver hammer in the Beatles song.

Later, in bed, Rachel's phrase birls round and round in my head:
*what happened was my punishment, what happened was my
punishment, what happened was my punishment what happened
was . . .*

26

I am waiting for the vet to ring. He promised. 'Tomorrow morning,' he said.

And now it's lunchtime.

I don't feel like food. Instead, I gobble several of Miss Chinese Crested's Belgian chocolates. They melt in my mouth, soothing and buttery-sweet. Too buttery-sweet . . .

I just make it to the sink.

Thank God Rachel is in her room. She'll be tapping away at her computer or dusting down the ancient heirloom tomes on Calvinism she brought back a short while ago, having spent all morning with my dainty neighbour, jabbering about God knows what.

I sound bitter even to myself. Bitter, and a little jealous.

My mother always said I had no ambition. Alan called it gumption. And Dafydd deplored my lack of endurance.

Dafydd was wrong. I have waited and hoped all my life. If that isn't endurance, what is?

But perhaps it is time to be pro-active, time to show some gumption.

Yes, I *have* waited long enough.

Yoyo first.

The receptionist at the animal hospital keeps me on hold until

I feel almost sick with premonition, then says she'll need to page the vet. 'He'll call you back, Mrs Fairbairn.'

I treat myself to an extra blood-pressure pill.

Five minutes later, Mr Stewart tells me that Yoyo is fine and can be collected from Summerhall Square after three.

My thank you comes out like a sob.

Then I just sit and smile into space. According to the kitchen clock, I have nearly two hours to kill.

So: one more act of gumption.

Directory enquiries can't find any Dafydd Colwyn in the Cardiff area. Maybe he really has died? I am about to hang up when I have an idea.

'Operator?'

'Yes?' The young man sounds weary. 'Name?'

'Same name, but listed under "Architects". In the *Yellow Pages*.'

A pause that seems weighted with a lifetime of waiting. Of endurance.

'"Preece Sandby Colwyn Architects" is the only one I can see here.' And he reads out a number.

My hand trembles as I write it down.

Should I or shouldn't I?

Show some gumption, Lizzie.

At my question, a secretary's lilting tones inform me that 'old Mr Colwyn' is only a letterhead now.

Suppressing a gasp at her casualness, I manage to reply, 'You mean to say that Mr Colwyn has passed away?' My heart has begun to thump and the kitchen tilts around me, tilting and turning into a blurry dimness.

From far away I hear someone say, 'Hello? Mrs Fairben? Are you there? Hello?'

I croak, barely. I'm clinging to the edge of the whirligig room. Clinging with my fingernails. Can't feel my fingers any more; they've gone numb.

'Not dead, oh no, Mrs Fairben,' the voice is saying. 'Old Mr

Colwyn has moved to Canada, to be with his son and family. Would you like to have the address?'

The kitchen slows to a standstill. Un-tilts itself.

But my courage fails me. Dafydd is alive and well, what more do I want?

Soon, in a few days, I shall dispose of his pastel-coloured letters mouldering away in my underwear drawer. For the moment, though, I am allowed to feel a little tired – tired and exhilarated.

I take a taxi to the Dick Vet's. I smile at the driver, smile at the rain sliding down the windows, smile at the ticking meter. I am half an hour early.

Yoyo grins when he sees me, wags his loo-brush tail, even tries to jump up. His left foreleg is bandaged from the IV-drip.

'He'll be fine now,' Mr Stewart declares.

'Me too,' I tell him, and he gives me a pitying look. He is too young to know any better.

I wish him a merry Christmas, then pay the bill ('money and fair words', as my mother would have said) and depart with Yoyo, a new muzzle and several tins of diet dog food.

The rain has petered out. There's a lingering brightness in the sky where the sun has set.

Arriving home after a gourmet stop at Victor Hugo's Deli for some Italian salami, stuffed Greek olives and a bar of Lindt's Lindor chocolate (a surprise for Rachel), I am puzzled to find the mortice locked. Where on earth is the lass?

Just as I'm slopping some of the gelatinous diet food into Yoyo's bowl, she comes rushing in – with a bunch of pink chrysanthemums and a rubber toy Christmas pudding.

John calls, then Ruth, to inquire after Yoyo. The family grapevine is flourishing, it seems. Feeling rather touched, I telephone Janice to thank her, but only get her answering machine.

The doorbell rings. Janice! I think. Yoyo runs past me barking, his hackles up. And *here*'s the Hawk, cap, boots and all, proffering a plastic bag.

'For Rachel,' he says.

'But she isn't . . .'

'Please.' He hands me the bag, then clomps off without a backward glance – as if it's him now that's trying to win a race.

'What did *he* want?' Rachel asks from behind.

Reaching into the bag, she brings out a small, square package wrapped in what looks like a purple paper napkin and sealed with yards of Scotch tape.

A Christmas present from the Hawk . . . I grimace as I make a mental note to buy chocolates for Doreen the Great Dane and a confectioner's box of candied fruit for Miss Chinese Crested. Rachel will receive her gift tonight. A non-Christmas gift to celebrate Yoyo's recovery and, I hope, the beginning of our friendship.

After a starter of salami and olives, with my vegetable soup bubbling on the hob and Yoyo fast asleep beside his new toy under the table, I hold out the two gold boxes. They aren't wrapped. But they are gleaming. The cigarette box is now filled with glacier mints, the matchbox with the Bengal lights I found in my odds-and-ends drawer. I had cried while polishing the enamelled bluebells, so vivid and true, cried at the memory of happier times . . .

'The boxes are yours now, Rachel.' I smile at her.

For an instant the dachshund eyes darken with suspicion. 'But you've already given me your radio.'

'This is different,' I say, still smiling. 'Take them.'

And then, next moment, she is opening and closing the hinged lids, brushing her fingers over the smooth metal, the enamelled flowers. 'They're exquisite, far too valuable. I don't deserve them.'

A Calvinist through and through.

'Of course you do. They were a wedding present from your grandparents, and I'd like you to have them.' I pause, wonder what to say next. 'As. . . a pledge. A pledge to yourself.' Another pause, but now the words come tumbling out: 'Forget about the sins of the fathers, about guilt and retribution, death and atone-ment. *Live*, Rachel. Forgive yourself. Use your head a little less and your heart a little more. Enjoy yourself. Enjoy the world around you, everything – the sky, the woods, the lochs and bens, the sea . . . For Marlene's sake, if not mine: *live*!'

Bravo, Lizzie old girl, that's quite some speech, I hear Marlene whisper. And all of a sudden I feel exhausted. Feel weak and exposed, as if turned inside out.

27

I wake to a sour aftertaste of my 'pledge speech' last night, my embarrassment so acute I pull the downie over my head and curl into as near a foetal ball as I possibly can without dislocating a limb. I feel a real hypocrite. Affirming life when only a few hours earlier I'd been wallowing in despair because of Yoyo. Extolling the virtues of free will when I myself have always relied on what Tinker Jeanie called 'fate'. . .

By the time Yoyo and I get back from a chilly walk around the Links, Rachel has left for the library. I peek into her room – to check the window is closed. The two gold boxes are displayed on her bedside table; the cigarette box is invitingly open, and I help myself to a glacier mint.

An hour later, after an unsuccessful attempt to get at the earth in my flowerpots, Yoyo wants to go outside, then starts rooting about under the hedge. I have to drag him away by force, pain zigzagging up and down my spine. Back inside, he keeps scratching at the vestibule door until I relent. It's diarrhoea – despite the diet food and muzzle. He dashes back in for a frenzied, sloshing drink of water before shooting out again, this time to be sick all over the path.

An elderly voice shrills from an upstairs window, 'A naughty wee fellow, isn't he?'

'Not naughty, Mrs McConnell. *Ill*! Yoyo is ill.'

At the Dick Vet's, Yoyo is sick twice more and they transfer him out to Easter Bush straightaway. 'We'll be in touch tomorrow,' they say. I only nod and hug my elephant skin.

The day passes, somehow. I am glad Rachel is away. When she returns, the pork medallions she cooks for supper congeal on my plate.

I go to bed at nine. But I can't sleep. The weather has worsened again. Gusts of wind and sleet make my window rattle. Rachel will be plugged into her digital radio, shutting out the rattling, though hardly the draughts. I ought to have had double-glazing put in years ago.

What will I do if Yoyo dies? Ask Rachel to teach me computer skills so I can get one of those virtual dogs or play virtual games of Patience? So I can surf the Internet for a community of virtual friends? Or will I end up wandering around the park with a dog lead in my hands, whistling and singing to myself, pretending I am not alone? A bit like that poor woman who haunts the neighbourhood with her pram and talks to the rumple of blankets inside?

How persistent that rattling is. *Rattle-rattle. Rattle-rattle.*

~

Willie outlived Alan by eight years and Julian, his biscuit-empire friend, by more than a decade. I still miss him. Miss our shared cups of tea. Our laughter.

Once he became less steady on his feet, I'd often take him soup or do his shopping. He couldn't abide his home help. 'Mouth like a mousetrap,' he used to say. But she seemed pleasant enough to me.

Three days after my fifty-eighth birthday, the telephone rang.

'Lizzie . . . I'm . . . very ill.'

I hardly recognised Willie's voice. It sighed and creaked and rustled like a tree in the wind. One of his dreaded angina attacks, I thought, and tore over to his flat.

He was slumped in his swivel armchair in the kitchen, facing the potted hyacinths on the windowsill. He looked terrified.

'We'd better call your doctor, Willie.'

The smallest of nods.

The doctor said he'd be with us shortly and would arrange for an ambulance.

I was in the bathroom gathering some toiletries when the rattling started in the kitchen. A flurry of April rain? But it was a still, cloudless day.

The noise was coming from Willie's throat, a low-pitched clicking and gurgling. As I approached, the chair suddenly swung round. Willie was dead.

Ten minutes later the doctor arrived. A quick examination, then the professional headshake. 'Let's wheel the old man through to his bedroom,' he said.

Willie's armchair was too wide for the door.

Pushing it back towards the kitchen fireplace, we bumped over some folds in the rug and next thing we knew, the body had slipped to the floor.

I swear I could hear someone chuckling. And it wasn't me. Or the doctor.

In fact, I'm sure I can hear someone chuckling now. Right here in my room. My bed. But I am not chuckling. Not chuckling at all.

28

Friday is another horrible day. Horrible weather. Horrible headache. Horrible waiting. I feel as if I am loitering in my own home. I switch the TV on – Christmas adverts, Christmas films, Christmas carols – and off. Then the radio – more Christmas carols. I water my plants, and the amaryllis flowers seem to darken to the colour of dried blood. I try to read the Rebus book. Stare at the crossword in the *Scotsman*. Christmas with its promise of happiness is light years away.

Eventually, at half past three, I call the animal hospital. Mr Stewart is off today and a young woman with a soft voice is in charge of Yoyo. 'I'm afraid your little friend will have to remain here overnight,' she begins. 'We've diagnosed pancreatitis, which is an inflammation of the pancreas, a gland behind the stomach. It's only potentially life-threatening and we have every reason to believe that your dog will recover.' Then she reassures me they're doing all they can – I should bloody hope so! – and will contact me tomorrow.

Poor Rachel. I'm not much company. She does her best to distract me. Tells me about her life in Switzerland, even about the Hawk of all people. Shows me his Christmas present – an anthology of twentieth-century German verse in the original and in translation –

and the letters he had enclosed with it, all the letters he'd written
to her, yet never sent, after moving back to Scotland. Apparently,
this is his way of saying sorry. At one point she recites a poem.
Something about a panther passing to and fro behind the bars of
a cage. 'A bit like Geoff himself,' she says. I know she means well.
But I can't help picturing Yoyo in his kennel out at Easter Bush,
drugged and fettered, hooked up to an IV-drip.

Later in the evening I hear her speaking to someone on her
mobile phone. The Hawk?

~

The Sunday morning after the Festival Fireworks, I was in the
Meadows walking puppy Watson, Mungo's successor, when a
rescue helicopter landed. As usual I hurried off as fast as I could,
hurried away from the rubbernecks, the police cars and the fire
engine, with Watson yapping and snapping about my heels. Long
ago my mother had instilled in me the superstition that if I lingered
at the scene of an accident, I would become tainted by 'the miasma
of misfortune'. But this time the ambulance caught up with me,
speeding past, sirens shrieking.

That evening Marlene rang our bell. Alan being Alan tried shutting the door in her face, and Marlene being Marlene simply planted
a foot inside.

She looked deranged. Sounded it, too. Kept tossing her head,
hair flying, eyes rolling like glass marbles, spittle-flecked lips drawn
back from her teeth. 'They've killed my son, Lizzie! They killed
him to get at me!'

I led her to the sofa, sat her down, then quietened her with
some brandy, which I fed her in the intervals between the mad
head-tosses. 'Who's "they"?'

'The goddamned Eliotts, of course. Who else? Couldn't wait
till Angus's twenty-first birthday. No, his uncle has to play Father
Fucking Christmas a whole bloody year too soon. Gives the lad
a bloody E-Type Jag. It's a killer on wheels, that car, and they

knew it. And now he is dead.' She wailed loudly. 'Dead! Died on the operating table. Dead! My son is dead!' More wails. Then a scream: 'Murdered!'

There was a cremation. Marlene did her utmost to ban her in-laws. Without success.

When Dr Stevenson went on her autumn holiday to the Isle of Skye the following month, Marlene began to haunt her favourite pub in Tollcross again. Two days before her employer was expected back, she ran into a former vet friend of Randall's and sat drinking and talking with him until the pub closed for the afternoon, then invited him back to 'my residence'.

As they lounged in Dr Stevenson's tasteful living room, helping themselves to Dr Stevenson's French Brie and biscuits and scoffing Dr Stevenson's whisky, the door suddenly opened and there stood Dr Stevenson herself, home early due to bad weather.

Marlene coolly introduced her as 'Dr Stevenson, my aunt'.

Even a kind, patient woman like the doctor had to concede defeat when it stared her in the face. She asked her housekeeper to leave. Politely, but firmly.

Soon afterwards, probably by bandying about the Eliott name, Marlene managed to secure a position with a 'highly connected lady' in Yorkshire – a breeder of Lhasa Apsos. Before her departure in November, she came round to say cheerio. And to moan about not having a posh enough outfit for the evenings at the new place, where there was bound to be 'superior society'. I ended up 'loaning' her my orchid-pink wedding dress from Phoenix Fashion. I knew I would never have occasion to wear it again.

She only telephoned me once from those kennels, the next spring, to say the job was too 'menial' for someone with her 'experience'.

Then, in the summer, I heard she was working as a hat lady at a private club in London.

By all accounts she hadn't lost her zest for life, not then and not two-and-a-half years later as she lay dying of throat cancer in a London hospital. Mrs Gray, frail from osteoporosis and old age, insisted on travelling down to be reconciled with her daughter. She told me that Marlene had craved 'fags' almost to the last, begging her visitors to put one between her lips whenever the nurses' backs were turned. And that not even the strong sedatives had stopped her, at the very end, from crying out, 'Not yet! Not yet!'

Thirty years on, huddling in my own bed, alone, I shiver. With envy.

29

In the morning Rachel announces she has decided to return to Switzerland. Before Christmas. Her father needs her. She is his only child.

She bites her lips and the silver ring trembles.

What about me? I want to shout. I'd like you to stay. Instead I say, 'What about Geoff? Your research?'

'Geoff?' She hesitates. 'I guess we're better off without each other, all things considered. And my research is nearly done.'

I play my trump card. 'What about Marlene? Don't you want to hear more about her?'

Now she relaxes, smiles. 'We've got a few more days, Lizzie. I won't be leaving until Tuesday.'

When Doreen appears at ten, I send her away with her Christmas box of chocolates and an hour's pay.

Every time the telephone rings I hope it's the animal hospital telling me I can fetch my scavenger home. Janice, Murray, Miss Chinese Crested, Ruth, John, Isobel, the friendly woman from Margiotta's, even old Mrs McConnell from upstairs: they all call to ask after Yoyo. And how am I? Do I need anything? What can they do to help? Their concern is very nice, but dammit, my head is thumping: Maxwell's silver hammer is beginning to feel more like a sledge hammer.

The hospital will be short-staffed at weekends, no doubt. But they did promise!

Rachel is out somewhere. Probably couldn't stand my fraying temper any longer. And I don't blame her.

Half past eleven. The ringing of the telephone sounds different this time. Louder. As if it's inside my skull.

'Mrs Fairbairn? Hello. This is Miss Rayner from the Easter Bush Vet Centre. I am afraid your dog's condition has deteriorated.'

I say nothing, just dig my fingernails into the upholstery of the rocking chair.

The unfamiliar voice continues, cautiously. 'He seemed to be improving towards evening, but during the night he had another attack. We will need to keep him under observation over the weekend. Not to worry, though. He'll be fine.'

Afterwards I stare at Rachel's chrysanthemums on the sideboard. They look stiff and uncompromising. Callous.

I stare at the TV screen opposite, blank except for a vague reflection of white hair and misery.

Stare at the coffee table. Isobel's visit today will have to be postponed.

Stare at the Advent wreath and the fallen needles on the shiny wood.

Stare at the fourth candle. Still unlit. What was its name again? Angels' Candle. No, not Angels' Candle. *Yoyo*'s Candle. If it is lit tomorrow, he will die. I know.

The candle slips off its spike easily. I hide it under the sofa, next to the toy Christmas pudding.

Once Yoyo is back, I shall light it.

Flames. My head bursts into flames. Red, orange, yellow, poison-green. Burning bright.

Bathroom. Painkillers, quick. Quick. Water.

Kitchen. Sit down, sit down. More flames . . .

Far away the telephone.

The front door.

'Lizzie! My God, Lizzie, what's wrong?'
  'Blinding headache. Can't see. Can't do a thing.'
  'I'll phone the doctor right away. Janice, too.'

More and more flames. Burning bright, and brighter.

'They've sent an ambulance. And Janice is on her way.'
  'Please. In my bedroom. Bottom drawer. Under lining paper.
Letters. Destroy. Please. Trust you.'
  'I will, Lizzie, I promise. Here's some ice now for your head.
Let me . . .'

Bright flames. Sick, so sick. Sorry.

Someone holding my hand. Rough skin, but warm, warm.

'Lizzie? Any news about Yoyo?'
  'Bad . . . he . . . is . . .'

Yoyo's candle angels flying happy Yoyo wings no pain

Lizzie . . .
    sing for company sing
    I've just phoned . . .
    a humming it fills me

the animal hospital . . .
fills me soothes the flames
and . . .
dwindling everything dwindling
Lizzie . . .
sing
they say . . .
not yet not yet
can you hear . . .
dark so dark
Yoyo is . . .
company sing for
better . . .
I feel light light light

Lizzie can you . . .